WHO ME 4GIVE?

WHO ME 4GIVE?

By: Jo Ann Felton Carter

Prospering Soul Publishing

Other books for you to enjoy by Jo Ann:

ABANDONED NO MORE

SHAME IN ME

SECRETS & THEIR LIES

WHO ME 4GIVE?

Published by Prospering Soul Publishing 14455 Gannet Street|
Corona, CA |92880 www.aprosperingsoul.com

Prospering Soul Publishing is totally committed to publishing
works that edify and exhort enabling the reader to prosper in
their soul as III John 2 states.

Copyright 2012 by Jo Ann Carter

No part of this publication may be reproduced, stored in a
retrieval system or transmitted in any way by any means,
electronic, mechanical, photocopy, recording or otherwise
without prior permission of the author except as provided by USA
copyright law.

This is a work of fiction. Any resemblance to actual persons,
living or dead, events, or locales is entirely coincidental. Names,
places and incidents are figments of the author's imagination.

All scripture is taken from the New King James Version except
where otherwise noted.

Published in the United States of America

ISBN: 978-0-9892671-2-0 book

ISBN: 978-0-9892671-3-7 ebook

Christian Fiction

CONTENTS

Prologue

Let me take a few minutes and explain why I write about issues we have that hinder us from maturing. After years of recapping my day every night to see if I had measured up to the Word, one day during my reading I stumbled on III John and realized my focus should be on getting my soul to prosper and not worry about if I had pleased the Lord or not. Understanding how the soul and the spirit entered into Adam during his making and that he died spiritually, causes you to understand the importance of becoming 'born again of the spirit'. Being born of our sinful nature, we are totally governed by our five senses; what we see, smell, taste, touch and hear. However we are not totally whole until His spirit dwells in us again. Some of us realize we are missing something at an early age, we just don't know what it is so we seek material things thinking once we achieve whatever; we'll be complete and content. What's missing is the image of God being awakened in us and after we are born again, our life of balancing the spirit and the soul begins.

Our soul houses our thinking and personality; who we really are and aligning who we are with who our Father created us to become is our life's journey and healing is very important. So, I am motivated to write about becoming healed of the issues we have in hopes of helping The Body of Christ.

III John 2 & 3, states **"Beloved, I pray that you may prosper in all things and be in**

health, just as your soul prospers. For I rejoiced greatly when brethren came and testified of the truth that is in you, just as you walk in the truth." The words, as your soul "prospers" imply an ongoing work in us and life itself produces situations that will cause us to work at having a prosperous soul.

Because the root of our understanding stems from our childhood and, our "method of reasoning" is also developed in our youth. I use childhood memories as the focal point of gaining understanding. When we become "born again" the "mind of Christ" must now become the root of our understanding. Applying the Word must become our method of reasoning. So be encouraged to spend time in studying the Word and, in His presence daily if possible so your love and relationship with Christ deepens and, your understanding becomes enlightened.

Trust Holy Spirit and give Him permission to counsel you; He knows your heart and intent even when you don't. **Isaiah 9:6** tells us; **"For unto us a Child is born, Unto us a Son is given; And the government will be upon His shoulder. And His name will be called Wonderful, Counselor, Mighty God, Everlasting Father, Prince of Peace."** Create an atmosphere of worship and wait for Him to guide you into your "counseling session" with Him. Be confident the Holy Spirit **will not condemn you.** He has a way of showing you yourself and not condemn you. Study the Word daily so when He speaks, you will know it is Him because He will confirm His Word.

Fiction is my choice of writing because it is so much easier to see the faults of others and not our own. In 2 Samuel 12:1-9 Nathan tells David a parable of a rich man taking a poor man's only lamb to serve as a meal for his guest. David was furious and stated the rich man should repay four lambs to the poor man and be put to death. Nathan told David **he** was the man in the story; only then was David able to see himself.

This topic on 'forgiveness' came about as a result of considering how some of us handle being wounded; and most times not too well. I have witnessed a lot of people leave churches because they were wounded by what someone said and or did. Don't feel bad if that's you. We are given hard places in our lives so we can learn how to handle them, it's all good, trust me. The Word comforts and assures us that ALL things work for our good, if we love Him and are the called! After having to deal with my own misunderstandings and several counseling sessions with Holy Spirit, not only did I receive total healing but I learned a technique to my ongoing healing when it comes to forgiveness. Remember the Bible states in **Matthew 18:7; "needs be offenses come."**

I must remind you, all stories are fictitious; they are not actual events that happened to neither me nor anyone I know. Enjoy!

Chapter One

The Invitation
Remembering how it all began

"Zinora"

As we rush to be seated in the sanctuary before the eleven o'clock service begins; Sister Hamilton was just wrapping up the Sunday School announcements. Today is Youth Sunday and because the youth choir is singing, we can hardly find a seat due to the choir members sitting in the pews instead of in the choir stand.   Finally we get seated and settled right at the moment Sister Hamilton announces that our church; Bethel Missionary Baptist, has been invited to render two selections at Praise Tabernacle Church's third Annual Musical Concert being held Saturday, May 19th. I felt my face flush as I thought, 'Oh great that's Nye's church; I'll have to play another game of hide & seek. This really needs to stop; I can't keep going out of my way to avoid him.'

Nye is my twin brother, Zinye Benjamin Rustin is his full name, and I am Zinora Ruth Rustin-Patterson, but all my life I have been called "Z." Today is March 25th and next month on the 28th Nye and I will be twenty four. That sounds like a blessing;

right? Well, it would be if only we were speaking to each other. This birthday will denote our 7th year of "rifting." Truth being told, the last time we said, "Hi" directly to one another was the day Wardell and I married; four years ago this coming June 22nd. I don't want to think about Nye right now, I need to concentrate on the Word this morning and not get worked up and leave church mad!

The youth did a great job today, and the music was outstanding. They rendered three songs and one of them was written by two of the Youth Choir members and it had a rap in the chorus. Young 17 year old Jonathan Moore did an excellent job bringing the Word. He taught from I Samuel 17:33; **"And Saul said to David, "You are not able to go against this Philistine to fight with him; for you are a youth, and he a man of war from his youth."** Jonathan went into detail explaining to us that as young as David was, God used him and caused His Super to come upon David's natural and Goliath was defeated. He encouraged all of us actually, not just the youth to seek after the Lord's will for our lives and for us to be obedient to the Word and the Lord will cause His Super to come upon our natural and we will do great exploits for God. He also encouraged us older members to pray and support the youth as they endeavor to do Gods work. We gave him a standing ovation; he was very inspiring.

After being dismissed, I briefly spoke with my Mother-in-love (law) Ma Patterson, and she mentioned to me how much she would love to hear me sing, "Endow Me," one of her favorite church songs. She reminded me that the very first time she saw me, I was singing that song and she has told me several times well over; how much she loves that song and the way I sing it. She hoped I would sing it at the Praise Tabernacle Musical in May and she was planning on being there in hopes Nye and I would do another duet. I informed her that the choir director chose all of the music selections. She gave me her famous grin while saying she would be praying I would sing a lead; the grin that makes you nervous because when Ma Patterson prays, well, let's just say things happen.

Standing here right now looking at her reminds me of Mama, she smiles at me like that when she talks about my singing. This reminds me we are having lunch at Mama and Daddy's today, always on fourth Sunday, so I had better get Nicki; our 2 year old so we can get going. The Sundays I sing in the choir and my husband Wardell works with the videography ministry, Vedette, one of his sisters, keeps Nicki with her during service and today even though I didn't sing, Nicki wanted to sit with Auntie Dette; as she puts it. I hug Ma bye and head towards the pew to wake Nicki up so we can head home and change clothes.

Wardell works with the church videography ministry one Sunday a month and today he's working, actually chaperoning the equipment while in the hands of our youth. He sees us and puts up his index finger, indicating to give him a minute; I nod back at him and smile. While waiting for him to finish up, Nicki indicates she wants to get down from my arms and join her cousins as they play "IT." Phoebe, another sister of Wardell, and I started talking and she also brought up the subject of the Musical and how she hoped I would sing a solo, however she didn't bring Nye into the conversation like Ma did.

I have the second and fourth Sunday lunch at Mama and Daddy's while Nye gets the first and third Sundays and we all do 5th Sunday's at our own homes. On the Sundays we have lunch with my parents, we go home after church, change clothes then head over Mama's with a dessert; usually something I made the night before. Today, during the drive home from church Wardell asked if I planned to attend the Musical at Praise Tabernacle and as I answered, "Yes," I looked him in the eyes. He gave me a long look while driving. I asked what the look was for and he replies, "Baby don't you think this conflict has gone on long enough between you and Nye? I think you should seriously consider calling him and make amends." I just sat perfectly still refusing to remove my stare from him while he turned to watch traffic. He knew I was staring at him but he ignored me. I don't want to get worked up in front of Nicki so I slowly turned my head towards the passenger window.

We don't argue because Wardell goes silent but; when it comes to the subject of Nye and I, well, I rant on and on about how nobody tells Nye to apologize; just me! I am known to slam cabinets when I get mad but for the most part; I am very mild mannered. Wardell and I talk about everything and the only time I even raise my voice is to laugh out loud or when the subject about ME apologizing to Nye comes up. Wardell never raises his voice, he just changes his tone to stern and believe me that works! I turned my whole body and faced my window, away from Wardell and even though my eyes were fixed on the people outside my window; my mind was prevailing over my eyes because I couldn't tell you what was going on. I was so deep in thought; 'dear, dear man, you've got it so twisted; I didn't do anything to Nye, he started this mess and he's the one that should break out the vacuum cleaner, broom and soft scrub to clean it up!' The rest of the ride home I thought about when all of this nonsense started, when we turned 17.

Mama and Daddy always prayed for us on our birthday and, because this was our 17th, Daddy had all four of us gather in the living room before we went to bed the night before our birthday. He told us we needed the Lords direction for our futures so he anointed both Nye and I with oil then they both prayed over us. We all felt the presence of the Lord and Daddy decreed the Holy Spirit to guide us into the lighted pathway we were predestined to take and he took authority over any spirit that would try to hinder the perfect will of the Most High God for our futures. I went to bed that night so full of peace. I just knew the Lord was going to direct me in my future and I smiled until I fell asleep. About three weeks later I had confirmation; I wanted to become a cosmetologist!

I remember being so excited that evening while we had dinner, I kept talking about how I have always loved to do hair and makeup for as long as I could remember. I explained to Mama, Daddy and Nye about how earlier that day, I heard a television preacher say most times our gifts and talents are known to us when we are children however, the devil has ways of making us belittle our thoughts. More than often we let the air out of our own dream balloon believing our negative thoughts instead of the Word of the Lord. The scripture he used was John 10:10, where Jesus was teaching, and it states, **"The thief does not come except to steal, and to kill, and to destroy. I have come that they may have life, and that they may have it more abundantly."** I leaped up off the sofa! I felt as though he was speaking directly to me; I was so happy I had confirmation on my future! After I shared that information at the dinner table, Mama said she was so proud of me because so many people spend years attending college and never use their credentials. Daddy smiled so big and told me he believed assisting others in looking better was conducive to assisting others in feeling better and, that could be a ministry in itself. not just a job.

Later, as Nye and I were drying the dishes, I noticed how quiet he was but I thought he was still thinking about what he wanted to do. When I asked him if he was okay, he sharply snapped back at me, "Shut up Z, just shut up!" And he threw the towel down on the counter and went to his room and slammed the door. I finished drying the dishes and before I went to my room, I softly tapped on his bedroom door and called his name. He abruptly opened his door and coldly said, "What do you want; I'm trying to finish my homework." "Nye, what's wrong, you wanna talk?" He gave me a blank stare and slammed the door in my face. I stood there trying to think of what I could have said to him that would have him so upset. I began rewinding tonight's events and conversations trying to make sense out of his reaction to me as I stood in front of his closed door. Walking across the hall to my room, I just couldn't figure out what was wrong with him and the more I thought about it the more confused I became, what just happened….. For the next week or so I tried to make conversation with him, but he would either stare at me, or roll his eyes and walk away.

About two weeks after he became distant, one evening Mama and Daddy attended a church meeting and we were home alone so I had made my mind up that I was going to get to the bottom of this distance Nye had caused between us; I was missing him something fierce. We were sitting at the kitchen table doing homework, I watched him real close to see if I could pick up something, anything that would give me a clue as to what was bothering him. I watched him looking for something and when he jumped up from the table headed to his room; I waited until he walked pass me and I quietly laid my book aside and tipped toed behind him.

He felt my presence and abruptly stopped. I walked around him, and got right in his face and he looked at me as if in disbelief I had the nerve to ambush him. I extended my neck and fixed a real serious look on my face; he slowly backed up as his eyes grew larger and larger. As I looked up smack dab in his eyes I could see his emotion turn from a question into fear and I stepped right along with him until he was pinned into a corner in the dining room then I sternly said, "Look Nye, tell me what's wrong with you right NOW!" His expression of fear slowly drained from his face, and he conjured up a smirk and said very calmly, "I'm the oldest even if it's only by three minutes; get out of my face before I hurt you!" I stood in front of him gazing into his eyes and in them was a look that gave me a chill. He was so cold and for the first time in our lives, I felt this disconnection I had never ever experienced before from Nye. I had never seen such coldness in his eyes before. As I stood in front of him I realized my heart was racing and for the first time ever; I was scared of my brother, really scared of him, so I backed away, slowly, in silence and, in disbelief. Nye had totally disconnected us, I mean….

I went straight to my room, closed the door, laid across my bed and cried; I literally whaled aloud as my heart ached from being severed from my best friend……. After the intense pain subsided somewhat, I had visions in my head of when we were very little and how I would follow him everywhere he went. I remembered how I could look into his eyes and know what he was thinking. Sometimes I would casually gaze into his eyes and ask without saying a word if he was alright and he would nod his head yes in reply to my question. I thought about how I would rest my head on his shoulder and he would say to me, "Thanks Z, I needed that." I lay across my bed crying as my heart ached for a conversation with him like we used to have. Or just share a deep gut felt laugh. I recalled how sometimes just the two of us would sit in the kitchen in silence reading and the only noise that could be heard was the turning of our pages. All of the things we did before had come to a screeching halt and, at that time, I had no clue as to why, and that alone was a stab to my heart. There really were no words to describe the depth of pain I was experiencing, not one word………

Well, we have arrived home from church, now to get changed and head over to Mamas; I am so hungry, man! I feel a little queasy.

While walking up to Mamas front door Wardell puts his arm around my waist and asks if I'm alright, I tell him yeah because I don't want him to know I'm thinking about Nye. He knows how thinking of Nye affects me and his response is always the same; I should be the one to end this madness and I really don't want to hear it, especially today. It seems since I heard that announcement about our church being invited to Nye's church; I've been kinda out of sorts as Mama would say.

Daddy greets us at the front door and grabs Nicki out of Wardells arms. She loves her grandparents and both grandfathers have this tickle game going on with her. She has the most infectious laugh, a gut felt laughter that makes any one hearing it laugh, and we all love to hear her bellow it out. Wardell was with me in the delivery room and as soon as she could be seen by us, he took one look at her and said, "Look at how hairy she is, and beautiful, she looks like a little kitten." So when Mama and Daddy arrived at the hospital, I told them what Wardell said and from that day to this, Daddy and Wardell call her Lil Kitten. As she leaps into Daddy's arms he says, "Hey there Lil Kitten, what you know good?" Then the tickling begins.

After I put my jacket on the sofa I head into the kitchen to help Mama get the foods on the table. We hug and for some strange reason it seems to me her hug is a little tighter than usual today. We end our embrace; I look deep into her eyes to see if I can read what's going on with her. Because Matthew 6 verse 22, states, **"The lamp of the body is the eye. If therefore your eye is good, your whole body will be full of light."** Nye and I were taught that scripture means the eyes are the mirror to your soul. We both have a lifelong habit of looking each other and other people directly into their eyes when we want to get an idea of where their heart is. So, because Mama gave me a tight and long hug; I wanted to leer deep into her eyes and see if I can figure out what was going on with her. I held her hand and looked her in the eyes and said, "Mama, what's going on with you today?" "Oh baby I miss having you around is all, mauh!" She hauls off and pecks me on the cheek. I love my Mama and looking into her big light brown eyes reminds me of how much she loves me. I gave her a big mauh right back and we both chuckled while headed to the sink to wash our hands and commence to putting the hot foods on the table.

As we ate our scrumptious lunch; homemade Turkey Pot Pie and fresh garden salad with our choice of dressings along with piping hot croissants plus iced tea with a hint of mint, we listened to Daddy as he tells us word for word, about the sermon today he and Mama heard. I found myself half listening and half reminiscing. I sit in what was Nye's seat while we were growing up, on Daddy's right. Nicki sits in my seat; on Mama's left, and Wardell sits on the opposite side of the table in front of me; on Daddy's left. Before we married, Wardell would come over on Sundays and always sat to Mama's right; across from me. So sitting here now reminds me of the dinners we had and how Nye would sit here silent most of the time after our 17th birthday.

I am reminded about a dinner we had a few days after Nye had quit talking to me. We were all sitting around this very table when Daddy asked Nye if he was alright; did he want to share anything. I think by now it was obvious to Daddy that Nye was not himself. My eyes were glued to Nye as I watched him politely rest his fork on his plate then turn his head and look directly at Daddy while saying, "I'm doing quite well Daddy; everything is going pretty good for me right now." He smiled and when Daddy smiled back and said, "Good son, just what I want to hear, that's real good." I noticed Nye turn from Daddy to Mama and give her a smile and nod and then he glanced my way and gave me a short cold stare. He calmly picked his fork up again and finished eating. I was sitting looking at him, trying to see if there was something, anything I could sense from him that would give me a clue as to what was it that had him so upset with me!

Nothing was what I got, nothing; it was as if he purposefully went void so I couldn't pick up on his emotions. At that moment I became furious with Nye for blocking me out, what has gotten into him? Then it occurred to me, 'maybe he's going through something he doesn't want me to worry about and he's protecting me in his own way.' It was then sitting at this very table, I decided to leave Nye alone, whatever was bothering him; when he was ready to talk to me I would be here to listen, so I decided to just watch him and pray for him to get over whatever it was bothering him.

Later that same night while I was getting ready for bed, Mama came into my room and asked me what was going on between me and Nye; something was off and she could sense it. I told her I had no clue and when I tried to talk to him about why he was so distant towards me, he shut me completely out. As I told her I thought he was going through something and didn't want me to be affected by it; I began to cry and she walked over to my bed, sat down and extended her arms out to me. I scooted over to her and allowed my mothers arms to console me while I cried. While holding and comforting me she rubbed my arm and after my flow of tears ceased, she told me she'd have Daddy talk to Nye and get to the bottom of this. She couldn't stand to see this space between us because for 17 years we have always shared everything and her heart was aching knowing we were detached.

I think a week or so had gone by when Daddy came into my room and asked what did I think was bothering Nye, and when exactly did I notice him becoming distant with me. I thought about it for a minute and told him it was the night I announced I wanted to become a cosmetologist. Daddy was standing in front of my dresser with his back up against it and both hands in his pockets jingling his change. He stared deeply into my eyes absorbing my every word nodding every so often. I told him about the night I cornered Nye in the dining room and when I told Daddy that Nye said he was the oldest by 3 minutes, his eyes became distant, as though he had just walked out of the room, and the pocket change jingling abruptly stopped.

I sat there on my bed holding onto my history book staring into his eyes, realizing he was not in the room with me mentally; I went silent, waiting for him to return to our conversation. A few moments later; as if he had woke from a sleep; he was back looking at me and calmly said he would talk to Nye. Then he smiled his warm Daddy smile at me and told me not to worry, everything would be as it was soon. He walked over to me and I got up on my knees in the bed, and my Daddy hugged me so tight. When he told me that he would talk to Nye and everything would be as it should and for me not to worry, water began to fill my eyes. His voice almost cracked while telling me he loved me and was so proud I was his daughter, and he quickly turned and left my room.

As I watched the door close, I felt as if everything would be back to usual soon because if Daddy says he will talk to Nye, and everything would be back as it was; I knew it would happen just as my Daddy says it would and I smiled so big, Daddy is taking care of the situation, ah, I can rest assured now!

Sitting here now as we finish eating the homemade Turkey Pot Pie Mama made, I realize I have always felt safe having my Daddy around, we all felt safe with him being our covering. You must understand; my Daddy is a strong, yet very sensitive man. He will fight any man to protect his family and pray in the spirit to fight the devil and every power and principality, however, he will get watery eyed when one of us is hurting. He is a Rustin force to reckon with when it comes to protecting his family though, I mean! In church he cries almost as much as Mama does; but don't get it twisted! He's no softie; he's just sensitive and compassionate, but my Daddy is every bit a man's man, believe you me. I tune back in on the conversation and Daddy is really into the recap of this morning's sermon. As I look at him and hear his deep voice I'm reminded of an incident that happened when we were about 6 or 7 years old.

Daddy's baby sister, Aunt Ruthie May came to spend a night with us on her way to Des Moines, Iowa. It was her first time visiting us here in Kansas

City, Mo. and Mama was so glad We must have cleaned every wall in the house and Mama cleaned mirrors and light bulbs in every room. Daddy's baby sister was coming and she wanted everything to look nice for her sister-in –law. We all went to the train station on a Saturday afternoon to pick her up and I remember witnessing Daddy grab a shoe shine man by the throat and I heard my Daddy say some real bad words I didn't think he knew. All because the man cursed in front of us. Daddy turned towards the man and said, "Hey man, there are women and children present, watch your language." The shoe shine man chuckled as he told Daddy, "Come on man I'm sure they have heard those words before." Daddy put a lot of base in his voice and said; "Maybe, but you're gonna respect my wife and kids, so apologize to my wife right now."

The man laughed as he threw the rag he had in his hand over his shoulder. The next thing I knew, Daddy grabbed him by the throat and lifted him up and off the ground. Mama pulled us close to herself and stepped back while shouting in a quivering voice, "DAVID, DAVID, honey stop before you kill the man!" Just like that; he let the man go and while the base was still in his voice he yelled, "Apologize before I make her leave!" The man held his throat while stretching his neck and chokingly said, "Ma'am; please accept my apology, I'm very sorry to have disrespected you and your kids." Then he looked at daddy and said, "Sorry man, I'm sorry." The shoe shine man collected his box and left, still rubbing and stretching his neck.   That was the first time I witnessed my Daddy in confrontation with another man. The last time was in church.

We were about 13 or 14 and by now Mama wasn't the pianist for the choir, she only assisted the choir by playing the organ on most songs but when the older songs or the hymnals were being sang, she would have to switch places at the piano with Sister Cheryl. Sister Cheryl Hall was young, like in her mid-twenties and she knew all of the latest fast singing choir songs and could play her heart out, I mean! Daddy always sat on the Deacons row which is to the right of the choir stand right behind the piano player. Well, one Sunday while we were getting our robes on, as soon as Mama left the room headed for the Sanctuary, Daddy entered the doorway and stood there looking around the room.

I thought he was looking for me or Nye because I knew he had to have seen Mama because she had just left so, as I zipped up my robe I watched him. He stopped searching the room and walked in and went straight to Brother Levi and said something to him. I know my Daddy and the way he was acting, his eyes were pierced as he eyed Brother Levi; I don't know how to explain it, but I felt something wasn't right with the way my Daddy looked at Brother Levi so I looked around the room for Nye and made eye contact and directed my eyes to Daddy then back to Nye and Nye gave me a nod. We both eased out of the room and followed Daddy and Brother Levi.

We were careful not to let Daddy know he was being followed. Daddy walked slowly and took a peek into a few of the classrooms whose doors were opened and the third door he peeked into he stopped and walked in and Brother Levi followed his lead. We stood completely still hoping and praying silently that he wouldn't turn around because we had no explanation as to why we were following them. Brother Levi didn't quite close the door all the way so we tip toed up to the door and listened.

Did we both get an ear full! Daddy said, "Take this as a warning, keep your eyes on my wife and I swear fo god I'll get up in front of the church and beat you till you can't see." We heard Brother Levi say, "You must be insecure having a wife that fine thinking every man looking at her is a threat." The next thing we heard was a thump on the wall and Daddy yelling, "I wasn't born a deacon, I'm a man. I see the way you look at my wife watching her every move." Thump! Bam! Nye pushed the door all the way back and walked into the room, I'm right behind him and by now some of the choir members are behind us and we are all stretching our necks trying to see into the room. When we step completely into the room we see Daddy bent over with some of Brother Levis' robe in his left hand and his right hand is bald up in a fist and up in the air. Brother Levi has one leg hanging over a stack of chairs lined up against the wall and his fist is up in the air aimed for Daddy's face.

As Daddy turned to face us, his eyes go directly to Nye's and immediately he says, "I was just helping Brother Levi get up, he tripped." Brother Levi co-signs the lie, "Yeah, uh, thanks, uh, I really appreciate it man." He gives us a fake smile as he stands straight up adjusting his choir robe. Daddy walks up to Nye and whispers, "Keep this from your mother, you hear me." Daddy has his head tilted a little and his eyes are roaming the room taking in who all is observing what just happened as he pushes himself through the crowd that has appeared in the classroom. I listen to the murmurings; "What you suppose that was about?"   "Yeah right, tripped my foot." "Deacon Rustin? They say you gotta watch the quiet ones." "Umm, something ain't right chile."

Nye walked to the door way of the Sanctuary and stood still. I had hold of his robe at the elbow and when he stopped, he turned, looked at me and said, "You heard him; don't say a word to Mama. Z, you heard him right."   He put his index finger over his mouth and turned from me and walked into the sanctuary, right up into the choir stand. The whole time we were in the choir stand my eyes were glued to Daddy and his eyes were glued to Brother Levi. The few times I glanced over at Brother Levi, he was staring straight ahead, not at anything or anyone in particular, just straight ahead like into space. He dared not look at Mama. Yep, my Daddy may cry in the presence of the Lord, but he is definitely a man's man, let me tell you!

That's why the night Daddy left my room I just knew he would straighten Nye out. In fact after Daddy left my room was the night I realized Nye was mad at me for making my decision about my future before he did! He's the oldest by 3 minutes, and is always bringing it up every chance he gets, I couldn't believe it; Nye jealous! He doesn't have a jealous bone in his body, I just couldn't see him jealous of me, it just didn't add up but the facts are the facts. I have always followed his lead and now I am on my own track and he can't deal with it. It's almost insulting to me; as if he thinks I can't do anything without him suggesting what and when I do something, ugh! The nerve of him! I feel Ms. Pissed waking up in me.

Okay calm down....alright she's sleep, where was I? Oh yeah, Daddy never did come tell me what he and Nye talked about, but after that night he would make Nye talk to me while at the dinner table. Daddy would say something like, "Nye, ask your sister to pass you the potatoes." Or, "Nye, tell 'Z' who won the game." That was the extent of Nye's conversation with me; necessary conversation only. No small talk or sharing his corny jokes, not even the heart to hearts we used to have. See, Nye would tell me everything and I felt like I had a sister most times because we were so close. He would be the first to say, "Did you see what she had on?" Or most times he would come to me and say, "Hey Z; let's split a banana split, or let's do this or what do you think about doing such and such." We really had the twin thing going on, yeah, we had it.... and now.... I am missing "US" so badly. Ooh I feel queasy.

Chapter Two

What's Going On?
Memories

Remembering Nye today for some strange reason has me really missing him and being here sitting in what was always his chair growing up; has me going down memory lane…. I started avoiding Nye just so I wouldn't miss him and my heart would ache so for a hug or just eye contact with him, especially at night when I was relaxed. Sometimes I would wake from my sleep crying and missing him so much. One night just before we graduated from High School, I climbed out of bed and glanced at my clock; it was 3:37 in the morning. I went straight to his door and softly knocked. I knew he wasn't sleep because he snores loud like Daddy and when I put my ear to the door there was no snoring. I knocked again and softly said, "Nye, I know you're awake, open the door." Silence; as I rested my ear on his door. It made me mad that I had reached out to him and he pretended to be sleep, so, that was the beginning of the end for me; forget being there for him when he was ready to talk! Avoidance was the role I'd play after that; after all didn't he start this mess!

I realize I'm sitting here upset and I feel myself squirm in my chair. I look up at Wardell and notice how engrossed he is in Daddy's sermonette. I glance over at Mama and she is having fun with Nicki at the table. So I divert my attention back to my Daddy and realize he reminds me so much of his father, our Granddad Rustin; because he sounds so much like Granddad. Daddy is a combo, he looks like both his parents. He has Grandma Rustins eyes, forehead and cheek bones but he is Granddads color, dark chocolate and has his shaped head, nose and chin, also he's tall and thin like granddad was but daddy has what Mama calls a pound cake belly opposed to a beer belly because he doesn't drink beer. And let me tell you he has Granddads deep voice which scared me so much as a child I hardly went around Granddad Rustin because of it.

If I were to close my eyes it would be as though I were sitting in Milo, listening to Granddad, I mean!   Our Rustin grandparents lived in Milo, MO, and I remember us taking what seemed like the longest rides to get to their house.   Granma Rustin's first name was Hope and she was brown skinned, about five feet five with dark brown eyes that were shaped like she may have had Oriental blood in her veins, they were so slanted. Most all of her pictures she looks like her eyes are closed because when she smiled her eyes almost closed completely; and she was almost always smiling. She was round and wore an apron all the time unless she was off to the store for something. It seemed as though she constantly cooked and her foods were so flavorful, ooh wee, I mean!   Mouthwatering good!   When she and Granddad met, she was 19 and he was 24.

She had a job doing day work for a nice family in Sheldon, MO, and he was working for the Buffalo Wallow Prairie Conservation Area, in Lamar, MO, as a handy man. He farmed, dug ditches, and fed the animals, whatever he was told to do. They both rode the same bus but never spoke to one another, just noticed each other in passing as they traveled to work in the mornings.   It wasn't until Granddad's church had a revival that they actually talked to each other. You see, Daddy's side of the family was raised Pentecostal, strict Pentecostal. So when Granddad saw Grandma Hope walk in his church, well, Daddy always told us that Granddad Rustin told him the story like this...

"When I saw yo Mama come a sashayn' down that isle in my church house, boy, I tell you; I saw her in a wedding dress marchin' straight to me. Show nuff, as soon as I saw her set foot up in Grace and Mercy Church of God in Christ; I knew she was da one." Whenever Daddy would tell us about what he called, "The Rustin men history," he always told us the same stories. The stories consisted of how Granddad met Grandma Rustin and how he met Mama, then he would always say, "The Lord knows how to match the Rustin men because we need just the right woman, the woman that was made from the Rustin rib." And he always made a point to eye Mama whenever he said that. Yep, whichever story he'd tell, it was always told the same way, word for word.

Granddad and Granma Rustin married only three months after the revival and right away they had Aunt Corin, Aunt Edna, and Uncle Phillip Junior; who we call Uncle Junior, then came Aunt Pauline and Aunt Ruthie May; they are all close in age however Daddy came along when Aunt Ruthie May was nine. His full name is David Phillip Rustin. Daddy said because of hard labor, poor living conditions and poor diets both of his parents died of some form of lung disease. Granddad was taken by TB and Grandma was taken with pneumonia. Like I said, I was scared of Granddad Rustin's deep voice, and, he was always serious, but Grandma Rustin, she was like putty in my hands and we loved each other something fierce. I mean! I don't care what I wanted, she would always smile real big and tell me, "Yes baby, you can have it."

Before Granddad Rustin died we went to Milo to spend the weekend. Nye and I were about seven or eight years old and we didn't know he was sick until we arrived and saw how thin and frail he was, but still we didn't know it would be our last time seeing him alive. That weekend Granddad coughed a lot and always had wads of tissue around him. After hearing the family conversations while we stayed in Milo for Granddads' home going; Nye and I found out he had tuberculosis and had waited too long to go to the doctor; there was nothing that could be done. The last time we spent with Granddad, Nye was chasing me and I ran into the living room and came to a complete halt when I saw Granddad lying back in his recliner. He raised his hand up and waved for us to come over to him. You have to understand that Granddad was not a man given to smiles, he was very serious even when he told a corny joke; and with his voice being so deep, well, for as long as I can remember I have always been afraid of him. So, as he lay there in his recliner staring at us I felt obligated out of respect to oblige him so I grabbed hold of Nye's arm and stepped behind him as he inched up to about a foot away from the recliner.

Granddad whispered in a raspy voice, "I love you." And smiled at us, I relaxed thinking how his smile was so unlike him, but it was warm and so much liked Daddy's. Then I noticed a tear fall from his eye as he leaned forward toward Nye. As Nye took a step closer to Granddad, by me having a good tight hold onto his arm; I felt him hesitate ever so slightly; oh my goodness! Nye is scared! Granddad leaned up close and grabbed Nye so fast and hugged him, and then he waved for me to step up to him. I just stood there as Nye stepped away giving me room to step up close to Granddad. I couldn't move I stood stiff as a board looking at the thin frail frame of my once healthy Granddad and the next thing I knew; Nye had his hand in my back, pushing me up into the extremely frail arms of our Granddad.

He hugged me and slumped back down in the recliner coughing something fierce. As I stood there staring at him I realized he was in pain, I could see it on his face. I stood there looking at him thinking; 'Why am I scared of him, he's not scary at all.'   What's so strange about that memory is, every time I remember Granddad; I remember how he smelled to me that day; the last time he hugged me, he smelled like vapor rub. Whenever I smell vapor rub, I remember Granddad Rustin, ump, guess I'll always remember him that way.

Grandma Rustin prayed and fasted for Granddad to be healed and when Granddad died; she was mad at God for taking her one and only love. That's what she kept saying over and over, "The Lord took my one and only love, all of the mean, selfish people I know and He had to take Phillip." The way she said it, was what scared me, how could she be mad at God; that's what I didn't understand. I had heard a lot of Preachers say that you had better not get mad at God cause if you do, His wrath would come down on you. I thought wrath was a piece of wood and it would fall on top of your head. I was so scared for Grandma Rustin and I loved her so much, I didn't want anything to fall on her. I was so scared for her I prayed and asked the Lord not to let any trees in their yard fall on her. Daddy drove us to Granddad Rustin's, 'Home Going' and we stayed with Grandma Rustin for almost a week. It seemed as though every time we were in the house, Daddy was on the phone making all of the arrangements.

Grandma Rustin stayed in her bedroom until someone came over and as soon as the company left, she went right back into her bedroom and shut the door. Aunt Corin and her husband, Uncle James stayed in the kitchen cooking all the time. Whenever neighbors or church members would bring food, she would smile and tell them thank you, but she wouldn't eat anything brought over, so she cooked. Uncle James made us biscuits every morning and they melted in my mouth, now that's one man that can cook! Their kids; Barbara Jean, James Junior and Stacey Rene', called themselves babysitting us. "Stay outa that house, stop running in and outa that back dough, (door). Git somewhere and sit yo tail down!" All they did was holler at us.

Now Aunt Edna, she was a crying mess. She screamed and hollered so much she got on everybody's nerve. When she parked her car in front of the house and opened the door; she'd start with the; "Oh lawd, what am I gonna do without my daddy?" Someone would have to help her sons; Andre, Clifton and Keith, get her up on the front porch and as soon as she would sit down; the whining would start. "What am I gonna do now, my daddy is gone." When we were all in the sanctuary for both the viewing of the body and the service, her sons kept trying to hold her down, she was popping up like a Jack-in-the-box hollering and screaming. She was divorced from Uncle Andre and when he walked in the sanctuary for the service; she eyed him up and down and I mean! She performed!

Uncle Junior and Aunt Marjorie have two daughters, Beverly Ann and Lisa Faye and they stayed in their room most of the time. I thought they were so pretty and Aunt Marjorie said they both have straight "A's" and all they do is read books. Uncle Junior and Aunt Marjorie sat in the living room all day and kept everyone company talking about the good ole days. Now Aunt Pauline and her husband, Uncle Leroy had two boys, Leroy Junior and Paul Michael, and they are just a year apart, talk about bad! They popped firecrackers under the front porch when people came over to visit, broke one of the back bedroom windows; throwing rocks at each other, can you picture that, at each other! And, they told me and Nye we were aliens and that's why we looked alike.

During the repast, they walked up behind people and made themselves belch real loud. Uncle Leroy took them out back several times, but before we knew it, they were up to something else. Now Aunt Ruthie May is married to Uncle Bernard and they don't have any children. At the gravesite Nye and I overheard Uncle Junior tell Uncle Bernard, "This is a good time to let you know, even though Daddy's gone, I happen to own a baseball bat of my own. Just want you to remember that in case your hand happens to find my sisters' face again."   Uncle Bernard began shaking his head, 'No' while telling him, "Ruthie May allowed me one mistake, and I have already made it." Uncle Junior looked real long at Uncle Bernard and said, "You remember what I said." And he walked away.

Yes indeed; Granddad Rustins' 'Home Going' is one I'll never forget as long as I live! Granma Rustin lived a few years after Granddad, then she took to pneumonia and we rode back down to Milo and again Daddy took care of everything, but that time Uncle Junior helped. What made Grandma Rustins' funeral so sad, and I do mean funeral; there was no rejoicing in the church that day and I think it was because Grandma Rustin had died still mad at God. The night before the service, after we came from viewing the body, Mama made Nye and I sit in the living room where Daddy was reading his Bible sitting in Granddads recliner. She pointed for us to sit on the sofa and with her Bible in hand, she stood over us and told us no one knows the heart of a person, but God, and because He is forgiving; she personally believed God gave Grandma Rustin another chance to reinstate her relationship with Him. Daddy never backed Mama with an, "Amen" like he always does, so I thought maybe he disagreed with Mama on that subject. Oh yeah, that was a sad funeral I tell you, sad….

Daddy doesn't talk much about his childhood or siblings, he says it's because they are so much older than he is, and they have very little in common. He and Uncle Junior are the closest because Daddy lived with Uncle Junior for almost four years, but what's so strange is; Uncle Junior does whatever Daddy tells him, like he's the younger brother and Daddy is the older, just can't figure that one out. He doesn't talk about his upbringing at all and Mama says he doesn't like to talk about his older sisters and brother because every time they all gather together, the conversation is always about how bad Daddy was as a child and he so desperately wants to forget his past. They don't call him, "Motor Scooter" for nothing!

Daddy was born and raised in Milo, and rarely left that little town. He said he had no intentions of getting married until he was well into his thirties but, he met Mama at a church musical. He was twenty seven and living with Uncle Junior who was not at all strict, and Daddy loved to play a game he called, "The Field." His story of how he and Mama met always went like this:

"There was a gang of people eating in the back of the church after the musical and your Mama kept walking pass me and I happened to notice how big her legs were and the fact she couldn't keep her eyes off me. So, I made it my business to talk to her after we all ate and of course when I flashed my Rustin smile on her; she begged me to get married." Mamas' story is a little different. She says her church was hosting the musical and she was one of the many servers that afternoon and he was the one watching her every move. She noticed him staring down at her legs and couldn't wait to tell him off after the guest churches ate. That was the only reason she considered even talking to him.   Well, as it so happened, all of the older crowd had left the room and Daddy decided to talk to Mama and when he walked up to her, she let him have it.

After he walked up to her and opened his mouth to speak, she raised her hand to him and told him real stern, "I do not appreciate you putting your eyes all over my legs. I am a respectable woman and if your eyeballs look like they want another peek at my legs, I'll slap your face so hard; you'll have to wear glasses, you hear me!" She said he looked directly into her eyes, smiled and said, "You are absolutely right, and I apologize, you are a lady, please; forgive me." He nodded and humbled himself so; Mama said her heart melted. She made him court her for six months before getting married, he was twenty seven and she was about a week from turning twenty two.

As I sit here looking and listening to my Daddy; I feel tears forming in my eyes, what's wrong with me. Now I have that queasiness again. I look down at my plate and realize I'm sitting in my big brothers chair, the place he should be sitting and I fight back tears. I glance up at Wardell and he's looking at Daddy so I excuse myself and hurry to the bathroom. I lock the door and turn the water on so I can cry. I realize coming over here today has me a little nostalgic and I really miss Nye. As I glance up in the mirror; I see Nye, we look identical. He's taller than me, 6 feet one and I'm 5 feet six.

Since I had Nicki, I have more hips now, and from the pictures I see of him, he is still pencil thin and, we have the same facial structure, features and coloring, which is caramel like Mama and our hair color is what we cosmetologist call, 'Dirty Brown." We both have light brown eyes like Mama's and smile like her too. What seems funny to me now is, we are a combo of Mama and Daddy, just as Daddy is a combo of his parents, ump, that thought puts a smile on my face. I hear a soft rap at the door and hear Wardell ask, "Baby you okay?" I smile real big as I turn the water off and unlock the door and say, "Yes, honey." As I open the door I wipe my face with my hands and, while I slump into his arms, I add, "I'm okay." And I bury my face in his big strong chest so he can't see the water in my eyes.

I hear Nicki whining as Mama tries to console her. I know she didn't finish her nap and is cranky so I grab Wardells hand and head back into the dining room. Daddy says, "We might have to have dessert later, Lil Kitten is sleepy. Z; what you bring us for dessert today?" As I pull Nicki from Mamas' arms and adjust her on my hip, I tell Daddy, "Today is Icebox Lemon Pie. I made two, so we'll have ours at home later." Daddy smiles real big and says, "Umm, one of my favorites." I take Nicki to the bathroom and Mama follows me asking if I was alright. I told her yes, just a little queasiness, and then I told her about the announcement at church today and that I was not looking forward to playing hide and seek with Nye. She stood there in the doorway with her eyes fixed on Nicki as I spoke, she never moved her eyes but she told me: "Think about being the first to bring mortar and pestle to mend the bridge."

She smiled while eying Nicki then she began clapping her hands and started praising her for being such a big girl going potty by herself. I stood there admiring my Mama, thinking; 'My Mama and her words!' Nicki is so sleepy and fighting it something fierce with the full fledge crying and now the falling out has started, so I get real stern with her and say, "Alright Emoni Nichole Patterson! There will be no falling out, you understand me?" Now she simmers down to a whimper but it breaks my heart to hear it, so we head for home to let her finish her nap. On the way I sit in the back seat with her lying across my lap belted in while I rub her precious little head.

When we arrive home, she is knocked completely out and Wardell takes her into her room and nestles her in her bed. I hurry loading the dishwasher and just as I take the broom from the closet, I decide to use the bathroom first so I prop the broom up against the cabinet and head to our bathroom. I'm humming as I walk down the hall back to the kitchen and stop in my tracks as I realize Wardell has swept the floor and is just returning inside from emptying the trash. He really is a good man; I'm blessed to have his last name. As I stand here watching him put a clean bag in the trash receptacle; I remember the day we met, just as my Mama and Daddy; at a Gospel Concert his family's home church; Bethel Missionary Baptist, was hosting.

For as long as I can remember Mama has always played the piano for our church choir, you know, the old folk church music and hymnals, and she made Nye and me sing in the choir. We didn't have a choice. We started singing with the adults at the age of 8, and we sang until Reverend Stephens started a youth choir with the handful of kids in the church back then. We attended Rose of Sharon Holiness Church of God In Christ all of our lives. Mama and Daddy still attend there. Daddy is 3rd generation Deacon and Mama is 4th generation Sunday School Teacher/ Deaconess, so we were brought up in church. Every Saturday morning in David and Eunice Rustin's house; you would get up at 8am and Mama would either fix waffles or pancakes or French toast or grits and for sure there was Canadian bacon and scrambled eggs on the table along with your choice of milk or juice for breakfast.

The next order of business was to get showered and dressed, and then head right back to the kitchen for a scripture study, which Daddy taught and Mama interjected. After scripture study, Daddy would commence to cutting the grass while Mama, Nye and I would march into the living room and rehearse before the three of us headed to the church house for choir rehearsal. Because Mama was the piano player; we had to know all of the parts to every song so that when the other kids would get off key, we would sing their note and get them back in harmony.

Daddy is an excellent teacher. His motto has always been; "In all you get, you had better get an understanding."   Proverbs 4:7, **"Wisdom is the principal thing; Therefore get wisdom. And in all your getting, get understanding."**   Mama's motto is; "Always, always rightly divide the Word, always." 2 Timothy 2:15; **"Be diligent to present yourself approved to God, a worker who does not need to be ashamed, rightly dividing the word of truth."** So, between the two of them we dissected a scripture verse every Saturday morning and you best believe we understood what it meant. By the time we were 12 years old we could almost finish quoting most Preachers scriptures and; we knew every church song there was, from hymnals to the, "Worldly Church Music," as Mama and Daddy would call it. Nye and I would sing all of the leads to the songs mainly because the other kids were too shy to stand before the congregation, but not us; we were used to singing. After all, we had been singing in front of people most of our lives.

Nye would bang on the piano sometimes and mock Mama and she caught him one day when we were 9 years old. He was just a banging and singing falsetto; mocking Mama and we didn't hear her come in the kitchen door. I was bending over laughing when all of a sudden we heard a real loud, "Oh, so you like the piano…" Nye started shaking his head, "No" and apologized, but Mama whipped off her sweater and threw it down on the sofa. She walked over to the piano and made him sit on the bench and watch her play. After that day she made him practice with her in the evenings and a few months later Daddy paid for him to take lessons. It turns out Nye is a gifted piano and organ player, he plays by ear and he reads music. At the age of 16, he started playing for the Youth Choir and sometimes at home, he would sit at the piano for hours and play melodies from his heart; just play what he felt, music that would have you worshipping the Lord and crying from the depths of your soul, yeah; I really miss that about him…

Anyways; I, on the other hand, love to sing, sing, and sing! I make up songs when I worship the Lord privately, Wardell loves it, but he loves to hear me sing. I could sing the alphabet and he would stand and applaud me. The April before we graduated high school, our youth choir was invited to sing at Wardells family's church, I did a solo and Nye and I did a duet. After the service Wardell followed me to our church van hollering, "Hey miss, excuse me, miss." I kept walking towards our bus; I had no idea he was referring to me until he said; "Miss lead vocalist from Rose of Sharon," I stopped, turned around and saw the finest man I had ever laid eyes on in my life!   He was slimmer then but still fine.

Wardell is a dark man with pearly white perfect teeth, 6 feet tall, and real tight curled hair that he has the wisdom to keep cut extremely short, and back then, he was not dressed the best, putting himself through college and all, but I could see a good hearted, loves him some Jesus, faithful and committed man! Whew, my temperature rises just thinking about my man! I never will forget that day, the day I met my Mr. Patterson. He was nervous but direct and as soon as I turned around and looked into his eyes, I smiled.

He extended his hand towards me indicating he wanted to shake my hand and as I extended my hand towards his, he blurts, "Hello, I hope you don't think I was yelling at you, I was trying to get your attention. You have such a strong anointing and a beautiful voice. Are you seeing anyone?" When he asked me if I were seeing anyone, his eyebrows jumped up as if he was surprised the words had left his mouth. He hunched his shoulders and realized he was still holding my hand and dropped it like it was hot. I laughed, and he smiled at me again and said, "Excuse me, I'm a little nervous, you are so beautiful, I can't believe you're talking to me, I mean, ah, that you're letting me talk to you. Can I call you sometime; I mean on the telephone, can I get your number?" Just that second Andrew, one of our choir's tenors, walked up behind me and said, "Z, we're waiting on you, you're holding the bus up, come on."

Wardell says to me, "Just tell me your number; I'll remember it, I promise." He smiles again and I commence to reciting my number as I back away from him, headed to the bus. When I reached the bus door, I glanced back at him and he has followed me, notices I see him and nods his head yes and gives me the thumbs up, as if to say, "I gct it." I smiled all the way back to the church, I knew in my heart I had just met the man I would have my first relationship with and he was so fine! His smiling face was all I could think about for the rest of that evening.....Ahh my Wardell.......

Okay, ok, back to rewinding; I had so much going on then and the first time Wardell phoned me, Mama answered the phone and because she didn't recognize the voice, she stood in the doorway looking in my mouth as we had our first phone conversation. Because Mama was standing there, of course I asked the appropriate questions. Are you saved, Holy Ghost filled, fire baptized with the evidence of speaking in tongues? I made a point to say, "Good," after he answered every question to insinuate every answer was a yes. He asked me, "What's fire baptized." But I played it off; I figured I would explain it to him later when Mama wasn't in my mouth. After that call I had Mama's phone approval and she allowed me to talk with him once a week.

Because of my homework, research and filling out forms for Cosmetology School, and of course I had choir practices and home chores, most nights I barely had time to get it all done and get to bed before 11pm.   Wardell didn't mind our phone time being so short because of his studies. He had just turned 20 and was in his 2nd year of college, majoring in Business Administration Management and a minor in Spanish.   He took both Computer and Spanish classes while working part time at the bank, plus he did videography at his church and all of that activity left him very little time for socializing. He told me during our second phone conversation that he really liked me and wanted both of us to stay focused on our schooling because he had a feeling deep in his gut, we would have plenty time later on to spend with each other. I just replied with a simple, "Okay, that's fine with me." Wardell always prayed for me before hanging up, he was so thoughtful and soft spoken with me, I knew he cared about me just by the way he treated me and that made me feel as though I could return the thoughtfulness but, as I said, we didn't have a lot of time to be with each other then.

After a month or so of telephone conversations, he came over to the house for Sunday dinner to meet my family. Daddy asked a thousand questions about his family and Mama watched every move he made while Nye was his usual introverted self, Wardell even picked up on it.   As I stand here gazing at my man; he walks up to me and holds me ever so gently and whispers in my ear he'll draw me a hot bubble bath, ah…, that's just my Wardell.

Today we spent the rest of our Sunday resting and I made us some Polish Sausages with Pork and Beans for dinner, then we watched a Disney movie. Wardell paid some bills and we relaxed some more. Before I dozed off, I felt this queasiness in my stomach again and I know it's because of Nye but I didn't want to think about him and get so worked up I'll be unable to sleep, so I snuggled up in my loving husbands arms and drifted off.

"Zinye"

"Okay, Nye what's going on with you, you've been quiet since church was over?" I watch my beautiful wife as she slides into bed and questions me about my behavior. "Um, I wonder how Z took the announcement of the musical today." "Babe, why don't you call and ask her?" "Von, baby, she doesn't want to talk to me, if she did, she would have called a long time ago." "Well, if I were as miserable as you are, I would call my sister. That's all I'm saying." As I reach for her she meets me half way and pecks me on my cheek and snuggles herself to fit perfectly in my arms. As I bring her close to me, I let her know, "Z no longer needs her big brother. Yes there was a time we were inseparable. Mama told us often that we were one child instead of two. When my little sister decided to become a cosmetologist, she made it clear to me that her big brother had no place in her plans. Von, it hurt me deeply, but she's her own person, and if I have no place in her life, then so be it."

"I understand your feelings in this matter Nye, I just think with you both being older now and having families, you should let the past be the past and allow our children to know their cousin. Maybe it's time to grow past the pain of your relationship being severed so abruptly. Forgive the pain of the past and live in the present. There are three little girls who are paying for their parents not speaking, and now that we're expecting another baby, think about the kids, babe that's all I'm saying." "All right I'll give it some serious thought. Come here Mrs. Sexy!"

Chapter Three

Neither One Of Us
It's on and crackin now!

"Zinora"

It's Monday morning and even though I don't take appointments until Wednesdays, through the week I get up at 7am with Wardell, fix him breakfast then study my daily Word and pray until Nicki gets up, which is usually by 8 am., this is my daily weekday routine. But today I overslept; I didn't even hear the alarm go off for Wardell and I only have ten minutes before Nicki gets up. I go to the bathroom and climb back in bed and as I lay here I get that queasiness again and my mind goes back to Nye and how he was the one to keep this conflict with us fueled.

After High School graduation, I decided to work while attending Cosmetology School, I figured I could kill two birds with one stone; I would check out the shop life and get some first-hand information about the hair business. Reading about a subject is one thing, but hands on, now that's the real deal. I became the Salon Assistant at every Salon I worked. I was responsible for shampooing, wrapping, mixing colors with supervision and general housekeeping. The first shop I worked was for Jackie Cole. She was owner/ operator of, "The Hair Specialist," over on Broadway and East 18th Street and believe me, I learned a lot. When I started Cosmetology School in July, Nye went to work for one of the exclusive hotels downtown as a dishwasher and we hardly saw him. He would get home most nights a quarter to eleven, however, he had Sunday's off and never stopped playing for church and never missed a Sunday dinner.

Sunday nights when we were settled in our rooms, he would get on the piano and softly play. I stopped counting the times I pulled my covers back and placed my feet on the floor, prompted to run tearfully to him and hug my only brother, but instead I would sit on the edge of my bed and weep. My heart craving to go sit next to him and lay my head on his shoulder as he emptied his heart on those piano keys. But he started this mess! Oh, I'm crying now thinking about how pierced my heart would be hearing him play from his.

Some mornings Nye didn't leave for work until after 8 am and I would hear him in the kitchen talking and laughing with Mama. A few times I hurried into the kitchen just to find out what was going on in his life but several minutes after my presence was known by him, he would go completely silent. It took me a minute, but I figured out exactly what Nye was doing. He was shutting me completely out of his life, as if I had done something to hurt him or purposefully said something hurtful to or about him. The thought of him putting the blame on me for severing our relationship made me furious! I mean! So, I decided to wait until after he left the house before going into the kitchen. Just to let him know I could care less about what HE was doing. He can't shut me out because I could care less! Ump, that's me, care less Zinora Ruth AND; if Zinye Benjamin wants me to know what's going on in his life, he'd better walk up to me and tell me like he has some sense! He's the one who started this mess!..... Oh lay back down Ms. Pissed!

The week before our 18th birthday, April 21st, I finished my Cosmetology courses, and on our birthday Mama bought us an ice cream cake and we all toasted with bubbly Apple Cider to my finishing Cosmetology school. Nye only hit Mama's glass, I guess he didn't want to make it obvious not hitting my glass so he avoided Daddy's glass also. He didn't fool me one bit! After Cosmetology school, I went to work at, "Dontes' Kutz Above," a barber shop in Sugar Creek owned by Donte' Klugh. While waiting to take my test I worked at, "Hair that Moves," for Cherie Sanders, her salon is in North Blue Ridge. I left there and went to Lykins, MO and worked with Bianca and her husband Roberto, at, "Hair Dimensions." Then I went to North India Mound and worked for Miss Mabel Mayweather at, "Good Hair Days." When I passed my test I prayed for direction and decided to keep working and learning while saving my money until I felt it was the right time to go on my own. I prayed for confirmation as to when it would be the right timing for me, I need to move in the right season. I kept my mouth closed and ears open and believe me, I learned a lot.

The last Sunday in May, Memorial Day weekend, was when Wardell surprised me and officially asked me to marry him at dinner in front of my family. It had been a little over a year that we had known each other and he had a year left in college so he thought a year was enough time for us to prepare for our wedding.   After that Sunday, all of our conversations consisted mostly about us getting married the following year, it was so much to do. That was the day I met the whole Patterson family for the first time. After Wardell proposed he told Mama and Daddy he wanted his family to meet me, until then I was known as the girl that sang lead from Rose of Sharon COGIC church. He had informed his mother and father he was going to pop the question today and they insisted he bring me by and before he knew anything his Mother had all of his brothers and sisters and their kids coming over to meet me and congratulate us. Wardell invited Mama and Daddy to follow us to his parents and of course Nye was welcome to ride with us; we would probably be there for a few hours at the least.

I immediately looked at Daddy and he looked at Mama and after reading her face, he told us to go on, him and Mama would have his parents over one Sunday and break bread since it was official now I would become a Patterson. Daddy directed his eyes towards Nye and said, "Of course I can't speak for Nye." We all directed our attention to Nye and he squirmed a little in his seat and managed to look Wardell in the face and say, "Today is a special day for the both of you, I'll wait with Mama and Daddy to meet your parents, but thanks for the invite Wardell, I appreciate it." When he said the word appreciate; he almost choked from sentiment. I almost said something to him but I was choking from trying not to cry, the moment was so tender. Instead I looked at Nye and to my surprise he stood up as he told us he had to run. When he pushed his chair in, he looked at Wardell and sincerely said, "Wardell, Z could not have done better by my standards, congrats man." And he walked over to Wardell and gave him a good heartfelt hug.

Mama and I sat there sniffing and wiping our noses, we were so full of gratitude because we both knew Nye meant what he was saying. It was so moving I was rendered speechless as I watched him hug our parents and walk over to me and place his hand on my shoulder. I know Nye; he was fighting giving me a hug, I could just feel it! Oh why didn't I just grab and hug my brother while I had the chance. I couldn't move I was so full of emotion, the man I love wants me to spend the rest of my life with him and my brother actually physically touched me after not speaking a word directly to me in almost 2 years, I was speechless and motionless, I mean! We all sat there silent, and after the door closed from Nye's leaving, Daddy suggested Wardell and I get going; his family was probably waiting for us.

I didn't get nervous about meeting his family until we were walking up to the door. He took me inside the house through the side door after parking his 1994 Ford Focus under the carport. He grabbed my hand and told me to just be myself and they will love me just as he does, then he gave my hand a slight squeeze. I was so scared, the room was filled with Patterson's, wall to wall and the noise, my goodness! Kids were running chasing one another, laughter and music in the background, I had a flashback of when Nye and I were little and we visited Mama's side of the family and with Wardell holding my hand, it was like Nye holding my hand and so; I relaxed and fell in love with the whole Patterson clan. I mean!

Later that evening Wardell dropped me off at home and as soon as I walked in the kitchen door, I was startled because Mama was sitting at the kitchen table waiting for me and she asked, "Well, tell me all about your future in-laws." Then she pointed at the chair next to herself for me to have a seat. She was so excited and wanting me to describe Ma Patterson so she could remember what she looked like; it had been a while since the musical. At first I thought Mama was trying to see if I had really met Wardells' family and had stayed at his parents the whole time we were gone, but when she began asking me questions about Ma Patterson, I realized she really wanted to know what kind of woman Ma was. I pulled my chair in close to Mama and described everything; giving her a visual as if she were there.

We laughed and talked so, it was like having Nye to talk to and before I went to bed she told me that she was so glad to have me for a daughter and Wardell has shown he was properly raised by Christian parents and she was actually looking forward to meeting all of the Patterson's. Mama had water in her eyes as she said that to me. She realized she had watery eyes and told me that if she had ten daughters, she would still experience sorrow watching me walk away from her and into my own home. "Don't mind me Chile, you will have to have a daughter to understand this mixed feeling a mother gets knowing she has raised her daughter for someone else's son. Oh my lord, what am I going to do when Nye gets a wife and moves out, Oh for heaven's sake!" As she patted her eyes and waved her hand around, we laughed not knowing Mama was soon to find out what it was going to feel like to have Nye move out....

The 4th of July is when my parents met the Patterson's. Ma and Pops had a big bar-b-queue at their home and we were told to bring a dish that could feed at least twenty people so Mama decided to make her baked beans. I think she was nervous because she changed clothes three times before we left the house and she checked the beans twice in the car to make sure they weren't dried out. We all had a great time eating, playing games and eating some more and the karaoke was hilarious! When they started dancing, Mama and Daddy headed home, but not before telling Ma and Pops they had a ball; and they meant it because Daddy hasn't been that tickled in a long while. He doubled over at one point during the karaoke, laughing so hard; I mean!

Sunday, July 8th, while we were all sitting around having dinner and commenting on how tender and delicious the roast pork was; all of a sudden Nye loudly clears his throat, smiles real big and announced to us he had found an apartment in Coleman Highlands and would be moving out on the 31st. I gasped out loud and when everyone looked at me, I covered my mouth and stared at Nye as he held his stare back at me. It was so quiet you could hear the electricity humming from the refrigerator all the way in the kitchen and I kid you not, my heart sank; to think I would never see Nye again hurt me deeply. I felt as if the doctor had just told me I was going to die on July 31st. Wardell broke the silence when he said, "Nye, do you need a roommate, that's high rent district isn't it?" Nye smiled and said, "Thanks for being concerned Wardell, but I make good money and can afford it." Mama began stuttering as she looked over at Daddy while trying to get her words out, "Nye, honey, um, now, um, you must come to dinner on Sundays so we can know all of the great things happening in your life, yeah, we want to know what great things are happening."

Her voice began to crack and she looked at Nye as if she was never going to see him again. Her eyes quickly glanced back over at Daddy and she composed herself and continued speaking in a low tone that was apologetic, "Now I don't want you to think I'm babying you, being my only son and all, but, I, I mean, we love you so much and you've got to come to dinner; Okay?" Daddy interjects, "Son you can come home any time, not just Sunday's for dinner and I know we'll see you at church, right?" I'm looking at Nye the whole time Daddy is speaking to him, and he has a genuine smile on his face; he is really happy! He responds, "Ok, ok, I'll stop by just because, and definitely be here for Sunday dinners and believe me when I say I have no intensions of not attending church; the Lord has been too good to me. Besides, I'm just moving out of the house, not to another state, come on you guys!" Nye is laughing, I mean sincere heartfelt laughter, I haven't seen him do that in over 2 years and my heart is deeply warmed. Why did he have to start this mess!

He glances at me and gets this sneer on his face like, "Nah, nah, nah, nah, nah," But only towards me. Oh now I feel Ms. Pissed Completely Off waking up in me! What is this vendetta really about, and why does he insist on keeping it going with me? I looked at Wardell and opened my mouth to say something, anything and he kicked me under the table while shaking his head, 'NO'. Later when Wardell leaves, as we hug bye, he softly says in my ear, "Don't let him move out with this grudge, Zinora, just apologize." "I'll think about it." Was what I snapped back at him. I was definitely going to think about it alright! Nye started this mess, why should I be the one to apologize? Didn't I try to talk to him? Didn't I? Ugh!

Well, sure enough on Tuesday, July the 31st Nye had two movers come and put his bedroom furniture in a short moving truck. After I heard the doorbell ring I came out of my room and went into the kitchen where Mama was on the phone whispering to Daddy that the truck was really here. When she heard me enter the kitchen she told Daddy she would call him back later. She was wiping her face off with her apron and she was, as she would say; "Jittery as a runaway slave!" I stand watching her as she pulls out some of her odd dishes and pots and pans and as she places each piece on the counter, she wipes her eyes, looks at me and says, "Nye might need these." I began to blink back tears, feeling Mama's heart hurting. She would jump every time one of the men walked through the living room as she turned to see if they were done. She says, "Nye might need some cooking utensils and giving him some of these odd pieces would help him save a...." She stopped talking because her voice started trembling and she turned away from me and pulled out a Kleenex from her apron pocket and held it over her nose. I just stood completely still, unable to move.

Nye was walking back and forth showing them what to take as he put his clothes from his closet into his 89 Chevy Short Bed Pick-up. When I was able to move, I positioned myself in the kitchen by the back door so I could watch everything and noticed Nye glancing into the kitchen each time he re-entered the house. I could tell he was worried how Mama was taking his moving out. She smiled whenever she noticed Nye looking at her but she was wiping tears off her face when he wasn't looking. It only took the movers less than forty-five minutes to load up his things; and they were gone. It seemed like only a few minutes had passed when Nye slowly walked into the kitchen. He stood in the doorway looking at Mamas' back, waiting for her to turn around and face him.

He glanced up at me and I could see the pain so obviously written on his face; pain he knew he had caused our dear sweet humorous mother because he has chosen to grow up and move out of the house we grew up in. She wiped her face and looked up into my eyes and smiled as if to say, 'Okay, now it's time for me to be a big girl; watch and see how it's to be done.' As she slowly turned she made every effort to stand as straight as she possibly could and she placed a smile on her face as her arms automatically extended out to Nye. He slowly walked into our mothers loving embrace.

As I witnessed this historic event, I felt tears hit my blouse as Nye embraced her and closed his eyes. When he started speaking, I moved to stand in the kitchen doorway purposely just to see if as he left, he would apologize to me for the 2 years of torture he put me through by not speaking to me. But as he hugged Mama and said, "I love you so much, mere words can't express how much." His voice was beginning to crack and he quickly let go of Mama and spun around and when he saw me standing there I jumped because I was standing behind him crying. I gazed real deep into his eyes hoping, praying he'd ask for forgiveness because I wanted so terribly to hug him and say, "I love you too!" But he quickly turned to leave…out of the back door instead of walking pass me. As I lay here I am crying uncontrollably. Remembering the disappointment I felt watching him avoid me and thinking, 'that stubborn Nye, he started this mess! This is so ridiculous!'

I hear the pitter patter of Nicki's little feet coming my way so I rise up and look towards the door knob for her to appear. Sure enough she appears in the doorway peeking around the doorframe at me. We both break out with our smiles as she runs to me and jumps up on my bed I extend my arms out to her. As we hug she says, "lub you Mommy." Her words cause me to lose it and I hug her so tight. "Gotta potty." Is what she utters as she squirms to get lose from my embrace. I get up with her and we go into my bathroom for her to use. As she sits with feet dangling back and forth she asks, "What's matter mommy?" I stand in front of the sink looking at my beautiful little baby and realize she senses my pain and I wonder if love is equivalent to twin intuition. I get her hands washed and we get teeth brushed and faces washed and off to the kitchen we go for some Monday morning breakfast.

While Nicki climbs up into her high chair, I phone Mama to get my Monday morning update while I fix breakfast for the two of us. Um, Mama's not answering. The voice mail recording comes on so I leave a message. "I'm calling a little later than usual because I overslept. Call me when you get this message, love you bye." Wonder where she went this morning, probably to the supermarket.

After Nye and Von eloped; Mama and Mrs. Gibson became close while planning a wedding reception for them since they didn't have a wedding the family could attend. I was still living at home and every time Mama would come home from wherever she and Mrs. Gibson had gone shopping for the reception; I would sit at the kitchen table and listen as she gave me every detail as to what had happened.

The reception was at the Gibson's and I dropped by their house and stayed for about thirty minutes then left. I was so emotional and people would pause or double take when they looked me in the face and they'd stand in front of me staring. I knew they were thinking, 'She looks just like Nye but with acne.' The thought of my twin and only brother and I weren't speaking was constant the whole while I was there so, I quietly left.

After Nye and Von changed their membership from Rose of Sharon, Von would update Mrs. Gibson on everything happening with them, then Mama and Mrs. Gibson would talk every Monday morning and after they talked, Mama would call me with the update. Von had the twins three days after we left for our honeymoon so a week after Wardell and I returned from our honeymoon, I received a Monday morning call giving me the full blown details on all that had transpired while I was away. After Nicki arrived Mama waited for me to phone her on Monday mornings when it's convenient for me so I can keep in the loop of things going on with Nye and his family. I kinda know what Nye is doing through Mama.... This nonsense needs to end, I miss him so much lately and don't know why....sniff, I have become a crying mess since Sister Hamilton made her announcement, where are the tissues....

While Nicki and I eat our Malt-o-meal and toast; I take another trip down memory lane remembering the Sunday Wardell and I told my family we had set our wedding date. It was the last Sunday in August after Nye had moved out. I was working in the local salons and Nye was still washing dishes downtown. Nye and Wardell came over every Sunday for dinner and just before we finished eating I said, "Ok, you know we have been making plans to get married so... we've put our deposit down to reserve our wedding date. It will be held at the Intercontinental Kansas City Plaza and our wedding is set for next year, the last Saturday in June, the 24th."

As Mama stood up to come hug me, she smiled and said, "I knew something was up with you two, I'm so happy for you!" Daddy smiled and nodded his head as he looked at Wardell, he feels like the Lord put us together besides; we met like him and Mama; at a church musical. Nye pushed his seat out abruptly and slammed his napkin down on the table as if he were going to storm out of the house, but Daddy used his base voice and said, "Nye! Sit your butt back down. Your sister and soon to be brother-in-law just announced they're getting married and you are going to be polite AND HAPPY for her; do I make myself clear?" By now Daddy has both hands on the table and is half sitting and half standing as if he were in position to grab Nye if need be.

I could see the veins popping out on the side of Nye's neck and he closed his eyes for a few seconds to compose himself as he meekly says, "Yes sir." While his eyes moves from Daddy he plasters a fake smile on his face, and directs his eyes to me and politely nods as he says, "I wish you the best Z, and you too Wardell." After he turns to face Wardell, then he directs his attention right back towards Daddy as if for approval. I knew the smile was fake he can't fool me. But I play it off and reach across the table and grab Wardell's hand and look at Nye and give him a fake smile right back, while saying sarcastically, "Thank you Nye." Mama started asking all kinds of questions about what we had planned while Daddy, Nye and Wardell just sat there listening; well Daddy and Wardell anyway. I glimpsed over at Nye a few times and he still had that fake smile but his eyes never left the table cloth.

As Wardell was leaving, I walked him to the kitchen door and he asked, "Baby don't you think you need to talk to Nye; he's your twin, maybe he needs to feel included in our wedding; AND…. You need to be the one to make him feel that way, huh, what you think?" He takes his hand and slightly lifts my chin and looks me in the eyes then add, "Give it some thought ok?" After I let out a sigh, I tell him ok, but I'm thinking, 'Nye started this mess!' But I smile, kiss him on the cheek and tell him bye.

Oh yeah, it was on and crackin now! Nye made it clear to me he wanted nothing else to do with me and my life; he can fool everybody BUT ME! I know him because I'm part of him. So, whenever he'd show up at the house, I would close the door to my room. Sometimes he would sit at the piano and play, and I kid you not; my heart would ache so, it was hard for me not to run to him and hug him so tight neither one of us could hardly breathe, but I didn't do anything to him, so he should be the one to come running to me! In front of other people he was polite, but when we were alone he avoided eye contact with me altogether. On rare occasions when our eyes would meet; I saw the anger in his and it infuriated me because all I did was make a decision; huh, not my fault he's a dishwasher because he doesn't know what he wants to be!

"Mommy's trying?"   Nicki has finished her breakfast and now, as I look into her little brown eyes, I feel as if her eyes are reading the hurt in my heart. I'm sitting here at the breakfast table crying as I think about how much I miss my brother, what's wrong with me?

I push my seat back and reach my arms out to my precious baby and hug her so tight. Her little tiny hands are patting me on my back so lovingly to console me. I was finally able to collect my emotions. I seem to be out of sorts ever since Sister Hamilton made the announcement about our choir being invited to sing at Nye's church. Looking at my precious little joy, I'm reminded she'll be turning 3 on May 1st, and, even though she looks like me; she has Wardell's ways. The whole Patterson clan is kind hearted, loving and tender spirited people. That's why I love them so and my two personal Patterson's, oh how my heart throbs at the sight of either one of them.

I take her little hand and open it then bring it up to my face and tenderly kiss it. I close my eyes for a second and when I open them I notice how long her fingers are. I truly believe Nicki will be tall like Wardell's side of the family even though she was only 18 inches long at birth, and 8 pounds, she came into this world looking like a little hairy butterball to me. I am 5' 6"; caramel color skin with light brown colored eyes; real thick sandy brown hair and my eyebrows are so thick I have them threaded every 2 weeks. My only physical flaw is I have very serious acne. Both Nye and I had it when we turned twelve, his cleared up but I couldn't get rid of mine no matter what I used and trust me when I tell you Mama and Daddy spent a lot of money on my face. I mean! The only time it cleared was when I was pregnant with Nicki. After she was born, most of the acne reappeared and I kept five pounds from the pregnancy weight, but being 110 pounds instead of 105 isn't too bad. Besides, Wardell loves the extra hips on me.

He's number six of nine children and they are all by the same mother and father, which is rare these days. The Patterson's are a very close family and they are the first family I witnessed being balanced in their lives as Christians. Me being raised Pentecostal or a Holy Roller, all of my childhood; when I became a Patterson and spent a lot of time with them, I realized not every Baptist smoked on the church grounds, drink liquor and cussed. They dance a lot when they get together, but when you think about it; so do us Pentecostals, we just dance in church!

Wardell has five brothers; Linell Jr., Ronald, Clarence, Earl and Sheldon. His three sisters are; Aretha, Phoebe and Vedette. Earl, Sheldon and Vedette are younger than Wardell, as a matter of fact, Sheldon is the baby in his family and he's 3 months older than I am and we all get along well. They all treat me like a sister and my mother-in-law, Denise; introduces me as her daughter-in love. When she makes her 3 and 4 way calls on the phone, I answer, "Yes Ma," right along with my sister in-laws. Yes indeed, my Patterson family is very loving and supportive of me and Wardell.

All of the Patterson children are tall like Mrs. Patterson. She's tall and heavyset now and Mr. Patterson is about 2 feet shorter than her, but neither one of them is bothered by it. His face still lights up when she enters the room, even after 33 years of marriage: I think that's wonderful!   Ronald, Wardell and Sheldon are dark skinned like Mr. Patterson. Phoebe is light skinned like Mrs. Patterson and the rest of his siblings are mocha brown, and they all have dark almost black colored deep set eyes with thick eyebrows. Nicki's eyebrows are a combination of mine and her Uncle Sheldon. They almost run together, there is very little space between their brows without hair. And, it's amazing how strong Mr. Patterson's genes are, all of the males are muscular and bowlegged like their father. All of the females are tall and thin like Ma Patterson was when she was young. All of my sister-in-loves have Ma Patterson's beautiful thick hair and pretty smooth skin. Hopefully Nicki will take after the Patterson females and won't have to live with this acne. She already has their loving, compassionate disposition. And I thank the Lord for that!

On Monday and Tuesdays after breakfast, I walk Nicki around the corner to our neighborhood park. So I clear the table and take the pork chops out of the freezer to thaw and Nicki and I head to my room.   She jumps up on my bed and watches the Christian learning channel while I get showered and dressed. After I'm ready, we go to get Nicki bathed and dressed, I grab our jackets and off we go. While sitting on the bench waiting for my baby to enjoy her play time, this car drives by with music blasting and it makes me think about growing up with Nye.

There were so many times Nye and I would be in our bedrooms doing homework and out of the blue he would go into the living room and start playing the intro to Tramaine Hawkins, 'Changed,' to get me to come out of my room. That was MY song! I believe I memorized the words in fifteen minutes when I first heard it, and for the next few months that song was all I sang. Every time I would sing it with the choir, the whole church would be moved. Nye knew that song touched my soul when I sang it and every so often he'd be playing a medley of songs and when he wanted me to come and sit with him, all he had to do was start playing the intro to 'Changed' and I would appear by his side. I miss him so much and for some strange reason, today seem to have me melancholy about my big brother....oh my goodness! I can't seem to stop the tears, what's wrong with me; man I feel queasy!

I reach into my purse to get a tissue and when I look up, I notice this van with Pet Grooming advertisement on it. That reminds me of the last Sunday in September, after we set the date for our wedding. It was the day before I put my deposit down on my shop; that was the Sunday the whole Gibson family joined Rose of Sharon Holiness Church. Mr. Walter Gibson, his wife Shelia and their four children; Yvonne, Richard, Kirk and Brian, had just moved to Kansas City, Missouri. Mr. Gibson had just moved his family here from St. Louis. He briefly testified after joining, about having just accepted the position on Thursday, becoming Assistant to the KC Insurance Commissioner. His daughter, 18, had just graduated High School and wanted to pursue a career in Radiology. Before service started, I was in the back choir room; by then I was singing in both choirs. Mama said she hadn't long sat down on her pew and gotten herself situated when she saw the reaction on Nye's face; as though he had been struck by lightning the moment he laid eyes on Yvonne.

Nye had been playing piano for the 8 am service at Praise Tabernacle Church for several months to fill in until they found a Minister of Music to replace their last one.   He would leave Praise Tabernacle and rush to our church to play the organ for the 11 am services. At that time Nye was Minister of Music for our Junior Choir at Rose of Sharon and when they weren't singing he would let Mama take a break from playing the organ. Of course he had his rush on as he entered the sanctuary after coming from Praise Tabernacle. Mama said when he entered onto the platform, she watched him as he walked to the organ scanning the crowd and when he saw Yvonne, he did a double take and the look on his face made her say aloud, "uh oh!" She turned around to see who had captivated her son. Nye couldn't keep his eyes off her.

Two months later, they eloped and, 8 months later their twins arrived, Rachel and Rebecca who are 3 years old and will be turning 4 on June 27. I've never seen them in person, nor have I had the privilege of holding and kissing them, I have only seen their beautiful pictures. In fact, I had some pictures of my own made from Mama's and they are displayed in our family room on the fireplace mantle.

Don't you know Mr. Gibson was furious with Nye for turning his only daughter's head from Radiology Technician courses to a wedding chapel in Las Vegas, Nevada? I believe Mama's exact words were, "Chile; he was HOT under his collar!"   By thanksgiving, Nye and Yvonne had changed their membership to Praise Tabernacle. Yvonne told her parents they decided to change membership because Nye plays piano there. But Mama said the real reason they changed membership is because Nye was growing tired of Mr. Gibson's snide remarks every time they all spent time together. Nye told Daddy he didn't want to disrespect Yvonne's father but Yvonne has asked her father to stop disrespecting her husband but Mr. Gibson continued to bring up their elopement. Daddy told Nye he understood how he felt as a man, and changing membership was a wise move, he should never disrespect his wife's parents, ever. He also told Nye to run his own house like the man he was; and show Mr. Gibson he loves his daughter by actions, not by exchanging empty words.

Here comes my baby, running and smiling to her "mommy, mommy." I reach out and lift her up into my arms and she grabs my neck so tightly, I felt warm tears run down my face. Her hug reminds me of Nye, and how we used to hug one another so tight, we could hardly breathe.

"ZINYE"

As I slide out of bed trying not to disturb Von, I start praying in the spirit. She needs all the rest she can get being pregnant. The girls keep her busy from the time she opens her eyes in the morning, until she closes them at night. I'm blessed to have a wonderful wife and she's such a great Mom. Being an only daughter, I thought she may be a little spoiled. Turns out my wife is attentive to those she holds dear in her heart. Oh yes, I truly found my good thing when I found Yvonne, thank You Jesus! I start back praying in the spirit.

I leave the bathroom and quietly head to the family room so I can meditate on scripture. I need guidance with this musical. The theme is from Psalm 34:3 **"Oh, magnify the Lord with me, And let us exalt His name together."** It's important to me that the music line up with the theme so I'm seeking Holy Spirit as to what songs need to be sung so He can minister to every heart that will attend. I'm not just praying for our choirs music, but that each church choir represented will be lead also by the spirit as to what songs to sing. I take being minister of music very serious.... I wonder if Z will sing a solo, my sister can blow. She has had a voice since we were very young. As a matter of fact, I remember her humming when we were very small. I have always loved to hear her hum, sing, whatever melody comes out of her mouth, I love hearing her. She has an anointing like none other I have witnessed. Lord, I miss my sister....... Who in the world is at the door this early in the morning?........... Mama!

As she enters the front door, she says, "Von asked me to come over this morning at 7:45, am I too early?" In comes two giggling girls. "Granma Rustin!" Is being yelled by them as they run up to Mama. While Mama hugs her grand daughters, Von enters the room and says how sorry she was for oversleeping, and for Mama to have a seat while she gets cleaned up. As she leaves the room the girls follows their Mom and I invite Mama into the kitchen for some coffee. She says tea is her preference so, I get her the herbal teas and honey and we converse while waiting for the Rustin ladies to get presentable. Von wants to tell Mama she's pregnant in a one-on one setting. Her pregnancy with the twins was a little awkward being we had to hurry and get married. This pregnancy is different, we have no shame nor embarrassment attached with this baby and we are looking forward to its arrival.

If I had my way, my daughters would have an older brother to protect them, but I'll take a healthy son and believe me, I will teach him how to protect his sisters. Wow, I feel myself smiling as I think of having a son. Mama is asking me, "Nye, have you considered calling Z?" She gently cups my chin while gazing into my eyes. Her warm, soothing smile appears on her beautiful face. My Mama, what can I say about her? She has beauty that exudes from her heart and filters through her soul. I can't say a word, I'm so captivated by the love I feel from her. After I soak up her love, I'm able to talk.

"Mama, Z does not want anything to do with me. If she did, she would have called me a long time ago. She has made it clear to me she has her own life and there's no room for me in it." "Nye, baby, do you hear yourself?" As she gives me a bear hug, in comes my three gals. Von says, "Mama Rustin, I am so sorry to keep you. I am usually awaken by your son, but today of all days he decides to let me sleep." She reaches towards Mama and gives her a hug. Now the girls go stand on Mama's side, after her and Von hugs. Rebecca is first to hug and kiss her grandma. Wow, I really am blessed. No hateful in-laws in our family. Mama and Daddy both love Von as if she were their daughter. I wonder how she and Z would get along.

Yesterday, while Von and I were getting dressed, she told me she was going to tell Mama she was pregnant. She told her mother the day before and knowing her mother can not hold water long, well, she wants to be the one to tell my mother she's going to be a grandmother again.

Von and Mama are pulling out pots and pans so I Kiss Von and ease into my office. I'll let them do their thang. I have not been able to get Z out of mind these last few days. I keep reminiscing times of our childhood. This twin thing is so strong. I'm reminded of how I protected my little sister like it was the most natural thing to do. Now I'm smiling again. Remembering an incidence of my being valiant. We hadn't started elementary school yet so I'm guessing we were about four years old and this particular day at church was like most services. Z and I were standing in the isle bouncing to the music while watching the grown ups dance in the Spirit. All of a sudden this boy, Tareek Hobson, runs up between Z and myself, and pushes her as hard as he could. I stood there watching my little sister back stroking, trying to catch herself from hitting the hard floor and as I watched her, something in me rose up. I clearly heard, "Hit him hard so he'll know she has someone to protect her."

I walked up to him and pushed him as hard as I could. He barely moved and it was then I realized he was much bigger than I. I had to bring him down. So, I took my foot and kicked him as hard as I could in the knee. That brought him down. I grabbed him by his shirt and told him he had better not ever hurt my little sister again. One of the Church Mothers, Mother Benson, grabbed me by my shirt collar and told me fighting was not godly! I thought, 'Where were you when he pushed my little sister!' I walked over to Z and as I hugged her, I asked if she were alright. She had such a worried look on her face as she told me,

"I'm just glad he didn't hurt you. Nye he is so big!" I told her, "Nobody, big or small pushes my sister, nobody!" Oh how I miss my sister. I think I'm getting teary eyed, man oh man.   Von is calling me to breakfast.

After we eat, I am instructed by my lovely wife to take the girls into the family room so the woman to woman talk can began. I did as I was instructed.

"Zinora"

As Nicki and I walk back to the house, I start reminiscing again... I felt confident that Holy Spirit was leading me to put the deposit down on the building for my shop. I had looked all over and the best deal was an older stand-alone building that had lots of character and in a good location, what was wrong with the building was its age, it was very old. I figured all it needed was a bright color trim on the outside to attract attention to it and, if I gave the inside a few coats of funky colored paint, some bright pictures and grandeur accessories, then Walla! I felt like I was ready to take, "Beauty by Zinora" off paper and make it tangible. I had worked with the best in KC and watched, listened and learned all I could, besides, people in this business tend to be tight lipped with giving you any information; I guess they're worried of more competition, like me.

The building had been vacant for several years and the rent was inexpensive. Daddy helped me negotiate the lease to make sure all electrical, plumbing and major maintenance repairs for the duration of the lease would be paid by the owner and not me. Wardell offered to help me when I had business issues to tend too, and told me where I could purchase used books to read up on that would help me know and understand the basics to running a business. So after studying up, I wasn't too nervous about opening my own shop, just excited.

I filled the paperwork out for the lease and took my cashier's check to the management company that Monday morning after the Gibson family joined church and I was told someone would phone me in a few days with the date I could pick the keys up. Two days later I get a phone call and I'm so excited because it's the management company. The young lady goes through the formalities of introducing herself and commences to ask me which property was my deposit for; the building in Beacon Hill or Coleman Highlands. I was startled at first and asked why she thought I had applied for a building in Coleman Highlands and she replied, "We have two applications; one in Zinye Rustin and one in Zinora Rustin. One deposit for a salon in Beacon Hill and the other for a barber shop in Coleman Highlands.   I only have copies of the deposits and need to know which cashier's check goes with what property; are you Mrs. Rustin?" I felt like I had been stun gunned, Nye was opening a Barber Shop! The young lady had to ask me again before I could answer, I was just that befuddled.

After my conversation with her, I went to the nearest store and purchased a newspaper and eagerly scanned the fictious name section and there was Nye's ad; Kutz by Ziggy; with scissors used to draw the letter 'K'. I folded the paper so the address was visible, and drove over to check it out. Talk about upper scale! This strip mall was painted in purple, green and gold and you had to wait for a parking space. I noticed the, "For Rent" sign in the window smack in between a sandwich shop and a pet store; 'um, Nye was smart to pick that spot.' As I left headed back to the house, I was asking myself; when did he go to Barber College, and why has he kept what he's doing such a secret? I decided to talk to Mama later to pick her brain, my, my, my; Nye a barber. I wonder did he copy me or did he have the same confirmation and wanted us to go into business together? Maybe that's what made him so upset, the fact no one asked him what the Lord had revealed for him to do or, maybe he got upset with me because I never asked him if he wanted to go into business together. Well, if he were speaking to me maybe, just maybe I could have asked! You know what, it really doesn't matter; all he had to do was say something! He started this mess… alright Ms. Pissed, calm all the way down….

Later that evening I started dinner for Mama; she had set out the ground turkey and tomato paste so I knew she planned on meatloaf tonight. I had just put it into the oven when she walked in the kitchen door. While we hugged I asked, how her day was and she told me she'd had better days. I asked, "Mama, did you know Nye went to Barbering School?" "No baby he's never said anything about Barbering School, and what makes you think he's attended?" I sat at the kitchen table and told her everything I knew. I even handed her the newspaper so she could see for herself. We discussed how evasive Nye had become and it was then Mama told me the conversation Daddy had with him when we were 17.

She said her and Daddy both thought Nye would see how childish he was handling this matter and that would be the end of it. "No one ever imagined he would make a full fledge vendetta out of it; especially when considering how close you two were." The night Daddy asked Nye what exactly was eating at him, Nye told Daddy that I had closed him out. He said that I started keeping things from him, like I didn't want him to know what it was I was doing. He thought I was in competition with him, so after a considerable amount of assessment, he thought it best to let me do my own thing. Perhaps we were too close sharing our every thought with each other and it was time for us to grow up and have our own separate lives. Daddy asked if he was angry with me and Nye told him no, on the contrary; he was happy for me. When daddy asked Nye had the Lord given him any direction about his future, he said Nye paused for a long while, and when he spoke he thought his voice trembled like he wanted to cry, but Nye looked him in the eyes and said, "No Daddy; I haven't heard one word."

I straight out told Mama that I thought Nye was upset at me because I had heard from the Lord first. He has always felt because he's the oldest, he should be the first in everything and I was expected to follow him like I had all of our childhood. This time, little sis heard first, and it made him mad! I couldn't believe Nye would twist this thing on me, no wonder Daddy let him act like he did and never made him apologize to me like he did when were little. Once again, Ms. Furious took the wheel and I gladly let her!

Chapter Four

I Wish
Discovering Nicki's talent!

Well, we have made it home and now it's time for soup & sandwiches and Nicki's nap. She's running down the hall screaming, "Gotta go pee, pee!" I run behind her, as I step into her bathroom unzipping my jacket, she makes it to the front of the toilet. The look on her little face tells me, she didn't make it in time. Her little eyes got so big! Now she's starting to cry. I get on one knee and as I remove her clothing I tell her that it's alright, she had an accident then I start a little bath water. She hates being wet, that's why it was so easy to potty train her. Once she's completely naked, she smiles and claps her little hands, she loves baths. We go into her room and pick out an outfit for her to put on and she smiles so big and runs back to the bathroom; she can't wait to get into the tub. After I mop up her accident I close the top to the 'throne' and take a seat. I'll watch her as she plays in the water for a bit. She's so engrossed in her bath; I take another trip down memory lane.

November 9th, was the Thursday I opened up my shop and it was GREAT! We scheduled our Grand Opening for February 9th, and that was even more successful. There are 4 of us in the shop and each one of the operators knows their stuff, and, is very confident doing it! Nate; 24 and our Barber, works Thursday through Saturdays and it is standing room only when he's there. Sherry, 29, and Le Shell, 21 and both of them love doing hair just as I do and most

Tuesdays you will find Sherry in the shop and almost all day. She has a son; Anton 9 years old, and being a single parent her older sister, Tawana helps her with him. Their arrangement works out for the both of them because Tawana has 3 sons of her own and their ages are; 12, 7 and 5. Because the sisters live close to each other there are no problems. Le Shell or "Shell" as we call her cuts and styles as if her life depends on it! She attends all of the big hair shows and keeps us abreast of the latest styles. Yeah, I must brag to say we have an exceptional and great team; and, we are like family. I am so fortunate to have them.

The beauty supply where I get supplies from is not too far from Nye's shop, so I kinda go out of my way and drive by his shop at least twice a week; just to keep an eye on him. I guess driving by is my way of being connected to my only brother. I really don't know why I do it, but somehow driving by his shop makes me feel like I'm not totally out of his life. He so happened to have opened his shop three weeks after we did, and the following month after our Grand Opening in March, was his grand opening. I have to give it to him; he included a local radio station just as we did but instead of the station being set up near the front door, he had them set up at the end of the parking lot and judging by how crowded his shop was; it looked to have been a great success.

I miss him so much and I'm really happy for his success, however, I feel as though we could have collaborated, but I guess Nye is right about one thing; and that is we needed to grow up and learn how to be separate individuals; he is not my twin sister but my brother; and we are different. I just wish I could talk to him, you know; he understands me like no one else does and… sometimes I just want to look into his eyes and see that affectionate "Yeah; I know what you're feeling," look in them. Nothing has to be said, there's that look. I guess if you're not a twin, it's hard to describe the feeling of oneness you share, I don't know how else to say it; but I sure do miss my brother….

"Mommy I pinish." Were the words that ended my memory lane trip; Nicki is finished. I wash her up and watch her as she gets dressed. These days she demands independence and it's easier to watch and suggest than to have whining contests with her. Watching her struggle to get her sock on, I remember Mama sharing with Nye and me about when we were toddlers and learning to become independent. She told us stories of how we didn't want anyone to help us do anything, however it was natural for us to help each other. Nye had a hard time with getting shirts over his head and Mama said I would stop whatever it was I was doing and help him by pulling the bottom of his shirt down just enough to get his shirt pass his eyes, and then I would leave him to figure out the rest. I had difficulty with buttons and Nye would make sure all of them were done before getting back to whatever it was he was doing. She said sometimes she would sit and watch us in amazement; we were almost one child split in two the way we would finish each other's tasks and without saying a word.

As I glance at my watch, I figure I had better help Nicki with her other sock so she can get an hours nap in. After we finish getting the Lil Kitten dressed, we go into the kitchen and have Chicken Noodle soup and half of a Turkey and Provolone Cheese sandwich for lunch. Now Nicki is yawning and rubbing her eye which is her queue for, "I'm ready for my nap now." I get her face and hands washed and she runs straight into her room and picks up the hot pink notebook off her table set and she stands there looking at me with the most precious smile while her tiny little dimpled fingers clutch onto the notebook. Her face is lit up and I don't have the heart to tell her there will be no bedtime story today, so I give out a long sigh and take the notebook from her little hands as she bounces up onto her bed.

This hot pink notebook holds a nicely written story her Aunt Phoebe wrote for her. Phoebe presented it to Nicki at her 2nd birthday party. The story is about a little African- American girl that moved from her house in South Dakota, to Kansas City Mo., with her mother and father to live with her Granma. Phoebe writes children's stories for each of her nieces and nephews. Each book is titled the niece or nephew's name, for instance this notebook is titled, "Emoni Moves to Grandma's House". The story takes you through the move, but through the eyes of 4 year old Emoni. As soon as I finish reading the second page of, "Emoni Moves to Grandma's House," the phone rings and it's Vedette on the line. She tells me that Clarence's birthday is next week and we will be celebrating him turning the big 3-Oh this Saturday, at the Myer Street den; her parents house, and for us to bring the juice and pop.

When Ma and Pops Patterson celebrate at their home, we all potluck, and because Wardell and I work late on Saturdays, we bring the juice boxes for the little ones and twenty-five of the 2 liters of soda pop for the adults. When we celebrate holidays I usually take baked beans or a Banana Pudding. Pops, Clarence and Wardell love my old fashioned cooked on top of the stove Banana Pudding, and I need a few days' notice to whip it up. I told her we will be there after 6pm, and I will be sure to drop off the juice and soda pop at Ma's on Friday evening.

I returned to Nicki's room to find her asleep, looking like an angel. As I placed the light blanket over her, I couldn't help but think of Nye. He would always fall asleep before me and I always placed cover of some sort over him, a jacket, blanket or a few times my robe as I just covered Nicki. Tears are flowing from my eyes now; I really am missing him a lot these days. I wonder why? And what's with this queasiness….

I go into the kitchen to call Mama before starting dinner. She picks up on the second ring sounding winded, as if she has been running to answer the phone. "Hello Mrs. In the streets early on Monday morning." I jokingly say to her. "Well, hello to you, Mrs. So busy you can't phone your Mama at the usual time," was her swift reply. "Mama I overslept this morning you know I wouldn't let anything stop me from getting my Monday update." She laughed and told me to sit down because it was good and juicy today!

As I pulled out a chair from the kitchen table, I asked what had happened that was so juicy and she asked if I were sitting down, and I told her yes. "Well, I'm going to be a grandmother again, Yvonne is expecting! She called me yesterday and told me to come over this morning for breakfast and while we had tea, she told me she had a surprise for me, and after a few sips of tea, I was informed of the good news." Mama's voice is beginning to tremble, she's so happy she can cry. "Oh 'Z', I'm so happy to be able to see more fruit of my womb. Maybe this will be their son, a man child to carry the Rustin name on. Oh thank you Jesus, more righteous seed in our family." I sit here with tears in my eyes. I am so happy for Nye, becoming a father again. I know how much he loves his family; I can see it in all of the pictures. He has such a deep love in every smile, and the way he gazes upon Yvonne; is pure love and admiration for her. I say, "Mama, I'm so happy for Nye and Von, and, I'm in agreement with you that this one will be a man child to carry on the Rustin name, Oh, what a blessing!" The only sounds to be heard now are sniffles as Mama and I shed tears of joy.

My heart is aching so for a hug from Nye right now. I close my eyes and remember how it felt to be hugged by my only brother, and I began sobbing. Mama asks, "Z; baby are you alright?" As I try to collect myself, I let out a trembling, "Yes, Mama, I'm ok. I really miss Nye a lot these days. For some strange reason I've been melancholy since yesterday when the church announced our choir will be singing at Praise Tabernacle Church May 19th." Mama says to me, "Z, why don't you be the one to call Nye, you know how stubborn he can be. This has gone on too long, baby; just call him, I'll give you the number." Before I could think; I said, "Ok Mama, let me get a pen." I went to the counter and retrieved a pen from the cup of pens and tore off a post it and I sat back down at the kitchen table and wrote Nye's phone number down. Crying as I jotted every number. It seemed something was breaking off me at every stroke of the pen. I thanked Mama and clicked the phone to, "off". I sat in that chair and cried like a new born baby!

My mind goes back to the last time Nye spoke directly to me, at my wedding. I was running late because we were told by the Hotel we could only have 1 hour before the ceremony due to us renting the facility for 6 hours. I didn't think it would be a big deal considering I was going to arrive at the hotel already dressed.   The wedding ceremony was scheduled for 2pm, and when Mama, Daddy and I left the house at ten minutes after one; I knew I was going to be late. I had plenty of time at 6:30 that morning but where the time went puzzles me to this day. How can you go from plenty of time, straight to being late in no time at all? I mean!

When we arrived at the Hotel Daddy parked in valet, and as soon as the man opened my door I took off running. When I hit the lobby opening, I had to slow down and get a better grip on my dress and while I was slightly turning towards the hall leaded to the Ballroom, I heard this familiar voice say, "Hi Z". I turned my head just as Nye placed the most warm and loving smile on his face and continued, "Wow, you look beautiful, stunning, amazing!"   I slowly turned my whole body towards him and Von as the biggest, brightest smile I could ever have appeared on my face. He looked like a proud big brother and I stood staring into his face and felt the sincerity of his words in my heart. I almost ran to him for a hug, but I remembered I was running late; so I raised my hand and waved at them and said, "Hi, thanks so much Nye. That really means a lot to me." I thought my heart would burst because at that moment I forgot about the distance that had been between us. I felt tears of joy coming up and thought, 'Oh forget it I'm getting my hug.'   When I pulled on my dress and turned headed towards Nye and Von; I heard Mama say, "10 minutes Z, you need to go left." Her and Daddy were behind me walking as brisk as they could.   I blew Nye and Von a kiss and quickly turned left, toward the Ballroom and I took off running again.

The wedding started on time and I was so nervous. The ceremony was absolutely beautiful and the spirit of the Lord was obviously in attendance, everything turned out perfect! Later, in the Ballroom, as we all sat to eat, I glanced over at Nye and Von and noticed how attentive he was to her. When he glanced up at me, I flashed him a smile, but he had that old too familiar distant glare in his eyes; as if he were looking *at* me, however, he really didn't see me. I was disappointed we were back to playing the distance game again, but I thought, 'You know, he's the one who started this mess, so let it be the way he wants it to be; let it go Z, you have your own life now, just let it go!' Later, before leaving to take Von home, he came over by us and gave a general, "Bye everyone, I need to take Von home. It was good to get her out of the house; however carrying twins is a load on her." I watched him hug Mama and the next thing I saw, was him gently holding Von's elbow as she very slowly wobbled towards the exit.

Today I find out Nye is going to become a daddy again, and I am so happy for him and Von. Like Mama, I hope this one is a boy. The twins look like Von to me, but I've only seen pictures of them, and wish I could hug and kiss their beautiful little fat cheeks. Hopefully this baby will look like Nye. Oh my goodness, why am I crying so much? I get up to go to the bathroom and as I walk down the hall to the master bedroom I notice myself in the vertical full length hall mirror. I realize my face looks like I don't have any pimples. I stop crying and stand in front of the mirror and I take a lengthy appraisal of my face. I have fewer pimples around my forehead where usually there are clusters. I start to think, 'Ok now Z, you've been queasy, crying easily and now your face is getting clear. Think! When was your last cycle?"

I'm trying to remember as I head for our bathroom; I go straight to the face bowl and open up the medicine cabinet mirror and as I look up, directly into the mirror, I realize; I am pregnant!

I place both my hands on my face and closely examine the areas that are now smooth places. I can see the dark discolored spots now showing where there once were pimples and a big wide smile appears…now tears are rolling down my face as I stare at my image in the mirror. The same day I find out Nye is expecting his third baby; I think I'm pregnant with my second. Lord, we are still connected, and that's why I've been missing him so much. I need to call him and apologize for whatever I've done to make him think this vendetta is needed.

I go into the kitchen and get the post it with his number then I pick up the phone to dial. As soon as I hit the "talk" button I think, 'What if Nye doesn't want to talk to me? What if he is so wrapped up with his life now that he has a family; he doesn't have space for me now?……' I quickly click the, "Off " button and slam the phone down on the table and think to myself; 'He's the one who started this mess! He should be the one to clean it up!'   After I come from the bathroom I decide to start dinner and settle in my mind that as soon as Nicki wakes, I'm going to drive to the nearest drugstore and get a pregnancy test and take it as soon as we get back. I can't believe I'm pregnant! Well ….. Nicki will be turning 3 in less than two months, so I guess that's enough space between her and her brother or perhaps sister. Man, I wonder what it would be like to have a son. Wardell will probably love it!   I had an easy pregnancy with Nicki so hopefully I'll have an easy pregnancy with this one.

While the pork chops are smothering, I get the potatoes out and start peeling them and my mind drifts again. I loved having a big brother and it's too bad Nicki will have to be the big sister and I really don't have a clue as to what it's like to be an older, or big sister. Looks like both Nicki and I will have to learn how to do that role, or, maybe this baby will be another girl, um, now that would be nice, having two daughters, just like Nye does.   Now that I have the potatoes ready to be boiled later, I place the spinach and corn into skillets so I can fry the corn and sauté the spinach later. As I place covers on everything, I remember where our baby pictures are and head for the office and as I pass Nicki's room, I glance in at her.

I decide to sneak a kiss from her. I tip toe to my baby's bed and stand there gazing at her. She is so beautiful to me, lying there looking like an angel so full of innocence and beauty at the same time. Ahh, I think I'm ready for another little one, and I really don't care if it's a son or daughter. I'm going to love whatever gender it will be. I just pray for a healthy, normal baby. Man I wonder what Wardell is going to think about another baby. I bend over and kiss our Lil

Kitten and as I straighten myself up, I run my hand across her soft cheek and tears began to flow from me.

All I see is Nye in my mind, we have never loved on each other's babies and here we are getting ready to experience parenthood again, and, at the same time or at least close to it. I slowly walk into the office, right to the book with our baby pictures and a frame with our baby pictures. I head to the family room while zeroing in on the pictures that are in a double frame, the ones of Nye and I and I study our facial features.   When I get the pictures of my beautiful nieces I sit down on the sofa and look closely at the resemblances; I can't believe this! Both Rachel and Rebecca have our shaped eyes. I remember Mama telling us that when we were babies, we both had a few strands of curly light brown hair on the top of our heads and people thought I was a boy until my hair finally grew longer than Nye's. She told us people were always complimenting her on our eyes, maybe because they're light brown like Mama's and slanted like Daddy's. I'm sitting here with tears in my eyes and a big smile on my face, like some pregnant lady. Do I really need to take a test?

I hear Nicki's feet hit the wood floors, and she's off to the bathroom. I sit the pictures aside on the sofa and head to my baby's aide. She sits there, feet dangling and the warmest smile ever seen on an angels face! "Lub you Mommy." "Mommy loves you too." We exchange dialogue as I assist her. While we wash her hands Nicki looks up at me and asks, "Mommy can me hab a tister?" I'm taken aback for a second and realize she must sense my being pregnant, so I smile at her, dry her little hands and lift her to my hip and say, "Would it be okay if you have a brother?" As she wrinkles her cute little nose, she says, "No!" And shakes her head no, "tister." I ask, "Baby, what's wrong with having a brother, aren't brothers' fun?" She pauses for a minute and very seriously says, "Bayan mean Mommy, I want tister, peas, Mommy peas." I laugh and hug her so tight, Bayan, as she calls her cousin; Jaylen, is also two years old and will be turning three in August. Tagging him with the word rambunctious; is really putting a mild description on him. He's the youngest male cousin and his older brother, Jared, is five and Jaylen mimics his older brother quite a bit these days.

I get her shoes and sweater on, make sure all the eyes are off on the stove and off we go to the nearest drugstore to confirm her having a sibling, lord I hope she gets her wish. I hate to admit it but both Wardell and I have spoiled Nicki. I can't help it, she is so sweet, and sometimes I look at her and see myself, and, what can I say, it's like I feel what she feels and give in to her wishes. I know I need to say, "No" to her more often, but honestly, it's so hard for me too.

I remember when Nye and I were small and Daddy would say to Mama, "Baby, you are going to have to grow some tough skin and paddle them, don't let them run this house, Unie, baby, can we agree to that?" Then he would hug her. Mama always had tears in her eyes when she scolded us. When I was pregnant with Nicki she told me so many stories of how it was rearing Nye and I, mostly stories of our infancy and toddler days. Most times we laughed about what she told me, but now, since Nicki has arrived, I can really relate to Mama, we mothers just have a bond with our babies and it's so hard to separate ourselves from that maternal attachment. Guess that's why the Lord provided a male to be in the house, otherwise all children would grow up to be spoiled brats.

Wardell is most likely to explain to Nicki why she cannot have nor do something instead of just outright saying, "No" to her. I guess it has to do with his upbringing. Ma Patterson still to this day will take her time and explain why her grandchild should or should not do something, and she explains it in a way that makes plenty logical sense, like Wardell does his Lil Kitten. She always hugs her grandchildren whenever they get scolded by one of us parents. There's one thing Ma and Pops Patterson both believe in; and that is for the parents to discipline their own children. Pops says; and I might add, loud enough for everyone to hear; "If you don't want the police to beat em, you'd better beat em yourself!" Both Ma and Pops will tattle tale before they themselves will do the disciplining.

Wardell told me that while growing up, Pops did the majority of the discipline in their house and they were all okay with it because he would whip them and that would be the end of the matter. His mother however, would fuss, whip, fuss, punish and whip some more. It took her a while to work up a whipping, but he said when she got there she was all the way there. They would go around the house singing Mc Fadden & Whiteheads "Ain't no stopping her now!"

Personally, I can't see Ma whipping anybody, fussing yeah, but raising her hand to a child, I can't see it, and she is so patient. When it comes to her grandchildren, she stands a few feet away from you while you do the dirty work, and after you scold, she comes right behind you and says to them, while rubbing their arms lovingly, "Now, now baby, it's for your own good. Tell grandma you won't do that again, okay?" Then she wipes their tears away and smiles at them before hugging them. Also, I can honestly say that I have never seen her make a difference with any of her grandchildren; she loves them all just like she loves her children. Sometimes Phoebe and Aretha talk about how Ma spoiled Sheldon, being the baby and all, but I have never noticed it, she loves and I think spoils them all, no wait, 'US' all. Now Pops, that's a whole different ballgame altogether!

He is a loving and gentle man when it comes to all of us, but, he has an essence about him when he interacts with the males. You get the feeling they respect him and his opinions. I remember at our wedding reception, just before we left headed to the airport, Wardell took me by the hand and we walked all over that ballroom, looking for his father. We found him sitting with his grandchildren, one on each knee and he was bouncing them and smiling so proudly. There was a line of jumping grandkids, yelling, "Do me next Granddad." As soon as he saw us standing there, he told the kids to give him a rest for a few minutes he had to talk to Uncle Wardell. He looked Wardell in the eye and said, "Son, let me talk to you alone for a minute." He nodded at me and stepped away and Wardell dropped my hand, turned to me and told me, "Wait here, I'll be right back." I thought his father was upset or something so I watched them. Pops stood up against the wall and he said something to Wardell, Wardell shook his head yes, Pops said something else, again Wardell shook his head yes. Pops stepped up to Wardell and hugged him, stepped back, looked at Wardell, said something else and nodded. Wardell turned to face me and had the biggest smile on his face, he hugged Pops and almost ran to me, he grabbed my hand and whisked me away, to begin our lives together still smiling.

While we were on the airplane holding hands, headed to the Ritz Carlton Hotel at Montego Bay, Jamaica for our honeymoon, I asked Wardell why was it so important for him to talk to his father before we left and what did he say to him. He told me his father just gave him some marital advice, he has a speech for all of his sons on their wedding day and none of his brothers would ever repeat what was told to them so he was anxious to find out what advice he would be given. When I asked what the advice was; Wardell kissed the back of my hand, smiled at me and said, "He told me to always remember, happy wife; happy life." "That's all he said?" Wardell winked at me and said, "Um, you'll find out later tonight what that means." Then he lifted his eyebrows at me. It took me a few minutes to get what he meant, and as soon as I figured it out; I snatched my hand away from his and turned my head away from him, I was so scared.

While dating we hugged each other when we left each other, but Wardell had only kissed me once and that was on accident. He stepped up to me to kiss my cheek and I turned my head to face him and he kissed my lips instead. I opened my mouth, he opened his and Wham, my body reacted as I put my arms around his neck. He jumped back as he pulled my arms away and said, "Gotta go!" And he almost tore the door off the hinge trying to get out of the kitchen. I was a virgin and had only kissed boys in the basement at the church when I was little. See, Mama has always been known to have dreams about things that happened to people, BEFORE it happens! And, I was too scared to kiss any boys, afraid she would see me kissing in her dream.

So, when I had my first experience with an open mouth kiss, whew; I took a cold shower that night. A few days later when we talked on the phone, Wardell talked as if nothing had happened, so before he prayed for me I asked him if we should talk about the kiss and he said, "Zinora I never meant for that to happen, it won't happen again until we're married, alright." "What if I want it to happen again before then?" "Okay, now you're talking like you're not saved. Trust me, it will be worth waiting for, now that's the end of this subject, okay? Zinora are you hearing me?" "Yeah Mr. saved, I hear you." That evening, sitting on the plane, on the way to begin our honeymoon, I was terrified.

That's when I remembered just a few days earlier, Mama had come into my room and sat on my bed and asked me if Wardell and I had discussed family planning. The way she looked at me I think it was her way of fishing to see if we had done anything yet. Her eyes almost smiled when I told her no, we had not discussed sex at all. Then she told me that the first time a female experience love making can be slightly painful but it was only temporary pain, when your husband knows what he's doing, you'll forget all about the pain, and then she blushed, smiled and fanned herself. I thought about the accidental kiss Wardell and I had... and understood her fanning. After she left my room I thought to myself, 'My goodness, as old as they are they're still having sex!' Right then, on the plane I smiled thinking about Mama and that's when I slipped my hand back in Wardells and reached up and pecked him on the cheek.

So....I remembered all that just to describe Pops Patterson and the type of relationship he has with his sons. He is different with the females though, he asks me every now and again, "Wardell treating you alright?" I always smile and say, "Yes sir, he's good." He responds the same all the time, "Alright, just checkin."   He never interjects into our female conversations, however, if something is said in front of him, a few days later Ma wants to talk to us about something a bug put in her ear. The conversation will be about what Pops heard. I think he feels it takes a woman to talk to a woman and a man to talk to a man, but he is always kind and loving, no matter what he hears in our conversations.

Vedette told me she once overheard Sheldon and Pops in the kitchen and the conversation went like this: Sheldon told Pops that he was 17 now and a man and that it was time for Pops to start seeing him as a man and not still his little boy; he was old enough to make adult decisions now. Vedette said after a few seconds of silence, Pops told Sheldon that a child becomes an adult when he or she can take advice and the next thing she heard was the back door closing. That's when she made her entrance into the kitchen and pretended she never heard a word; Sheldon had simply left the room.

Having a close relationship with my sister-in-laws make me think it will be good for Nicki to have a sister; Nye was close enough to be my sister until he started this mess between us..... I wonder if he wants a son...

Oh well we've made it home from the drug store with the test in the bag. It is after 3pm., so I'll spend some time with Nicki teaching her the alphabet. She is so quick to catch on, and she loves learning. Oh, let me get the phone... it's the bank. "Hello there handsome!" "Hello to you, gorgeous and sexy." "Oh..., Wardell you still think I'm sexy after almost 4 years of marriage?" "Yeah baby, you will always be sexy to me. Hey I've been thinking...when was the last time your friend visited you?" "Man, you are really one with me, I just walked in the door from picking up a pregnancy test, I'll take it later, but ... I don't think I need to take it to know what the result will be." I'm crying now and can't get any more words out of my mouth.

Wardell asks, "What's wrong baby, you're not ready for another Patterson in the house?" I sniffle up the last of my tears and get a napkin off the table and blow my nose. Finally I say, "No Wardell, I want another Patterson, I'll have all the babies you give me. I, I...I miss Nye like something crazy." My voice is trembling and I hold my breath waiting for him to tell me to call Nye and put an end to this. "Wardell, you still there?" "Yeah, baby, just call him and put an end to this craziness. Look I had a few minutes between interviews and thought about my girls; how is my Lil Kitten?" "She's good, want to say hi?" "Not now baby my next appointment just walked in the bank. I love you, see you at five thirty." "Okay, love you too." Wow, that's almost some twin oneness right there, or maybe love is just that strong.

I remember when Nye and I were twelve, about to turn thirteen in a couple of months, and Nye asked me if I were having some pain in my lower abdomen. He placed his hands on his lower abdomen while asking me. I told him yes I did and when I told Mama, she said it was probably my reproductive organs getting ready for my menstrual cycle. He said Mama never told him anything about a menstrual cycle. I laughed and told him only females have one so they can carry babies. His eyes got so big and he was so serious as he said, "I'm having pains Z, you think I might be able to have babies too?" His question made me think, 'I know Mama told me only females had reproductive organs, but the look on Nye's face; scared me.' He was having pain, I didn't have to show him where, maybe, Oh lord, I said as I ran to get the phone, "Let's call Mama at work and tell her." Mama told me to put Nye on the phone and she talked to him for a few minutes and he hung up. "What did Mama say?" Nye told me she said I was not to worry; only females can have babies and Daddy was going to have a long talk with me tonight when he gets home.

Yeah, oneness must be linked to love. I lay the phone down and see the pictures sitting on the sofa and I long to hold and hug my nieces so bad. I feel tears coming and Nicki comes over to me and points to the picture as I sit down, she says, "Shell." As she points to Rachel, then as she points to Rebecca she says, "Becca." She gives a deep hardy laugh as if her love for her only cousins on her mothers' side of the family is deep. I lose it; I cover my face and cry like a baby. I can feel Nicki's little tiny hands rubbing my head as she asks, "Mommy trying?" My heart aches for Nicki because she has never seen nor hugged her mother's twin brother's daughters. Then I realize she doesn't even know she has an uncle on her mothers' side of the family. As I cry; I shake my head thinking, 'Now that's just a shame!'

Nicki climbs up on the sofa and tries to console me by stretching her tiny short arms around me and squeezing me as tight as she can while telling me not to cry. The whole time she's consoling me I'm thinking, 'This stupid mess is all because of Nye, he is so stubborn!' I turn around and hug Nicki and reassure her that Mommy is alright. She looks me in the eyes, smiles and asks, "All better, huh Mommy?" She sounds like me when I'm asking her the same question, I can't help but laugh as I reply, "Yep, it's all better baby, all better." I pick her up and head to the kitchen wiping my tears away with my hands.

I remove the tray to her high chair so I can sit her down in it, but she will not let go of my neck. I try to reassure her that Mommy's alright now but, no way is she letting go of me. I take a seat and she's still holding onto me but now she's in my lap. So I start talking to her. "Baby, Mommy is sad right now because I miss my brother." "Butter?" "Yes, baby; Mommy has a brother?" "Butter mean to Mommy?" WOW! A light just came on…the scripture that says in **Matthew 7:12; "Therefore, whatever you want men to do to you, do also to them….."** Flashed like a banner across my mind.

I need to be the one to extend the olive branch to Nye, after all I'm the one crying and walking around like a pitiful mess with my baby clutching onto me for dear life because she thinks her Mommy's crazy! I get up from the kitchen table and go to the family room to get the phone…again I chicken out. What if he doesn't want to talk to me? I couldn't bear the thought of Nye not answering the phone. I had a vision in my mind of Von handing the phone over to Nye while saying, "Its Z". I could see Nye take the phone from her hand and hang it up, right in my ear. Having that little vision has Ms. Pissed waking up again, so I throw the phone back down on the sofa. Nicki is still hanging around my neck so I say, "Mommies all better now, let's make Daddy some cookies, kay?" I feel her arms loosen from around my neck as she says, "Yey, tookies!" As we head back into the kitchen.

We put the first batch of cookies into the oven and I make a pallet on the floor for Nicki and turn on the oven light so she can watch the cookies. I get the potatoes going while she lies on her stomach making her little feet sway in the air. She stares into the oven, saying, "Grow." I get the corn started and feel that queasy feeling again. I can't figure out if it's my being pregnant, or Nye. Anyways; Nye takes the lead in my mind. I smile; he loved taking the lead when we sang duets. I always told him that women and children are supposed to be first, but he would, "Demand, the man to be first!" I laugh aloud as I think of that. Nye would look around the room, for a table to pound on as he were saying the word, 'Demand', it would always make me laugh because he looked so ridiculous! Him demanding something with his skinny behind; Ha! I realize my ha was aloud while a smile is planted on my face.

Nicki mimics my, "Ha," and, as I look down at her, I think how much fun she'll have with a sibling, sister or brother. I think, 'um, that's funny, she said, "Ha" in the same note I did. I wonder if she has an ear for music. So I say, "Yea, aah" in "b flat". I hear "Yea, aah" in "b flat; right back at me! Lord, my baby can sing! I remove the skillet with the corn off the stove and reach down and pick Nicki up while I sing, "Dear Jesus I la, ah, of you," I get it right back, run and all. I start smiling and hugging Nicki, she can sing, my baby can sing, who'd a thought!

I set the timer on for the cookies and sit Nicki on top of the counter and we sing up a little storm. She mimics whatever I sing. I change notes; she change notes. Some of her words are not clear, but my baby has some pipes! Wait until Wardell hears her. Oh, Wardell! Let me finish cooking, we have been singing and I finished the cookies and turned off the potatoes and thought I was finished cooking altogether. Wow, I remember the days!

After school Nye and I would play around while he would be on the piano and we would sing so; I would forget to start dinner and Mama would be on fire when she came home and catch me at the piano with Nye. Neither chores nor homework would get done, we would just sing and forget time existed, like I just did today. I hear the garage door. Wardell is entering the garage and I haven't sautéed the spinach nor mashed the potatoes yet. I feel my heart racing as if Mama will be the one coming through that door. Ooh wee!

I'm so excited I pick Nicki up and stand straight, like at attention as Wardell walks into the kitchen. He stops in his tracks, looks me in the eyes, then his eyes moves down to Nicki and the biggest smile burst through and lights his whole face up like a candle. I dash towards him as tears are running down my face. He meets us half way and chuckles as he says, "So the test is positive hey." He hugs both of his Patterson girls together, then slightly moves his upper body back to look me in the face and asks, "So; do I have to paint a room blue?" Now he takes a step back and rubs my belly and continues, "For our son this time?" Ooh, ooh, ooh; I love this man!

He takes Nicki from me and asks her what have we been up to today and as Nicki tries to give her daddy a play by play of today, I go to the bathroom; with my test in hand, and come back to the kitchen and finish dinner. After I take my last bite of dinner, I tell Wardell about our daughters' gift to sing and he's floored. He sits at the table and stares at Nicki with his bottom lip hanging almost on the table. He is speechless as his eyes goes from Nicki, back to me, then Nicki, and back to me. He puts both elbows on the table and folds his hands together; then, commences to pounding on his mouth. I notice he's blinking his eyes so I get up and stand behind him, bend over and hug him while I whisper softly in his ear, "If I didn't know you; I'd think you are about to get emotional on me." He slightly turns around, grabs me by my waist, turns his whole body, and lays his head on my stomach and squeezes me so tight.

"Zinora, baby; I love you so much." He buries his head in my stomach and says. "I love you baby, I do." All I could manage to say was, "I love you too." And I burst out crying. Nicki burst out crying, I have startled her, Wardell jumps up and runs to her rescue. I'm wiping my tears away with my hands as I rush right behind him. Wardell laughs as he takes Nicki out of her high chair and says, "Man! I sure hope this is a one-time occurrence. Who's pregnant; me or you! It's okay Lil Kitten; Mommy is alright baby, its okay." Now Wardell is hugging both his girls again and Nicki starts rubbing her little eyes, indicating it is nite, nite time for Nicki.

"ZINYE"

"Alright girls, as soon as we get home I want you to allow your mother to get some rest. Okay, you agree to let her rest?" "Yes, Daddy, we agree" I get the duet reply from them as I look in my rear view mirror and watch as they move their heads up and down. We just told them they are going to have another sibling and Rebecca asked if it were going to be twins again. These kids are so smart for their age. I hear Mama and Daddy say that so much when they are around our girls, but I'm starting to notice it myself. I took them out to dinner to an Italian Restaurant because Von had a taste for some good lasagna. Daddy knows the owner and the food is great. The girls took the news pretty good I think. I hope they allow another person in their world. They are so close, almost one person and that scares me, to think how dependent they are of one another. I can only pray they love the new comer and welcome them into our family. Too bad Z and I didn't have another sibling, it might have been easier for us to live our separate lives if we knew how to share one another.

While driving home I passed the main street used to get to Z's house. I immediately thought of how she's taking the news about the musical. Last year she avoided me like the plauge. She sang Yolanda Adams' "The Battle Is Not Yours", and my Lil Sister tore it up! The whole church went completely off with praise. I was so proud of her. I sure hope she renders another song that leads the congregation into praise again this year. It would be great if I could get her to help me with this musical. Nah, she probably won't have anything to do with me the way I have treated her. I never dreamed she would allow us to go without talking this long.

I just thought she would have told me off by now and made me talk to her.   When we were growing up that's exactly what she would do if I gave her the silent treatment. She was always laid back. I was the one to suggest doing things. Seldom she would say, "Nah, you go ahead, I'll pass on this." She was my anchor and if for some reason she refused to follow my lead; I would wonder why, what was wrong. To tell you the truth, when she refused to follow me, it was then I would examine the consequences. She would make me mad when she didn't follow my lead and I would give her the silent treatment.

Z was the cautious level headed one, and I was the risk taker..... She would give me a few days to allow me time to sort out my feelings then she would walk up to me with that stern look on her face and say something like, "Okay, you've had time to get over whatever you need to get over. Now, let's keep it moving brotha." But she has never confronted me this time. Maybe its because she has her own life now and has no time for her brother! Leave it be Nye, just leave it be!

"ZINORA"

I tell Wardell that I'll help Nicki get her pajamas on. He tells me that he will clear the table. After wrestling with Nicki to help get her pajamas on, I get her toothbrush ready and stand her on her step stool and I rush into my bathroom. As I reach my hand out to retrieve the stick, for a few seconds I stand completely still…hesitant to pick it up, the stick that will confirm what I already know; I'm carrying another Patterson. As I lift the stick up, I see the plus sign…I don't know why; but…my heart is pounding so fast, and, my hand is shaking….I am so scared…I'm having another baby! As I place the toilet top down to have a seat, Wardell shows up at the bedroom door and asks, "You take the test?" I can't answer him, I can't move for some reason. Now he's standing in the bathroom door with both hands holding onto the sides of the door frame. "Baby is something wrong?" He asks me this while his forehead wrinkles.

I sit unable to speak; I'm scared and sit frozen staring at him. He gets a serious look and walks up to me and gently takes the stick out of my hand. He looks at it; then up at me. "What does this plus sign mean?" First his eyes look into mine, I still can't speak. Now his eyes are moving around my face, he's looking for some indication of my mood, happy, sad, disappointed, he can't see scared. Nicki yells, "Mommy!" As though she's in a panic, Wardell quickly throws the stick on the counter and takes off running to her bathroom. When he gets to the door to our bedroom, he glances back at me while yelling, "Daddy's coming Lil Kitten." I'm paralyzed with fear. What am I going to do with two babies, a husband, and, a business. My perfect life as I know it, is going to change!

I'm sitting here thinking about some of the stories Mama used to tell me about raising twins. How hard it was having to feed, bathe, clothe, cook for and do laundry for two babies, and keep her husband satisfied, house clean…I start to shake my head, "No," I don't think I can handle this, just thinking about it makes me tired. What am I going to do, I never thought about birth control. The night Mama asked me if we had discussed having a family right away or planning to take birth control, she told me after we were born she took birth control pills for five years and when she stopped taking them, she never got pregnant again. Because she had a daughter and a son; she was satisfied with having two children; she just happened to have had both of hers at the same time. When I talked to Wardell about when to start a family, he said whatever I wanted; he would be in agreement with it, because I had the shop and could work at my own pace. He was making good money as Assistant to the Bank's Branch Manager, and has never relied on my money, so we just let the Lord have His way about our family. But now…I'm just not sure.

I stand up and look at myself in the mirror. To look at me you wouldn't think I was 23, about to turn 24 in a month; I look more like I'm 18 or 19. People are always asking me how old I am because I look too young to be married and have a two year old. I think it's because of my pimples; I look like some teen with acne. Most venders that come to the shop don't believe me when I tell them I am the owner; they say I look so young. But as I stand here looking at myself, I'm thinking another baby will age me, I'll be too tired to sleep. Oh no! What about Nicki, will she be jealous of her brother or sister? Will I have to give up my shop? Will I get fat and Wardell run off with some secretary at the bank? What if he doesn't find me sexy anymore while I'm pregnant and wants a divorce? Oh my goodness, what am I going to do without him and two babies to raise...

"Let's talk to Mommy; Mommy, where are you?" I hear the patter of Nicki's feet on the floor, Wardell must have put her footed PJ's on her. She's following her Daddy looking for Mommy and a smile automatically breaks out on my face. My heart is so warmed knowing she's my baby, I love her so much. It's hard to think what our lives were like before she came into it. I twirl around and as I bend over to pick Nicki up; she leaps into my arms. Wardell stands in the bathroom door way and ask, "What does that plus mean." I look over at him and he is serious, almost worried, so I say, "It means... you are going to be a father again." I stare at his face to see how he's going to react to another baby. He smiles so big and starts to back up, so, holding onto Nicki, we follow him and watch as he plops on the edge of our bed and sighs. "Baby, you had me scared for a minute. I thought something was wrong." I walk over to him and plop Nicki onto our mattress and as she bounces, she laughs so hard, from her gut and it makes both me and Wardell laugh.

I lie on the bed on my side and laugh until I cry. Wardell crawls over behind me and wraps his arms around me, I feel so safe wrapped in his arms; like everything is going to be alright. Nicki crawls over to me and says, "Mommy don't try." She has her little forehead wrinkled and is rubbing my face with her tiny little hand and I cry as I reach and pull her into my stomach and squeeze her so tight. "Daddy, why

Mommy try?" He pulls her closer to me and hugs the both of us and replies; "Daddy thinks Mommy is scared just a little." "Mommy scared ob da boogeyman?" Wardell jumped straight up and grabbed Nicki while he asked, "Who told you about the boogeyman baby?" I sat up and wiped my face with my arm, "Yeah, who told you that?" She sat there in her Daddy's arms looking scared she had told a secret. She started fidgeting with her fingers and looked at the both of us, hesitant to speak. I say, "Nicki, baby you won't be in trouble, who told you about the boogeyman." I stroked her face and she burst out crying as she reached out to me. I grabbed her and hugged her so tight she started twisting to break free from my arms. I fought back tears, I love my baby so much and just this instant, I realize; I will love her sister or brother just as much. I don't care what it will cost me, or us. Lord, please let this baby be healthy and an asset to our family, please!

We all crawl to the head of the bed and as Nicki lies across my lap, I rock her and Wardell lies on his side by her and gently kisses her forehead while rubbing her hair, she falls asleep within a few minutes. Wardell tells me he'll put her down for me. I grab a pillow and curl up as I watch him leave the room carrying our baby to bed. I'm thinking this will probably become our routine for a good while. I hear him checking the doors and turning out lights and when he comes back to our room and stands in the doorway. I raise my head up and ask, "Wha?" He stands there and begins to wave his tie up and down and says, "I'm gonna have to remember to take my expensive work ties off before assisting our children with brushing their teeth, look at this; toothpaste everywhere." He smiles and raises his left eyebrow at me. I know what that gleam in his eye means and as he closes our bedroom door, I start peeling off my clothes.

"Zinye"

"Alright girls, while I clean the kitchen your Dad will supervise your bath, okay?" "Kay, Mommie!" Comes from both girls, sounding like a duet; Rachel an alto and Rebecca soprano. Lord I thank you; both my daughters have singing voices. I am reminded of Z when I hear them sing. My sister has a range on her! I remember when we were little, how she would close her eyes and sing whatever the latest song Mama had taught us to sing for our church choir. For as long as I can remember, Z has always loved to sing....just like my girls....Wow, my sister Zinora.

As I multi-task, siting watching the girls wash up in the tub and reading my newspaper, my mind drifts to when Z and I were little and we did everything together. It puts a smile on my face just thinking of it. I decide to put the newspaper down and ask the girls if they want to sing one song before I wash their ears. Wow what a joyous response, "Ooh yes, can we Daddy!" My reply is, "Okay, what do you want to sing for Daddy?" Rebecca glances at Rachel and we both look at Rachel as she stares at Rebecca for a few seconds then says, "Ordinary People!" And she smile her mothers beautiful smile. Man I love these girls! Before I could agree, they start singing, "Just ordinary people..." I sit back and listen to their heavenly voices.

As they bellow out the last verse of the song, I watch Rachel open her eyes and Rebecca allows her sister to finish the lead as she sings, "Little becomes much... Oh yes, little becomes much, when you place it, in the Masters hand, and, and. Now Rebecca joins in on the last note as they harmonize, "Hand!" While they hold the note, I stand and give them an ovation. "That was great, now for the ear cleaning." "One more song Daddy, please." "Okay, but make it short and sweet." Rebecca starts, "Yes Jesus loves me, oh, ooh, oh, ooh, yes Jesus loves me, yes Jesus loves me, for the Bible tells me so." Rachel sings the same chorus and I dry them off and wrap the towels around them while they sing the song together in harmony. Now its time to go into their room and get them in pajamas.

I love to hear them sing, and they love to sing in harmony. When I teach them a song, we sit at the piano and I go over their parts. It's amazing, they each know one another notes and will sing it to get the other one back on key. Kinda like how Z and I did when we were young and had to sing in the choir for that very reason; to keep the adults and the kids on key!

While they get lotioned, in comes Von. She sits on Rebecca's bed and hands the girls their pajamas to put on. I get the Bible off the end table so I can read a scripture to them. Growing up in the Rustin home, it was a part of our life, having Daddy read us scripture every Saturday morning. Because I work on Saturdays, I decided to read the Word with my family Monday through Friday nights before bedtime. I choose to read Proverbs and Ecclesiastics and only two or three verses. Even though I use the Quest Bible, I expound on it so they'll have some sense of understanding. I know they are young now and it may not make much sense to them, but as they grow, it will come together. The Lord has truly blessed me with a good wife and two precious daughters. Now that we're expecting another baby, I am so grateful and I know this child will be a blessing to our family also. When I think of God's goodness towards me, I can't help but smile and give God praise!

I read Ecclesiastics 3:1-8 and the girls said their prayers and now it's Mommie and Daddy time! Oh bless the Lord oh my soul.....

"Nye, babe what's wrong?" Von is questioning me as I slide into my side of the bed. I don't want to let her know I'm thinking about Z. She'll tell me to call her..... oh well, here goes. "Okay, I must admit Z is heavy on my mind. Von; I can't seem to stop thinking about her and missing my sister. Baby, you do understand don't you? I mean, she's not just my sister, we're twins and our bond is strong."   As she slides next to me, she gently strokes my face and says, "Nye, we have twins, I understand baby! What you need to do is pick up the phone and call your twin sister."   I grab her and reach for a kiss but she hesitates and says to me, "Nye, you have never told me exactly what happened between you and Z. I'd like to hear what happened."

"Now? You want to hear what ripped our relationship apart now? Von, baby, its love time!" As I gaze into her eyes, she is as serious as a heart attack while she blandly says to me, "Yes, Nye I want to hear what happened from the horse's mouth, right now." She sits straight up with her back against the headboard and as she folds her arms, she looks me directly in the eyes. I can read them; no lovin; talk!

So, I take in a deep breath and sit straight up, and start.

"After Daddy prayed for us the night before we turned seventeen, I went on about my daily routine. I never prayed for direction because I believed the Lord would guide me to where He wanted me to go. About a week later Z asked me if the Lord had given me any direction as to what He wanted me to do and I told her no He hadn't. She never said anything else to me and I didn't bring it up again.   Von, you have to understand, she told me everything, I believe we were each others filters, you know. She would run her feelings and thoughts by me and vice-a- versa. Well another week or so went by and she just blurted out at the dinner table that she knew what the Lord wanted her to do! She never ran anything by me. She didn't even ask my opinion! She just slapped the news on me like my opinion didn't matter to her.

I felt betrayed. How could she determine what the Lord had in store for her without running it by me like she always did? I'm the oldest and she would usually get her confirmation from ME! I felt she closed me out, she no longer needed me anymore, she was going out on her own, all by herself. Besides why would she go to the front of the line and get her orders and not tell me what she was doing? She broke the twin code! I know it sounds stupid, but we talked EVERYTHING over." As I hear myself I feel like a child, a selfish spoiled child. I look at Von and reach for her waist and draw her close to me and finish talking, "Baby, I felt betrayed, by my best friend." ......

Von slides herself close to me then as she climbs to straddle me, she says, "Nye, you owe your sister an apology." I open my mouth to speak and she places her finger over my lips and continues. "Babe, you are a born leader and when those you lead are lagging, you can get pretty stubborn. I'm not beating you down Nye, listen to me. A great leader is one who mentors followers into becoming great leaders. Baby that's what you did for your sister, you helped her learn how to hear from the Holy Spirit and then you felt betrayed when she did. I think you hurt Z. You should have been happy for her but instead you shut yourself out of her life, the life you were a great part of." Von leans down and pecks me on the lips then she smiles and asks, "Are you mad at me?" I hesitate to answer. I know she's right, all these years I've never thought about how Z felt, I knew I hurt her, I just thought she would come to me like she always did and tell me we are going to start back talking and that's that! But she never did, then I was hurt.

"Ok, Mrs. Rustin, you are right. I owe my only sister an apology, where do I go from here? She has her own life and it doesn't need me in it." "Nye, you have been moping around here for almost a week over missing your only sister. Drop your pride and let her know you love and miss her. Ask her to forgive you for being young and foolish. She loves you, she'll forgive you and our kids can have a relationship as cousins should that live in neighboring towns. That's just my opinion, I hate seeing you miss her so much it hurts YOU, that's all." She leans in and kisses me with a kiss that says, "Lovin Time!" I reach over and turn off the lights, as Teddy Pendergrass would say.

Chapter Five

Good Morning Heartache

Mama's Empathy

TUESDAY:

"Zinora"

I woke up late again and queasy. Oh my, I guess I'd better get used to this. I have heard a lot of conversations being in beauty shops for four years. Now I'm reminded of all the women that shared how each pregnancy is different; just like the child coming will be different. Now I understand what they meant. I had an easy pregnancy with Nicki. I didn't even know I was pregnant until Wardell mentioned to me how we had made love every day for 45 days straight. I was never sick until my labor started, then I threw up like a pregnant woman, man oh man, I mean! I had a trash bag with me in the car on the way to the hospital and, in the labor room. Well one thing's for sure; this baby is definitely going to be different.

Different, now that reminds me of when Nye and I were getting ready to start kindergarten and Mama took us shopping for school clothes and as soon as we walked into the mall, there was a group of Scottish people at a booth, and there were so many people standing around. Some were signing papers, some were talking to the men with skirts on and some were gawking at the men, just like Nye and I. Mama had to call for us to catch up with her, she had walked right by them, we were so amazed to see men with skirts. Men! While we were in the girls department, Nye picked up a skirt and held it up to his waist. I laughed and pointed my finger at him and said, "You look funny, like those men we saw." I laughed so hard and loud, Mama had to tell me to quiet down.

Nye threw the skirt back onto the pile real fast and jotted next to Mama. He didn't open his mouth the whole while Mama picked out his clothes. After the shopping was done, Mama asked who was hungry and I shouted "I am!" Mama gave Nye a funny stare and grabbed his hand. When we were seated at a booth; Nye and I sitting on one side and Mama on the other, she asked Nye if he was alright. He said, "Yes Mama," and sat up real straight. Mama asked, "Nye why are you sitting so straight is something hurting you?" He replied, "I'm keeping my legs closed." "Why?" Was her question back at him. "So my pee, pee won't fall off like Z's did." Mama gets up and sits between Nye and me.

She leaned down towards Nye and asked; "Nye, who told you Z's pee, pee fell off." He says, "She broke hers, I'm not gonna break mines." Mama sat straight up and put her hand over her mouth, as her whole body shook, she was laughing so hard, she couldn't hold it. She shook her head and laughed out loud. She waved her hand around in the air and stomped her feet under the table. She laughed for a good three minutes. Nye sat there looking like he didn't care she was laughing at him; he was not going to open his legs. I sat there looking at both of them for a few minutes, then I looked up at Mama and I got so tickled watching her rock back and forth, waving her hand; I joined in on her laughter.

I glanced at Nye as I leaned forward, and his face was void of any emotion. I knew he was mad we were laughing at him, but I couldn't help myself. Mama's laugh was infectious, if he weren't so mad; he would be laughing too. After she was able to collect herself, she told him that even though we were twins; we were different, I was a girl and girls are not born with pee, pees. It was okay for him to open his legs. Nye never moved an inch.

When we left the mall, the crowd had thinned around the Scottish Booth and Nye walked straight over to one of the men with a skirt and asked real loud, "Did your pee, pee fall off?" Mama ran over to Nye, shoved the bags under her arm and snatched him up and pulled me by the arm right out of the door, but not before I heard people giggling. That was the day I learned girls and boys were born different. Um, my pregnancy's different, maybe th s baby will be a boy.

I miss Nye so much and to think both of us will have our second pregnancies together; makes my heart ache for his company. The doorbell rings. I raise up to glance at the clock, its 8:22 am, who in the world is at my front door at this hour. I jump up and grab my robe and house shoes and I literally run to the front door. I look through the peep hole and it's Mama. I open the door and ask if everything is alright. She hugs me and comes in all out of breath as if she ran to the door. "Mama, what is it, are you alright, is it Daddy, is he alright, what's going on?" She grabs hold of both my arms, and smiles while saying, "Z, baby I was just over this way and thought I'd stop by is all." As I close the door, I take in a deep breath, I know my Mama and when she smiles that smile; something's definitely UP. I grab and hug her then take in a few more deep breaths so I can calm myself down and wait until she's ready to spring whatever it is on me.

In the room comes Nicki, smiling and when her eyes sees Mama, she yells, "Gam Ma! Gam Ma!" Now her arms are extended out for her Gam Ma. Mama sweeps her up and off the floor. I watch them as they embrace each other around the neck, I can't help but smile. I realize I need to use the bathroom quick… off I run to the bathroom hollering; "Ooh, I'll be right back!" I see myself looking like a giant version of Nicki as I'm running to the bathroom, hoping to make it in time, I mean!

After I wash my face and brush my teeth, intending to return to the family room, on my way I hear Mama and Nicki in her bathroom so I stop to take a peek at them. Mama has thrown her jacket over the doorknob and she is sitting on the edge of the tub watching Nicki on the potty as her little tiny legs swing in the air. She is telling Gam Ma about how good she can sing with Mommy. She uses her hands to show Mama how her daddy moved his hands to his mouth after he found out she sings. It is so funny; when she removes her hands to do her demonstration, she slips downward and quickly grabs hold to the sides of the toilet seat and the cutest "Wooh" comes out of her little mouth and Mama's hand immediately covers her own to keep from laughing aloud. When Mama removes her hand from her mouth, she's sporting the widest smile, a smile so full of pride.

I walk into the bathroom and Mama looks at me and say, "Oh, Z, she reminds me of you so much! She's as sweet as peach cobbler, oh; I could just eat her up! Then Mama stands up and kisses Nicki on the forehead, and asks her if she is finished now. I reach down and stop up the tub for Nicki's bath and Mama tells me she will be happy to bathe her grand baby this morning. I stood there and watched Mama assist Nicki out of the bathroom and into her room to pick out an outfit to wear. I get her toothbrush ready and decide to take advantage of Mama being here with Nicki.

I go take my shower while Mama attends to Nicki. While showering I wonder how Mama's going to feel having two new grandchildren at the same time. It would be a lot easier if Nye and I were talking to each other. I want to hold and kiss my nieces so bad; what if both of us have sons' together, wow; that would be a blessing. Wardell and Nye taking their sons to games together, cousins growing up together; now that would really be a blessing!

I go into the kitchen where I hear laughter coming from both Mama and Nicki. Nicki has Cheerios stuck to her nose for Mama to eat off and every time one is removed; Nicki sounds out her hearty gut laugh and it makes Mama double over with laughter. I join in the laughter and suddenly I remember Mama laughing with us when we were little. In fact I remember laughing a lot while we grew up. Mama looks at me and her smile vanishes. As she stands she asks, "Baby, what's wrong?" She walks towards me and opens her arms so wide for me, I cling to her and start crying; "Mama I missNyesomuchand I'mhaving anotherbaby, Idon'twantthisrifftogoonanymore."

"Slow down Z; what are you saying, baby?" She leans her upper body away from me and rubs my upper back while saying, "Take a deep breath, now start over, slowly this time, okay." I follow her instructions to a tee. "Mama I miss Nye. I want to end this feud, today! And you're having another grandchild, I'm pregnant." Mama reaches for my face with both her hands and as she gently holds my face, she kisses me on my cheek and says, "I know Z, and don't worry baby, everything will work for the good, watch and see." I stand looking at her asking myself, 'Now, why am I surprised, Mama has probably had a dream.' I watch my Mama as she pulls out a chair. She points at it; meaning for me to sit down.

After I'm seated she leans in close to my face and tells me; "You know I'm one given to dreams. I saw you and Von; both pregnant and at the park with the girls." When I called you yesterday, I thought you were going to tell me about being pregnant, but I decided to come over today so you could tell me in person. Baby, I'm so happy for you and Wardell. Both of you are great parents; and you make such beautiful grand babies for me and your Daddy to love. Now when do you want to go over too Nye's? I think today is good; what you think?" Mama is smiling, but I know that smile; it's a not so sure one. I look into her eyes and she starts again; "Now Z, you will have to be the one to extend the olive branch, your brother will deny anything is wrong before admitting he's at fault." All I could do was stand up and grab hold of Mama and hug her while tears ran down my face. I know she's right; she has always been right.

"Alright Mama, let me eat something and get out of these sweats. I go get myself a small bowl for my Cheerios. Mama goes into the foyer and I hear her on her cell. "Good morning Yvonne, how are you feeling this morning; …and the girls? Ahh huh, I'm over Zs' right now, and was wondering; are you going to be home for a while, I might stop by before heading home. Okay, call me if you have to leave, alright honey, bye." I watch Mama as she enters the dining area. She gives me a quick glance, but I know my mother; her brain is click, click, clicking! She takes a seat next to Nicki and glances again, real fast my way. "Okay Mama, what do you have cooking in that head of yours?" She sits straight up and without looking at me says, "Why Zinora Ruth; what on earth are you referring to?" I don't want to play her game, so I quietly finish eating my cereal while watching her and Nicki interact.

Nicki is finished and Mama takes her into her bathroom to get cleaned up. I place my bowl in the sink and think, 'Am I ready for this today?' I feel my pulse began to race, I am so nervous about mending this almost seven year rift between Nye and myself. I keep thinking he has a good life now, a life without his little sister wanting to know his every thought. After all; he has a wife now to share with, why would he need me now. Maybe I'm the only one missing our childhood together. I decide to ask Mama about Nye, she seems to be our common thread, even now. As I walk down the hall towards Nicki's room; I hear singing, Nicki is auditioning for Gam Ma. Mama is singing, "This little light of mine" for Nicki to follow her lead. Nicki sings the same notes Mama is singing and I can hear the excitement in Mama's voice.

As I enter into the room, I see Mama on her knees with her hands glued to her thighs while in front of Nicki. Nicki is standing in front of Mama singing and Mama's mouth is moving along with Nicki's as she mimics her singing grand daughter. I'm standing in amazement, watching the two of them, so happy my mother is able to enjoy her grandchild. My heart leaps inside as I share the joy with my mother of having this wonderful experience of pure, unconditional love from a precious child. Nicki finishes her line and Mama grabs and hugs her real tight as she says, "Oh baby, you have such a beautiful little voice; Gam Ma loves you so much!" I feel warm tears drip down my face as I beam with love for both females on the floor. I turn around to go get dressed; sigh…it's time to make things right between Nye and I.

I changed clothes three times. Mama and Nicki came into my room, sat on the edge of my bed and watched me as I find fault with every outfit. Nothing looks like it fits right to me. Finally Mama tells me it's my being pregnant, so just keep on what I have on, and let's go.

As we walk out of the kitchen towards the garage, I feel as though my shoes are made of cement, my feet can barely move. I stand in the door and as I push the button to open the garage door, I say to Mama; "I don't think I can do this Mama, my legs feel like lead." "Okay, baby; I'll drive. Just let me get Nicki's car seat." She walks around me to get her car and she pulls it up to the garage, right behind my Onyx Black Metallic Chevy Tahoe. I can't make a move; I just stand in the doorway with my legs shaking as I watch her take the car seat from my vehicle, and put it in hers. Nicki is standing right by my side, watching Mama's every move just as I am.

"Okay, ready!" Mama hollers out in a false, forced happy tone. As if on cue, Nicki grabs my hand and starts to pull me saying, "Tome on Mommy, let's go!" Instantly I have a vision of me looking like I'm the 2 year old and Nicki has become the 23 year old. I don't want to look childish; so I make a move forward. I feel the bottom of my legs shake as if I'm wobbly, but I say to myself, 'Okay, you can do this.' And I continue to place one foot in front of the other. I open my car door and reach up and grab the garage door opener. I really don't want to do this! I've made it to Mamas' car and I just stand still, staring at her. She gives me a quick smile; you know the kind you rush on your face when someone you don't know walks briskly by you. She climbs in the back seat with Nicki and helps her get the seat belt on and locked.

As I climb inside the front seat of Mamas' Lexus LS, I wonder if I'm going to need a trash bag, I feel really queasy. "Mama, I'll be right back!" I climb right back out of the car and head to the shelf in the garage that stores our different size trash bags. I spot the small ones and pull a bag off the roll. I'm thinking, 'I don't think I can do this, not today anyway.' I turn around and my eyes meet Mamas'. She says, "Come on baby, this you can do with your eyes closed." As I walk towards her car, headed to the passenger's side; I fight back tears. I really don't want to do this!

While putting my seat belt on, Mama says, "Now Z; you have always been the one to forgive easily. Nye has the tendency to pretend there's nothing going on to forgive. But you, let's just say, your heart has always been the most tender between the two of you." "Mama, I know, it's just…I don't think I can do this now, not right now." I hurriedly put the bag in front of my mouth, I feel it getting watery. I'm breathing heavily trying to keep the queasiness to a low. Mama gets out of the car and comes on my side and opens the door and bends down beside me. She places her hand on my thigh and starts praying: "Father in heaven, I thank You that Your ear is always open to hear the cries of Your children. I come before You now placing a demand upon the powerful, Holy Spirit to touch and heal my baby of this morning sickness; right now! In the Name of Jesus, I decree it to be so, Amen." She rose up and kissed me on my cheek and said, "Come on baby; we'll do this another time, okay?" I tucked the bag in my purse and unlocked my seat belt.

I stood at the hood of Mamas' car while she loosed Nicki and I said; "Mama, I need to ask you some questions, wanna come in and I'll make us a batch of pancakes while we talk?" She lifts Nicki up on her hip, slams the rear car door and says, "Yep that sounds good." Nicki says; "Yey, pan ie cakes, yey!" While clapping her little dimpled hands together.

I throw my jacket over a kitchen chair, wash my hands and put my apron on then I gather all of the ingredients for the pancakes onto the counter. Mama sits silent as she watches me. Very calmly, she came up behind me, untied the apron and said, "You have a seat and let the pancake expert do this." She pointed to the seat next to Nicki for me to sit in. "Mama, has

Nye ever asked you anything about me, I mean, about what I'm doing or my family?"

She never looked up at me, but she talked the whole time she cooked. "No, he hasn't; but Von has. It took me a minute to figure out it was Nye asking through her; kinda like when you two were little. At first I thought she wanted to hear another side of the vendetta story, but then, I figured it out. Nye was hoping I would assume that's what was going on, and would spill the beans to Von that way he knew where your head was. Z, I always thought you would wake up one morning and say to yourself, 'This is ridiculous! I'm putting an end to this.' But, you never did and when I would bring the subject up, you would get mad as fire and rattle off how Nye started this mess. I grew tired of upsetting you, so I just left it alone." "Mama what was it that made you figure out Nye was using Von, you know, to ask questions he wanted to know about?" "When you were pregnant with Nicki, she asked me one day if you were glowing being pregnant; that was the question that made me think, now why would a woman want to know if another woman was glowing or not? That was the day I began telling her everything about you and your family, just like I tell you about Nye and his; this way you both know everything about each other." Mama stops what she's doing, looks at me, smiles and says, "Chile, I don't know what I'll do with my time when you and your brother makes up, I declare I don't." We both throw our heads back and give out a loud hearty laugh.

Just as Mama sits her plate down on the table to eat she says; "Z, I must make a confession to you. I really didn't want you and Nye to be as you were before. When the two of you first disconnected from each other, I prayed for you two to mend your relationship. Seeing you ripped apart like that made my heart weak but, baby I found a friend in my 17 year old daughter. I like you as a friend and dreaded losing your friendship. I really never put my foot down nor did I make David put his down and make Nye apologize and I owe you an apology for that. Still friends?"   I was so moved; I extended my hand towards hers and smiled as Mama put her hand in mine I said, "Always and forever!"

I can't figure out exactly what it is about a mothers cooking; I set out all of the ingredients for the pancakes, but Mamas' taste so much better than mine; just don't get that! The three of us ate pancakes and drank some ice cold milk with sweat dripping down our glasses; well, Nicki had her Sippy Cup. After eating, we all walked straight over to the sofa. Mama sat on one end while Nicki and I took the other end and we each grabbed a pillow. I hit the remote control to the television and it was on the music channel and because smooth jazz was playing; I just lowered the volume. Nicki ran into her room and returned to join us with her doll, "Missy." She jumps up on the sofa between Mama and myself, talking to Missy. Mama took her shoes off and grabbed the throw that was on the back of the sofa by her and curled her feet up. I kicked off my shoes, removed Nicki's and put my feet up on the sofa and covered our feet.

"So, tell me about how you feel having another baby." Mama says. I looked at her, wondering if I should tell her what I really felt. Mama has always allowed Nye and me to speak our minds, she's never freaked out by anything we have told her. Most times her reaction was one of laughter, judgmental or critical has never been her response to anything Nye or I have ever told her.   She listens and gives us her advice, but she's always made us feel it's alright to have our own opinion, as long as we're respectful sharing it. I just felt so guilty not wanting this baby; even if it was briefly. So, very slowly I began, "I was happy thinking about it, but Mama, I was so scared after I took the pregnancy test; when I saw that plus sign… I had second thoughts about another baby."

I start to cry, I feel so guilty; not wanting this baby, even if it was for just a minute and a half. Mama rubbed Nicki's arm and said to her, "Let's take Missy in your room and you can read her a bedtime story, she'd love that. Ok? Come on, I'll help you find a book Missy would enjoy." As Mama stood, Nicki responded with an excited, "Kay, I read to Missy!" I wiped my eyes as I observed them headed to Nicki's room. When Mama returned, she walked over to me, sat down, covered her feet and began to rub the blanket where my feet were. I grabbed a few tissues from the box on the end table next to me and blew my nose. I looked at her and she had a serious look on her face. She looked down on the floor and softly said, "Z; I had a miscarriage when you were almost ten months old. My mouth flew wide open and I heard, "Wha?" Spill out of it!

"Your Daddy was working 10 and 12 hours a day trying to bring home enough money to provide for the two babies we brought home instead of the one we were ready for; and I had the full load of nurturing the both of you on me. Chile, I believe I cried more than you and Nye did back then. We lived in those low income apartments over on Locust, and it seemed every time I would get the both of you to sleep at the same time, someone would turn their music up sky high, knock on the door or our phone would ring. All four of us walked around with black circles under our eyes for so long; they called us, "The black eyed Rustin's," when we went to church. I was running so much I didn't realize I was pregnant again until I started spotting."

Mama stopped rubbing on my feet and started rubbing her hands together. She looked me in the eyes and said, "Baby, I think I might understand how you must have felt. I thought the same thing when I came out of that tiny bathroom and sat my tail down on the used tattered love seat we had. All I could think about was if I had another baby now; your father would come through that door and find me on the floor dead! Me and my saved-self did not want another baby; not then. I sat on that love seat and prayed and cried asking the Lord to please not let this baby I was carrying make it to this world through me. I was so scared I didn't move except when it was absolutely necessary.

When David came home he was so tired, and when he didn't smell any food cooking, and looked around the room and saw it was a mess; he became flaming mad! The dishes from breakfast were still on the table, every toy you and Nye owned was all over the floor and to make matters worse, as soon as he closed the the door behind himself, I started crying right along with the both of you. He stepped in the room looked at the toys on the floor, then at me and said, "I'm dog tired Unie, I need some sleep, what have you been doing all day!" Mama was speaking in Daddy's tone of voice; she stops rubbing her hands together now and smiles while staring down at the coffee table. "Chile, I was mad enough to cuss that day, oh my goodness. I stood to my feet and yelled so loud at him. I said: 'Mr. Rustin; you stay here with your cryin, peein, hungry babies and I'll go to work for 15 hours and let's see how much you get done!' I tell you his eyes got big as skillets. He stood there staring at me for a few minutes, then he took inventory of the room again and this time he walked over to the kitchen table and sat his lunch pail down. Then he walked over to me and reached both arms out to hug me and I hauled off and slapped his face. I told him to never lay another hand on me as long as he lived and I ran into the bathroom and slammed the door.

I was too mad to cry. The words he spoke, 'What have you been doing all day,' were ringing real loud in my ears. The nerve of that man talking to me like that! I stood with my head rested against the bathroom door and I heard him began talking to the both of you. He asked, "What did you two do to your mother. When I left this morning my wife was sweet and loving; I come home and I don't know who she is..... Well now... what shall I do to the both of you? Maybe I'll just spank your butts; yeah that's what I'll do, teach you both to mess with my wife." I came out of that bathroom so fast, he was standing there; smiling. I looked around the room and the two of you were looking at me all wide eyed. I burst into tears, and David walked up to me and put his arms around my waist and gently asked, "Baby what's wrong, something happened today?"

I rested in his arms and softly responded; 'I'm pregnant again and I'm spotting.' I raised my head to see his reaction. He swallowed real hard and stood there for a minute staring blankly into my eyes. Then he dropped his hands from my waist and said, "Well, no wonder you don't want me to ever touch you again." And your father smiled the most handsome smile ever! I chuckled and felt a weight lift off me. Nye crawled over to your Daddy and as he bent down to lift him up, he said, "Well little man; you might have a brother to even out things around here while I'm at work." David looked over at me and noticed I wasn't smiling. "Unie, you'd better sit down, I can't have you losing my baby." As I sat down, I told him that I didn't want another baby right now, the timing wasn't right. He walked into the kitchen area, put Nye on the floor, rolled up his sleeves and started making dishwater. I sat on the love seat and watched him wash dishes, boil some hot dogs for our dinner and bring me a glass of water; and, he smiled the whole time doing it. He was dog tired and yet he took care of me, us actually. As I sat on that tiny, used love seat looking at your father; I made a silent vow to myself, to never complain to him ever again.

A few hours later I started hemorrhaging. I cried, but it wasn't because I lost the baby; Z…it was because I was relived. That following week, I went to the Family Planning Clinic and started taking birth control pills. For almost a month after the miscarriage I was so full of guilt…. Baby; I might know a little of what you felt." As I looked at Mama, I noticed she had water in her eyes, yet she was smiling at me.

For some strange reason; as I sit here looking at my mother; she doesn't seem as old as I thought she was when I was younger…

My home phone rings and Mama runs to the kitchen counter to get it. "Hello to you too Wardell, hold on." As she hands me the phone, she whispers, "I'm gone, talk to you later." She slips into her shoes, grabs her purse and jacket and blows me a kiss. "Hi handsome" I say, as I watch my loving mother walk out through the garage door. "Hey baby, just calling to see how my girls are doing, Oh wait; I have to remember to say family now. You might be carrying a little bowlegged Patterson in that sexy body of yours!" "Alright now, you keep that kind of talk up and I might be carrying twins." Silence... "Baby that might not be a joke you know, that is possible. Hum, I'll take twin boys." I can hear Wardell grinning through the phone. I remember what Mama just told me and I see myself laid out on the kitchen floor dead! Without thinking I blurt, "Love you, and see you at five thirty. Bye." Click. I am not claiming, nor am I receiving "Twins" oh no, not this Rustin female!

I sit here and think about Mama, and how she never complained when we were growing up. I thought parenting was easy because my parents made it seem that way. I remember her getting teary eyed whenever she scolded us. When I was little, I thought she was so mad at us that she wanted to cry. however, the older I became, I realized my Mama does not like to hurt people for any reason, her persona is very sweet and quiet. My Mama, like her Mama; very seldom raises her voice. Hearing her explain how she felt when she realized she was pregnant again after we were born; makes me not feel so bad about the minute and a half I had doubting whether or not I wanted this baby. I'm going to have this baby and love it! I feel tears running down my face and I push the blanket back and began rubbing my stomach. I hear words coming from my heart, straight out of my mouth; "You are already loved, and when you get here; we will celebrate your life, your wonderful, love filled life!" I smile and think of my Mama, my sweet, wonderful, Mama.

She has the personality like her mother and she's thin bodied with large legs like her mother; Grandma Campbell, but she looks like Granddad Campbell with the exception of his facial scars due to him having severe acne and shaving. He was real light skinned, his nickname was, 'Redbone' and he smiled all the time. He was short for a man, about my height; 5 feet 6 and round like the Pillsbury dough man and I mean he could dance! He moved like he was skinny on the dance floor. Oh yeah, we loved to be around our Granddad Campbell he was so much fun to be with and he always told us stories about when he was a young boy. The details he would tell us made it like actually being there with him and he would explain his emotions and the atmosphere in the places he talked about; our hearts would race and we would get out of breath.

It was as though we lived an adventurous life through his. He was so outgoing and fun to be around and when we were younger he always had a cigarette lit in his hand or in a nearby ashtray. Every time we visited them someone would always stop by just to say, "Hey". Granddad and Grandma Campbell always had company over and the rooms were filled with laughter and usually it was from something said by Granddad. When we were around 9 years old; we realized Granddad Campbell was a character as a child, he was some kinda bad!

I'm sitting here smiling as I can see in my mind's eye the first time we saw Granddad dance and it was a big deal because he and Grandma Campbell sorta tricked my parents into being in attendance; knowing Daddy had turned Mama into a holy roller by then. If my Grandparents thought Mama and Daddy was going to join in on the party, the plan they devised backfired because they stayed inside their bedroom the whole time the party went on. It was Nye and me that kept going back and forth to the bathroom sneaking a peak at the partying, I mean!

We had to have been about seven years old then because I know we were well past kindergarten and this particular Friday evening we arrived in Nevada just before dark. Granddad escorted us through the kitchen as usual into the front bedrooms. Mama and Daddy were in their room unpacking for the weekend and Nye and I were in ours; he was trying to get the T.V. on because they only had a few channels that weren't fuzzy in Nevada, MO. Grandma called us for dinner and when we arrived in the kitchen Mama asked Grandma why'd she cook so much food. Grandma made the shush sound while putting her index finger over her lips as she winked. While we ate Grandma disappeared but no one noticed because we were busy eating and having our usual conversation about how good the food was when the doorbell rang.

Now, we are used to company being at the house when we visit in Nevada; but tonight when Granddad opened the front door we heard, "Hey Redbone, you ready to party!" Nye and I looked at each other as our eyebrows skid all the way up to the top of our foreheads! Mama and her sister; Aunt

Daphne talk on the phone about the parties they have and some of the stuff they talk about that happens; well we were so glad we were going to get the chance to see a Nevada party first-hand tonight!

All of a sudden we heard this loud music; "I WAS BORN IN LIL ROCK, HAD A CHILDHOOD SWEETHEART…" Stevie Wonders 'I Was Made To Love Her' was blasting! We all jumped from our seats and ran towards the living room to see what was going on. I mean! Granddad was popin his fingers and swirling around as he had his upper body bent over and his eyes were closed. His feet were gliding on the wood floors; up, down, up, down, he was grooving to the music. I stood there watching him; so amazed he could really move with his big self! As I stood in the doorway I took inventory of the living room all fixed up with ashtrays and bowls of peanuts and potato chips on every table. There had to have been ten people in the room, some were taking off hats, some were hugging Grandma and a few others were hunching their backs and moving their necks side to side to the groove of the beat to the music. Daddy turned to Mama and asked if she knew about this party and she answered, "You know I wouldn't be here if she had told me about this."

A few minutes later we heard Daddy call us; telling us to come back into the kitchen. While finishing my last few bites of food I was hoping Mama and Daddy would go into their room and leave us in the kitchen so we could go sit on the floor in the hall and watch the Nevada party, but you know that didn't happen, right! They made us go to our room and told us not to come out of it except to use the restroom.

While Nye and I inched our way from the kitchen to the bedroom, Uncle Delbert and Aunt Thelma came in the front door and we had a chance to stand in the living room and watch more of the party while they hugged us and told me and Nye had they known we were going to be here; they would have brought Delbert Jr. so he could spend some time with us, he was spending the night with some friends of his tonight.

After our conversation with our Uncle and Aunt, we lingered and watched with our mouths wide open. The music was loud and fast! The room was smoky and crowded with people bobbing their heads, shoulders moving side to side, hips swaying, I mean! My eyes moved on Granddad and Grandma dancing in front of each other and he still had his eyes closed and was he git'n it! Grandma was moving gracefully swaying back and forth smiling and popping her fingers to the beat.   Here comes Aunt Esther and Uncle Marvin. They hug almost everybody in the room before seeing me and Nye; and did their faces light up. As they approach us Daddy stands behind me and says, "I thought I told you two to go to your room a while ago." Nye spoke right up, "We were on our way and Uncle Delbert stopped us to say hi."

Aunt Esther grabs Nye and hugs him real tight while yelling how happy she is to see her sisters' twins! Uncle Marvin nods at Daddy and Mama comes into the room and Aunt Esther grabs me and began hugging me so tight I can barely breathe. She tells me how much I look like her sister and makes me turn around so she can see my legs; if they're big like Mamas! We have to move into the hall now because more people have arrived and the dancing is getting crowded in the living room. The front door keeps swinging open as the guest arrive. Nye and I are grinning, so happy we can be a part of this party and praying someone else we know comes through the door so we don't have to go into that room. Oh well; Nye took me by the elbow as we took small, teeny tiny steps walking backwards to our room. Later Aunt Daphne and Uncle Wayne came into our room and asked us about school and our grades. Yep, that was the first Nevada party I remember and the first time seeing Granddad Campbell 'cut a rug'.

Now Grandma Campbell was thin like Mama, short maybe 5' 3" brown skinned and Mama took her big legs from her mother. Grandma Campbell was so sweet; love and affection just oozed out of her, the only time she raised her voice, was to call Granddad. Lying here, a smile appears on my face as the memory of this one trip to Nevada comes to mind. We had arrived at their house after dark and Granddad came to the back door to let us in and he disappeared. When Grandma came into the kitchen, she asked each one of us to let her see the bottom of our shoes. After inspecting all of our shoe bottoms, she said, "uh huh, just as I thought." She walked to the doorway that led to the dining room and yelled, "Robert Earl!" She put her hands on her hips as she stood waiting on Granddad to come to the kitchen. As he approached the dining room we heard him say, "My sweetness, what is it you need daddy to do for you." We watched him as he approached Grandma.

He extended his hands to hold her face, like he always did, and she said, "You been outside in my rose bush again, I don't want your stinking cigarette smelling hands on my face." She's saying this to him as she gently removes his hands from her face, he says, "Awl baby, what makes you think I been smoking." She turns around to face us and says, "Man, when you gonna learn I know everything you do? Now go outside and clean the bottom of your shoes, you trackin mud in my house." She walks to the broom closet and takes out the broom and dust pan, and heads towards the dining room. As we follow her, we see the big black footprints Granddad left for her to clean. Yep, the only time she ever raised her voice was to call her Robert Earl.

Grandma and Granddad Campbell had 4 children, Uncle Delbert, Mama, Aunt Daphne and Aunt Esther. Uncle Delbert married Aunt Thelma and they only had Delbert Junior. Aunt Daphne married Uncle Wayne and they had two boys, Dewayne and Donavan, and let me just say; the both of them are some kind of bad just like granddad was. They're in and out of jail as if it has a revolving door. Mama told me a few months ago that Donavan finally gave his life to the Lord this last time he was released, so we are all praying he stays straight and finds himself a wife and settle down. Dewayne is still serving time; he should get paroled in 2 years. Aunt Esther married a preacher, Uncle Marvin, and they had twin girls; Eva and Myra, then when they were 14, here comes Little Marvin Junior and he puts the 'B' on the word bad!

All of Mamas' family still lives in Nevada, Missouri where they all grew up. Grandma Campbell's maiden name was Turner before she married Granddad and her family had some land that was willed to Grandma, so she and Granddad raised their family in the Turner house, as they call it. Growing up, we always spent Thanksgiving there. Granddad passed when Nye and I were 14. He was involved in a head on collision just a few blocks away from the Turner house. It was hard for Grandma Campbell for months every time she heard sirens because she was home the day of his accident and heard the sirens and had no idea they were ringing for her Robert Earl. Now that was another home going I'll never forget, talk about beautiful!

When Mama received the phone call we were all getting ready to sit down and have dinner. Grandma Campbell had sent Granddad to the store to get some vanilla flavoring so she could make him a Coconut Cake and it was on his way home from the store some man crossed the double line at high speed and hit him head on. The Turner house is off a two lane highway because it's in the rural part of Nevada. The good thing about the accident was he went instantly but we had to have a closed casket ceremony. There were so many people in attendance of Granddads' funeral, the church had to put chairs outside and still people were standing around. So many came up to give a 2 minute remark, the Pastor had to cut it off. People were crying at the church, the cemetery and at the house and commenting about how much he was going to be missed. One of the Deacons had people in the dining room take turns telling us how Granddad Campbell helped them.

So many young men told us how the words Granddad spoke to them helped change their lives. Some of the women shared how their husbands changed for the better after having classes with Granddad; he was one of the church most liked Deacons. Grandma Campbell was so happy to hear all of the kind words spoken of her Robert Earl; she cried tears of joy right along with the rest of us. Yep I will forever remember my Mamas' Daddy. Grandma Campbell says the Turner land is willed to Mama and her siblings and hopefully Nicki will own it one day and leave it to her children.

Now Granddad Campbell is from the north side of Nevada and because he was 6 years older than Grandma he never knew she lived only fifteen minutes away from him. When Grandma and Granddad had their 25th wedding anniversary, Granddad told everybody the day he met Grandma was the day his whole life changed for the better. He had been honorably discharged from the Army for three weeks and was living with his Uncle Jon. The night before, Uncle Jon sat him down and told him very sternly that if he didn't work next week, he wouldn't be eating next week. Granddad Campbell decided to go job hunting the following morning. He walked to town and was headed to the supermarket to get an application for box boy and when he walked into the supermarket, there was Grandma Pearl standing in line waiting to pay for her few groceries. He said what caught his attention was her big beautiful eyes and the way she was staring out of the window, as if she didn't have a care in the world.

He went back outside and stood at the door and watched her and decided to approach her when she came out of the store. Granddad smiled real big as he told us, "When she came in full view, wow, my eyes almost popped outa my head! What a fine container she was to behold." While telling us this, he walks over to Grandma and extends his hands to gently cuddle her face in them, then he gives her a peck on the lips, gazes into her eyes and jumps and shivers as if he had been shocked by electricity and everyone in the room laughs. He continues, "Oh where was I, oh yea baby see what you still do to me, okay let me get back to my story. Now I knew she was a lady and I couldn't just pounce on her, so I walked up to her and said excuse me miss, and I reached into my pocket and pulled out a dollar and asked, 'Did you happen to drop this?' She looked at my hand then up at me and said, 'You know I saw you take that out of your pocket, man you need to go home and take your medicine.'

I said, what medicine and she said, 'For your mental illness because you must be crazy if you think I'm falling for that line.' I stood still and looked into those beautiful sparkling eyes and said, 'Ok, I'm crazy about you but the only medicine I need is for you to go on one date with me." She gave me a look and started walking away from me. I thought I'd never see her again if she got away so I started walking behind her and blurted; "I know you're a lady and I had to come up with some excuse to talk to you but…" She stood completely still and when I stepped in front of her, she looked me in the eyes and said, 'Here' and as she handed me her shopping bag she said, 'Walk me home.' I asked her what her name was and told her mine and we walked to the Turner house and I declare I had diarrhea at the mouth, man I couldn't stop talkin.

I went back to the grocery store and got the job as box boy because Pearl was my lucky charm." Granddad smiles extra big while saying those words and looking upon Grandma so lovingly; he continues, "She made me court her for nine months before she kissed me and the next week I proposed. I tell you that fifteen minute walk to her house seemed like only five when I arrived at Pearls' house and looked into those big pretty brown eyes. So, everybody, let's toast to my good luck charm; Pearl, baby, happy anniversary!"

I guess you could say I'm blessed to have grandparents and parents who love one another very much after being faithfully married for a lot of years; what a wonderful pattern for me to follow and, its a blessing!

Grandma Campbell is a petite, milk chocolate shaded woman with big round warm brown eyes. Her eyes make you follow her around the room when you first meet her because they are so round. To this day she is still a beautiful woman, she has a little stomach on her, but she still wears a size 8 and she can show you how designer clothes should be worn with shoes, purse and hat to match and, don't forget the gloves! Yeah, Grandma Campbell gets down when she steps out! I mean!

Yep! That's my Mama and her roots. Lord I thank you for my Mama and Daddy, the best parents ever! They demonstrated work ethics to us also. Mama always worked part time while we were growing up and after our graduation from high school she went full time at the church school. She has always been a good role model balancing home, work and church. I never knew how tiring being grown and a parent was until I became grown and she does everything herself, no cleaning lady, laundry helper or groceries delivered. She only works to pay her car note and she loves what she does.

Rose of Sharon Church has their own daycare and she teaches the toddlers on Wednesday Thursday and Fridays. Believe me when I say teach, because that's exactly what she does and she's a natural with little kids. The schools administrator is the first lady, Sister Odette Stephens, and she offered Mama a position helping the teachers with the older children because the kids listen to her but Mama says the older children talk back too much and besides, she loves to watch the little ones learn, it makes her heart warm, my Mama and her words.

When we were little every New Year's Day while we were having dinner, Daddy would tell us the story of how him and Mama made their exodus from Nevada because it was too difficult to get a steady job there. They stayed with Uncle Junior after they were married and back then jobs for black folk were only temporary, no full time work was available and you had better not fix your mouth to ask for benefits. You had to work with no days off with pay, no paid holidays, and you did good to get a break. Daddy said Mama was doing day work for a few months and one morning he woke to her throwing up, and he thought she might be pregnant, so he needed to get a job with benefits.

Turned out Mama had only eaten something that didn't agree with her but that made him decide to look outside of Nevada for work. Scanning the newspaper, he found janitor jobs listed in Kansas City, so he prayed and told the Lord if he applied and was hired here in KC, it would be all the sign he needed to move his wife. He was hired as janitor for Hy-Vee Grocery Stores and worked there until we were in first grade then he went to work for MGE; Missouri Gas

Energy, and he's still there. He started as a maintenance worker and when an opening came for a meter reader, he checked out some books from the Public Library and studied every night there was no church, and passed the test with high scores. Now, he supervises 8 employees and makes some good money.

Mama worked as Cashier for Gas-N-Stuff when they first moved here for a few months then found out she was pregnant and she worked there until the store told her she had to go on maternity leave, they didn't want her to become a liability. Her and Daddy thought they were having a big baby, at least the doctor told them the baby was big, turns out we were stacked on each other and only one heartbeat was heard.   When they told Grandma and Granddad Campbell Daddy had a job in Kansas City, Granddad was real mad and told Daddy he couldn't believe he would take Mama and uproot her from all of her family. Daddy told Granddad he had a good paying job with benefits and vacation pay. All that information did was silence Granddad, he was still mad. So, Daddy made sure to keep the rent and phone bill paid so Mama could talk to her parents and sisters every day, if she wanted.

You know thinking about this, makes me remember how Daddy told Nye to *show* Mr. Gibson he loved his daughter by actions, and not get into word tussling with his wife's father. I guess he was teaching Nye what he knew for certain worked. Wow. I'm 23 years old and I'm still learning from my parents. I wonder if Nicki will still be learning from me when she's in her twenties, oh my goodness; to think of her being grown... that thought makes me shake my head! My baby grown? I mean!

I 'd better check on her and Missy. I smile so big, my baby is so precious to me, and to think there will be another precious one running around here, ah, it makes my heart flood with love...

"Zinye"

"Yeah man, They had those same shoes on sale last week at the mall. You know that shoe store next to J.C. Penny. Yeah, Martin's Shoes, that's it! Oh yeah brother man how much do I owe you for the hair cut?" As I tell him twenty-five dollars, I'm hoping he forgets how to get back over here. I can tell he's not from this area. This man is so full of the streets! "Twenty-five you say?" Now he's whispering, because he probably only has a twenty in his pocket. Now the man is motioning for me to come close. "Say brother man, I'm short five dollars, can I drop it back by later?" I look him in the eye and let him know, "Man, the prices are on the wall big and clear, If you can't read, ask somebody." "Man I'm good for it, here take the twenty and I'll drop the five off later. What time you close?" "How about you don't ever come back, how's that?" "You can lose customers talking to me like that. I wanna speak to the owner!" "You're speaking to the owner." "Yeah, well take the money man, bye." As he walks out, I shake my head as I watch him leave. Drew, my right hand man looks at me and shakes his head along with me. As I sweep up I wonder if Z has people that don't want to pay for their services in her Salon. This twin thing is really bothering me. I need to read up on the Siamese Twins language, something must be going on with her.

Sometimes I drive by her shop to see if her Tahoe is there, I've memorized her plate; how crazy is that! I want to see if business is good over there. I am so proud of her. She does real good in that building and the way she fixed it up makes it stand out and she keeps it clean. Mama says her and Wardell are doing well financially. By him being in banking they probably save some money and knowing my sister, it's cash and carry with her. They are blessed and I must find a way to talk to Z and let her know how sorry I am for being childish. I just can't figure out why she let me go so long without talking to her. She tried to make me tell her why I was mad at her when I first stopped speaking, but... hey maybe she never figured out I was angry she betrayed me by shutting me out of her life. She didn't run her decision to become a cosmetologist by me at all. And, I felt as though she cut the line hearing from the Lord before me, I'm the oldest not her. I need to hear from her. I'm being eaten up inside missing her. She probably doesn't want me in her life now, Lord if she does, let her call me.

Alright, another walk-in. Let me take care of him and call Von to see how she's felling and what she wants for dinner.

"How are you. I'm Nye, what can I do for you today?"

Chapter Six

I'm Gonna Rap On Your Door
Can't nobody do you like Jesus!

"Zinora"

I throw the blanket back and go to Nicki's room, no Nicki, just Missy on her bed with cover over her. I look in her bathroom and she's trying to reach the facet so that she can turn the water on to wash her little hands, oh no, she's trying to reach the cold water! After I get her hands washed with warm water, she starts singing as we walk down the hall into the family room. This little light of mine has never sounded so sweet to me as it does now, my baby sings, thank You Jesus another praise and worshipper in the family!

My cell rings and as I go to fetch it Nicki grabs the remote. It's Ruby Adams, my regular Wednesday morning client. She tells me she'll be about 30 minutes late in the morning; she has to take her son to school before seeing me.   It seems he has a problem going to the 10th grade without a chaperone. The school notified her he has been skipping school and is being suspended for 2 days so, she has to see the principal about her being notified whenever he is absent from any future classes. I immediately phoned Aretha, Wardells' sister, to let her know I'll bring Nicki in a little later tomorrow morning. Aretha has a Day Care, "Sugar Plums Learning Center," and she watches Nicki for just a hundred dollars a week. She didn't want to charge us anything, but Wardell insisted we pay her something, because Nicki was only five months old when I decided to go back to work and infants require a lot of work. I feel so confident she will get the love, attention and care she deserves having family nurture her. Aretha has two young ladies that help her; Desiree Braxton and September Houston; and while helping her, they earn credits towards their degrees in Child Psychology.

After getting off the phone, I notice Nicki has turned the channel to Nickelodeon, I consider that as my queue to get some office paperwork done. I pull out the Italian Sausages from the freezer, hug Nicki and tell her that I'll be in the office and head down the hall. I sit down and pull out my laptop and as soon as I turn it on I hear water running from the refrigerator door and I get up and run back into the kitchen. Nicki is on her tip toes trying to get water into one of the glasses me and Mama left on the table. This girl is working too hard on this independence; she's not even three yet! 'Well, at least she's chosen water as her preferred drink', I think to myself as I get her Sippy Cup and rinse it out. I decide to cook the Spaghetti now, and make a salad and garlic bread, one of both Wardell and Nicki's favorite meals. This way little miss independent won't be in here by herself. I'll get the bills for the shop paid later while the clothes are in the washer.

WEDNESDAY:

"Zinye"

"I'm home" I yell out as I enter the family room. Silence, um where is everyone. I see movement in the back yard so I open the french doors and hear the duet, "Daddy, daddy's home!" As I close the door behind me, four arms are wrapped around my legs. I pick up the girls and get hugs and kisses from them and here comes their lovely mother with her sugar for me. Umm, I am so blessed! "Hey Baby, what's going on?" "Oh your mother called to tell me your sister is pregnant." "Wha! Z, again. Wardell knows what he's doing. Wow, did Mama say how far along she is?" "Nope. Apparently she just did an over the counter test, she'll know more later. Come on in I have your lunch ready, just get washed up." The girls are already headed to the bathroom to get ready for lunch. I am a blessed man, Thank You Lord!

While we are eating, Rachel asks, "Daddy, are we going to have a brother or sister or two brothers and two sisters?" Well honey, because the baby is inside Mommy's tummy right now it's too small yet to tell. But when we find out, we will let you know what to expect, ok?" Rebecca asks, "How did the baby get inside Mommy's tummy?" I looked at Von and said, "Your turn!" Without skipping a beat, she says, "The same way you two got into my tummy." The girls laugh and Rebecca says, "We were in your tummy." Rachel asks, "When?" Von tells them, "Just like this baby. As a matter of fact all babies start in their Mommy's tummies first, and when its time for the babies birthday... the baby comes out."

"We like birthdays! Yey, birthdays are fun!" Says the duet. Von says, "Oh yeah, fun." While looking at me like Whew, we just dodged that bullitt! The rest of the lunch conversation was about the fun had at birthday parties. I tried my best to get Von in the bedroom with me for a few minutes before my returning to work, but she said the girls were too worked up and there was no way they would sit still long enough for us to enjoy ourselves. She almost ushered me to the back door. Man I have got to get her away from the house so we can have some play time. Guess I'll have to wait for bedtime, yeah, come on bedtime!

"Zinora"

It was extremely busy for a Wednesday when I arrived at the shop. Miss Ruby walked in as soon as I put on my smock. I had her sit at my station and as I scratched her scalp, she filled me in on her son, Bryant, and became angry all over again while telling me verbatim how the Principal talked about Bryant's behavior as though he were some sort of criminal.

While Miss Ruby was under the dryer, Shells' client was on her cell phone and said she needed a few minutes so I asked Shell if she would thread my eyebrows; she is the only one in the shop that knows how to thread and threading seems to last longer than waxing for me. Sherry was in the back at the bowl rinsing color out of Ella and she hollered; "Z, who else in your family has those thick eyebrows?" I hollered back, "My twin brother Nye and we took them after our grandfather." I heard the water stop and Sherry yelled, "Girl! You have a twin brother?" By me sitting at my station, I could see in the mirrors the surprise expressions everyone in the room had. Shell's client's eyes bucked as she held the phone down while her mouth simultaneously fell open. Sherry's client, Ella popped up from the sink staring at me and Shell was getting ready to place the thread on my brow and stopped with her hands in midair, threads hanging while she gawped at me as if in total disbelief with her mouth wide open.

I felt so uncomfortable watching all of the stares and open mouths; not even thinking I replied, "We aren't close." What! Did I just open my mouth and insert my foot! There was this strange silence that fell on the room, the kind that made the words I had just spoken hang suspended, hovering over the whole room. I saw the look they each gave to one another before resuming what they were doing, the look like; 'can you believe this mess.' I felt a tugging in the pit of my stomach and then, that queasiness came over me again. I wanted to rewind the whole conversation, back, back, back….but I can't, they know now, so I just lay back in the chair as Shell slowly and silently threaded my brows. The silence was dreadful, I was so glad when Shells' next client walked in and said something. Once again I thought, 'These people don't understand, Nye started this mess and he should be the one to end it. I did nothing to him. He owes **me** an apology. Oh lord; put it on his heart to call me and apologize, you know he started this mess!'

It was 4:52 when my last client, Regina Womack walked out of the door. As I combed her out; I was praying for no more walk-ins. After I swept my area, I plopped myself down in my chair and thought about how completely out of gas I was. As I slt here I play a short movie trailer of all the things I have to do in my head. I saw myself picking Nicki up, fixing something for dinner, cleaning the kitchen and getting to Choir Rehearsal by 7pm, and I really believe I made myself dizzy! Having all this Nye stuff on my mind and so much to do…well, it's tiring, that's all I can say, just down right exhausting.

"Zinye"

It was so busy in the shop that time just zipped right on away. A young man brought his two sons in for a haircut and I thought about Z. I remembered the first time Daddy took me to the Barber and she had to stay home. I was so confused as to why she couldn't come with us, we did everything together. During the drive to the Barbers, Daddy told me that girls get their hair pressed and boys get their hair cut. He asked if I ever wished I had a brother. I thought it was strange he would ask me that. I always saw Z as my best friend, in my head the fact she was a girl had nothing to do with anything. All I knew was she was always with me and we shared everything. I guess when you're young, gender doesn't really matter.

I wonder how she's taking the news about the musical. Lord, please make her call me. I know this rift has swollen up into a big matter, and I had no intentions of it ever getting this big. She has always, always been the one to bring peace to any situation, so let her call me, please. I miss her so much lately. Maybe she's going through something right now, yeah that's probably why she's heavily on my mind. I pray in the Name above all Names, she is comforted and finds solace in what she's facing right now, in the Name of Jesus!

On my drive home I think about how Z and I have always been connected. The twin thing was really strong with us. I never knew our bond was stronger than other brother and sisters until we started school.

The first day of kindergarten, we were in the same class and the teacher kept watching us. The next day Mama had to take us to school again and while we walked to school, she told us we were going to have separate classes. I thought she meant Z and I were going to be in a class separate from the other kids, it wasn't until we were told two different class numbers that I understood Z and I were being separated. She has always been quiet and needs me to help her get moving. I guess you can say she has always been the cautious one, and I have always been the risk taker. For as long as I can remember, I have had to take hold of her elbow and guide her along the way. Yeah, I smile while thinking of that......

Mama took Z to her class first and as all three of us stood outside the classroom door, Mama told both of us Z was going to have her own class and make friends, and I was going to have my own class and make friends as well. I couldn't figure out why we had to have our own classes and told Mama so. I grabbed Z and we hugged while I told Mama she was not going in there by herself! Mama had tears in her eyes while telling me, "Nye, honey, try it. Who knows, you might like having new friends! You can compare notes later about the new people you meet here today. Come on let's take your sister inside her new class. Come on honey." She pried us apart and all three of us inched our way into Z's class. I looked Z in the eyes and thought, 'I'll come get you if you need me, okay?' While she looked me in the eyes she shook her head yes. Her teacher took her hand from Mama's and Mama directed me away from the classroom. I wanted to bite Mama's hand and rescue Z, but she had a tight grip on my arm.

As she dragged me to my class she explained to me that I was the oldest and had to be strong so Z would be strong. She told me that we had plenty time to be with each other when we get home from school, and we could tell each other about our experiences. "It'll be fun, you'll see honey." My teacher, Ms. Moore, took my hand also and asked me where would I like to sit. I scanned the room and found an empty spot and pointed to it. When I turned around, Mama was gone. It wasn't until I sat down that I realized I didn't know how to get to Z's class from here and I spent most of my time in that room trying to remember the steps Mama and I took from Z's class. She might need me and I don't know how to get to her.

When my class lined up and marched to the gate after class was over, I saw Z in line. She was talking to a girl in her class. I was so relieved, she didn't need me after all! Mama walked over to Z's class and talked to her teacher, Ms. Franklin for a few minutes and then her and Z came over to get me and Mama talked to Ms. Moore. During our walk home, Mama asked us to tell her about our class and what we had learned today. I told her I wanted to be in Z's class and she explained to us, how we were twins and must learn how to become separate like other children. Mama told us this was new to us and that we will get used to being separate, it was going to take time, but you will like it, just wait and see. It was then I realized I was going to have a tough time separating myself from Z. Man, it's still tough........

THURSDAY:

I woke before Von so I decided to get some prayer in this morning. I need guidance for this musical. I feel as though the Lord is going to set a lot of people free and hopefully some salvations will occur. This year Holy spirit instructed me to have only four choirs render 2 songs instead of the six choirs rendering 2 songs. We as the church need to magnify the Lord more than our situations. I need all the guidance I can get. It would be nice if Z could help me. One thing about my sister, she can praise and worship the Lord from her heart like nobody else I know can. She has always had a pure praise. The more I meditate in the Word, the more I understand it's the pureness from our hearts that invoke the presence of God.

As I get cleaned up I remember the first time my sister ushered in the presence of the Lord at our church we grew up in; Rose of Sharon Church Of God In Christ. Z has always been sensitive to the move of God. She could tell when the mood was shifting in the spirit, even when we were young. The more time I spend with Holy Spirit, the more I realize He has to have a pure heart in order to summons His presence and, I realize us Rustins are chosen (selected), not just called (invited). That's why it puzzles me as to why she hasn't made me put and end to us not talking. I just can't figure it out.....

As I enter my study, I can see in my minds eye that Sunday so clearly in my head....

It was a rainy overcast Sunday, the kind of day you want to stay in the house and watch cartoons while Mama popped pop corn and made her magnificent home made chili and her sweet cornbread. None of us could seem to get a move on except Daddy. He kept saying, "Come on, let's get a move on. I hate being late!" We made it to church on time but we were still dragging ourselves around like we were weighted down. People at church were yawning and slow moving also. It wasn't just us Rustins minus Daddy, it was the weather that had us moving in slow motion. We had already sang our first song we rehearsed, and it was offering time. We were waiting for Mama to end playing the introduction to, "In some way or other, the Lord will provide."   This was one of our usual offering songs and Mama loved playing it. All of a sudden Z   stepped forward. closed her eyes and bellowed out, "**Praise Him, Praise Him, Praise Him in the mornin, Praise Him in the noon day, Praise Him, Praise Him, Praise Him till the sun go down**!"

She started clapping and modulated as she repeated her words. Mama immediately switched songs and the choir joined her. People in the congregation walked by the offering table and after putting their offering in the basket, they started clapping and dancing in the Spirit. It was amazing how she sensed the move of the spirit. I couldn't believe she stepped up like she did, she was always so shy. The whole church was caught up in praise unto the Lord and Pastor Stephens even changed his sermon. "Give us the garment of praise for the spirit of heaviness." Isaiah 61: 3. Man, did he preach!

When we were home eating, Daddy asked Z how she felt when she stepped forward and began singing. She told us she felt a large hand in the middle of her back gently push her forward and she closed her eyes because she had no idea what was going to happen and she didn't want to look at the people. When she opened her mouth, she was just as surprised as we were at what was coming out. All she knew was she had to let what was inside her come out. Daddy explained to us how the anointing will find a yielded vessel to use so he can comfort and guide His people. "Baby the anointing is an endowment, its an equipping to produce His presence. He only produces His presence for His glory. You are blessed to be used and I am so godly proud my daughter is being used by the Lord, and you're what, eleven years old? You are a Rustin and we are part of the chosen, the remnant. Remember that okay baby, remember who you are and Whose you are." Daddy pointed towards heaven when he said "Whose you are." I felt as though he were talking to me too. Yeah, my little sister could usher in the presence of the Lord.... I sit here in my study smiling while picturing Z's face in my mind. Lord, please make her call me.....

"Zinora"

Man It's Thursday already, this week is moving along. While scrambling Wardell some eggs, he walked up behind me and whispered in my ear; "Baby, what's bothering you?" I knew exactly what he was referring to; I tossed and turned all night. I couldn't say anything, I just kept scrambling the eggs and shook my head 'No'. He twirled himself around and put his back against the kitchen counter and slightly bent his upper body in front of me and said, "I do know the first trimester is supposed to be stress free, right?" I reached around him and took a plate out of the cabinet and placed his eggs on it then grabbed the toast from the toaster and buttered it. We both walked over to the table and he sat down, still looking at me.

So, as I placed his breakfast on the table I pulled out a chair, sat down next to him and I told him about what had happened at the shop yesterday and how sad it makes me feel. Of course he asks, "Then why don't you give Nye a call, and ask him to forgive you, if you've done anything to offend him?" I placed my hand on his and sincerely said, "Baby I know you're right, (sigh), Mama gave me his number, it's over there on a post it….. I'm seriously thinking about giving Nye a call. He smiled that, "I'm so proud of you," smile at me and said, "Now that's my girl!" Then he winked at me and had me blushing….ooh, ooh wee, I loves this man!

While taking Nicki to Aretha's I thought about what I would say to Nye after all these years of being silent…I need a real unique ice breaker, something that will make him not hang up on me….. Maybe I should do as Mama suggested, just pay him and Von a visit, besides this way I can get some hugs and kisses from my nieces. Now I'm envisioning my arms around Rachel and Rebecca and while I'm kissing and hugging them; they throw their little arms around my neck. I think of how Nicki's little, warm, tender arms feel around my neck and tears begin to form in my eyes. Oh I just know their little fat jaws are so soft and sweet… I glance in the rear view mirror at Nicki as I wipe away the tears that have begun to flow down my face. Yeah, I'll become a walk in, as we call it in the hair business, just so happen to drop by Nye's…….

After dropping Nicki off, I make a stop at the Beauty Supply. My client this morning needs a color touch up and I need to pick up additional cellophane.

I pick up my supplies and without even thinking, I find myself driving by Nye's shop.

This is insane! I have got to stop doing this, I feel like a stalker, and what's so crazy is… this is my brother! Come on Z, get it together, you've got clients waiting…stalking your own brother, girl……I drive to my shop; shaking my head at myself all the way.

Ivy James was waiting for me when I arrived and the shop was jumpin all day, but I did manage to call and make me an appointment to see my doctor next week, Wednesday. I also made a few calls to rearrange my appointments and before I realized it, it was after five, so I got my rush on. Tonight is 7pm Bible Study and for us not to be late, I need to push it!

When I went to get Nicki, Aretha wanted to talk to me for a minute. I followed her into the kitchen and she pulled out a chair for me and she sat across the table. She had such a serious look on her face; I was a little worried something had happened to Nicki but she read the fear on my face and said, "Z, nothing's wrong. I want to inform you about Nicki's behavior. She's telling everyone she comes in contact with that she's getting a sister. Yesterday she told a few of the children here she's getting a sister, but today she has run up to a few parents and shared with them that she is getting a sister. I need to know if you or Wardell has told her she's having a sister, because I don't want her telling stories and if I need to sit her down and explain the difference between pretend and real to her I will need you and Wardells' support with me on the subject. I want to run it by you first so we can work on her imagination together.

I was shocked at first that Nicki was telling anyone about having a sister, and then I thought it sounds like she's looking forward to a sibling, and I was glad about that. What I can't figure out is how she knows, I never said anything to her and Wardell didn't mention to me that he had talked to her. While I'm sitting here thinking all of this, Aretha is staring at me, waiting for me to respond. I open my mouth to tell her what I'm thinking and she starts smiling and as she tilts her head she says, "You're pregnant aren't you?" I sit staring at her thinking, 'Now how did you figure that out?' She jumps up from her chair and comes around the table so fast; I barely had a chance to turn around in mine.

Now she's grinning and saying, "I'm gonna be an Auntie again! Oh Z, congratulations, when are you due?" She reaches her arms out to embrace me and I'm still in shock! "Aretha, how did you figure out I'm pregnant?" As we end our embrace, she continues her grin as she says, "Daddy used to tell us every time Mama was pregnant and when we were grown someone asked him one day at the dining room table, how did he know when Mama was pregnant and he said whoever the baby was at the time would follow Mama around like she was the mailman and they were waiting on a check. Daddy told us that babies can sense those kinds of things, just pay close attention to them. Besides, you are glowing!"

"Well, I just took the over the counter test and it was positive so I'll know more after my doctor's visit. I can't figure out if Wardell told Nicki, cr if she sensed it, I haven't said anything to her. Oh, but you know, she did ask me if she could have a sister, yeah, she did ask me that. Wow, it's amazing how small children are so discerning, wow!" "Oh Z; I'm so happy for you; I just pray the baby is healthy, we know it will beautiful and spoiled, boy or girl." Aretha hugs me again, this time real tight and don't ask me why, but I thought to myself; 'This should be my brother hugging me', and I started blinking back tears. As we walked out of the kitchen, Aretha yelled for Nicki to get her jacket, it was time to go with Mommy now.

As I fastened Nicki into her car seat, I asked, "Nicki, baby, do you want a baby sister?" As her little brown eyes lit up, she exclaimed, "Yes Mommy, wittle tister!" She clapped her hands and smiled so big, I found myself smiling and thinking how wonderful my life will be having two precious children to love and spoil, Oh…I'm so blessed!

Well, we were fifteen minutes late getting to Bible Study, even with me pushing it. Wardell put Nicki's pajamas on her and supervised her teeth brushing while I cleaned the kitchen. Usually one of us stays home with her on Bible Study night, but tonight is special, we have a guest teaching so both of us wanted to attend and the rubbing of the eyes and whining had started before we left the house. I only pray she'll go to sleep in the sanctuary and both of us can enjoy the teaching.

Our Reverend Hall is married to Francis Atkins-Hall and she is the youngest of her family. Her oldest brother, Reverend Emmet Atkins is our guest speaker tonight. He really is more of a Teacher than a Preacher, and both Wardell and I love his messages and we're excited to hear what he is teaching tonight. He's a tall, thin man and looks nothing at all like Sister Hall. He is brown skinned, with large brown eyes, thick eyebrows and grey all over his face, eyebrows, mustache, head; all white as snow, but his teaching mesmerizes you. You find yourself hanging onto every word that comes out of his mouth and I know he has a Word for me tonight, I can just feel it!

Oh boy! Reverend Atkins is requesting our choir to sing "Grateful," by Hezekiah Walker. I hope Nicki doesn't cut up while I sing, she's clutching onto me real tight tonight. Oh my goodness, Wardell had to take her out into the vestibule; she just about had a conniption when I stood up to leave her!

Well, the congregation was definitely in worship mode when Reverend Atkins took to the pulpit, the anointing was so thick, it could have been cut with a knife! Ooh wee... He paced back and forth in front of the pulpit under the anointing, and kept saying, "Yes" as he moved and finally he told us Holy Spirit had changed the direction of the message and he was going to share with us some scripture on FORGIVENESS. I felt my jaw drop...

Want to hear something that will make the hair stand up on the back of your neck? Wardell returned to the sanctuary with Nicki as I left the choir stand to return to our pew and she leaped into my arms. I sat down and laid her across my lap with her feet on Wardell's lap. As I began to rock her she tossed and twisted so, however; I kid you not, as soon as Reverend Atkins said the word forgiveness; Nicki went limp on my lap, out like a light by its switch! I knew right at that moment this message was intended for me; and so... I listened.......

He quoted **Luke 6:37**; **"Judge not, and you shall not be judged. Condemn not, and you shall not be condemned. Forgive, and you will be forgiven."** As he walked to the pulpit, my eyes were fastened on him. It was as if Jesus was talking to me through him. I no longer saw Reverend Atkins; I saw The Word, heard The Word, and yes, received The Word as HE was standing right here speaking to me!

As I heard the Word, I could see in my mind so clearly Nye and myself. I saw how every time I wanted to reach out to Nye; I either judged or condemned how I thought he might respond to me, ultimately putting the responsibility of apologizing on him. All these years of judging and condemning has caused me to construct walls of un-forgiveness around my heart. Me; the person who was minding my own business when, suddenly one day, my only brother pushed our relationship aside like an old rusty bike that was no longer appealing to the rider. I heard myself whimper….

Wardell handed me some tissue and put his arm around me and began to rub my arm. I could actually see the Word being spoken so clearly to me, and, at the same time the fallow ground of my heart was breaking. Lord I love You and need You to help me with this! I heard Reverend Atkins say; **"If someone says, I love God, and hates his brother, he is a liar; for he who does not love his brother whom he has seen, how can he love God whom he has not seen?"** Reverend Atkins was quoting **1 John 4: 20**, and did that Word show me, me!

Reverend Atkins elaborated on how forgiveness, in its purest form; is unconditional, just like love is. The same way we are capable of loving someone who does not necessarily return the exact measure of love; the same conditions are attached to forgiveness, it doesn't matter if the person we forgive, forgives us, we simply forgive because... **we** have been forgiven! **Matthew 18: 21** and **22** reads: **"Then Peter came to Him and said, 'Lord, how often shall my brother sin against me, and I forgive him? Up to seven times?'   Jesus said unto him, 'I do not say to you, up to seven times, but up to seventy times seven'."**

After Reverend Atkins explained the just of the rest of the chapter, he wrapped it up by saying; "So, our heavenly Father does not want this horrible tragedy of not forgiving you because you refuse to forgive, to happen to any of us! BUT... He said while holding up his index finger; it will happen, if we are not practicing forgiveness. As he closed his Bible he asked us all to examine our hearts and if there is any indication of un-forgiveness, simply come to the altar and get it right; no one judging, lest they will be judged. I slipped Nicki over onto Wardells lap and went to the altar. I humbly went to my knees and cried as I prayed for the Lord to forgive me for not being forgiving. It really didn't matter who started this feud or why; right now; I'm sorry for whatever; I want my brother back......

While kneeling at the altar, I allowed the un-forgiveness to flow out of me through each tear that fell; it was me and the Lord and I told Him exactly how hurt I felt being pushed aside by my only brother and best friend... I wept as I felt the pain surface caused by the way I had been treated...The hurt swept, and swept through my heart..... I pleaded for Holy Spirit to give me a clean heart, a heart that would not judge, condemn nor harbor anymore un-forgiveness. A heart that forgives. I WEPT.   When there were no more tears for me to shed; I stood up and to my surprise, I had to avoid stepping on so many hands, the altar was full! Yes indeed, the Lord Himself spoke to Bethel Missionary tonight!

During offering and benediction, only a few choir members were able to sing; the rest of us were still under the influence of the anointing; He was still speaking to our hearts; telling us how to come correct at those who had wronged us and to humble ourselves because we had done wrong ourselves. How do I know this was the move in the sanctuary... the people were walking over to one another weeping and asking each other for forgiveness, almost everyone in the room was weeping, it was awesome observing the move of God, all I could do was shake my head, it was just that awesome!

During the ride home Wardell kept looking over at me but he didn't say anything. When he pulled into the garage, he said, "I'll put Lil Kitten to bed, go let the Lord finish what He's started." I unbelted Nicki and when Wardell opened my car door the tears continued to flow. I ran a bath and sat in the tub while the water was running so I could listen to Holy Spirit. I heard so clearly: 'Nye misses you as much as you miss him. You have always been first to reason, he needs to know you will forgive him, he is saddened you have allowed this to go this long, he needs his little sister.' I was rested against the back of the tub, my head on the pillow and shaking my head yes, my way of letting Holy Spirit know that I understood what He was telling me as tears streamed down my face. To think Nye was just as tortured as I am; made me want to apologize to him so he could feel better. When I opened my eyes Wardell had closed the bathroom door so total healing could be ministered to me. He didn't even turn the television on to distract me. Ooh, ooh wee! I love this man!

I began to sing unto the Lord from the depths of my heart. I sang words that expressed how much I love and appreciate Him, I felt the warmth of His presence flood over me and the smile in my heart produced a gratifying smile on my face....I began thanking Him for being so loving and tenderhearted towards me and before I knew it....I was clapping my hands and praising the Lord. I stood up and stepped out of the tub and did my holy dance; the dance Nye and I used to do when we were growing up. I mean I danced and shouted, "Thank you Jesus!" Until I was totally out of breath. I have never done drugs in my life but I tell you! I was floating when I came out of that bathroom, you hear me! I felt just like a gliding cloud!!!

I crawled into bed and Wardell held me in his arms until I dozed off.

FRIDAY:

I overslept again! This time Nicki woke me. When I saw the clock, I jumped out of bed and was running like a fast forward movie. This is the Friday my client Faith Griffin comes and she is always punctual and gets an attitude if she has to wait her turn so I know she's going to be mad at me this morning because there's no way I'll be there before her. Oh lord, slow time down for me this morning, palee-z. Okay, okay, think....think Z.....if I don't fix something for us to eat, I can save time and possibly get to the shop before Faith does, yep, I'll take Nicki a packet of instant oatmeal and have Desiree make it for her. That should put me on schedule, yeah, that should do it!

Just as Nicki and I enter the garage I get that queasiness again and immediately think of Nye. Now I smile. I'm thinking of telling him I forgive him and how it's going to free us both up, I'm so glad I'm saved!

As I pull up into the Salon parking lot, Faith pulls up right beside me. I glance over at her and she gives me this look! Oh boy…it's going to be attitude and we haven't even said good morning! I think of some scriptures to put my mind on Jesus, I have no intentions of going to attitude city today at all. I am blessed, and repel stress; she can take that trip by herself…… as I close my car door I pleasantly say, "Good morning Faith, looks like it's going to be a beautiful day, wanna come inside and make the day come in second to your beauty?" I smile at her but she slams her car door and arms the alarm. Stepping up onto the curb she states; "Zinora, are you always this chipper in the morning? I don't think I have ever seen you sad or mad. How can you be so happy all the time, I need to know your secret." As I hold the door open for her I state, "Well, come on in and I'll be more than happy to tell you!"

Sherry has already set the tone in the shop for the day. Her worship music was on with the volume low and she was reading her Bible while Ms. Hathaway was under the dryer. After we all spoke to one another, I asked Faith if she really wanted to know how I stay so happy. She looked at me in the mirror and flatly said, "Yeah." I grabbed my smock and a comb and while I scratched her scalp, I shared how allowing Jesus to have the reigns to your heart frees you to be happy and full of joy. I told her when you do that; the circumstances surrounding you can't penetrate your emotions and allow negative thoughts to rule your thinking. You simply see what's happening and know within your heart that the Lord has your back and you trust He will guide you in the right direction; unless you just don't want Him too.

She listened and when I asked if she was ready to go to the bowl, she asked, "How do I give someone full reign to my heart when they might jack me up, how can I trust someone I can't see? The people I do see have done a job on my heart already." I was looking at her while she spoke and she was not being sarcastic, she was sincere, she had no clue. At that moment I was so thankful to have the parents I have. They raised us up in the fear of God and, taught us how to embrace the Word and they didn't stop there; they also mirrored how to love the Lord to us. I motioned for her to walk with me to the bowl and as she relaxed, I shared the love of Christ with her and then I expressed in detail how someone who would die in your place can totally be trusted! She was real quiet so I covered her head to allow the conditioner and the Word to penetrate, and I left her at the shampoo bowl alone.

Faith stood up to leave my chair and Trisha walked over to the chair to sit down. Faith stood still and looked at Trisha as if to say, "Don't rush me!" Then she walked away from the chair and allowed

Trisha to sit down. I thought Faith was taking a long time to retrieve her money, so I draped Trisha and started applying oil before the relaxer. Faith walked up to me and pulled out her cash and handed it to me. As I thanked her, I reached for the cash and she held onto it, looked me in the eyes and asked me where I attended church. I told her, she released the cash and simply turned around and walked out, never said bye or anything, just left the room as I said to her back; "Have a blessed day." I made a mental note to add her to my prayer list this week; she was troubled, more than usual today.

When Ms. Reeves came in, she had a breakfast sandwich and the odor was divine. I remembered I hadn't eaten yet and was feeling light headed so I asked if anyone else was hungry hoping someone would jump at the chance to go get us something to eat. All I heard was, "No, I'm good" all across the room. Now I was trying to figure out when was I going to be able to leave and where would I be able to go that was close, and, what was I going to have…. I sighed out loud.

Well thank the Lord for Shell. She arrived with a bag of drive thru breakfast food and when she went through the bag, there was an extra sausage sandwich and I believe it was put in the bag just for me! After I ate I had energy to pop the ladies out, one, two, and three!

Another day whizzed by and before picking Nicki up I need to stop by the store and get the drinks for the birthday party tomorrow night and drop them off at Myer Street. Ma and Pops will have a fit if I drop off the drinks without Lil Kitten. As I drove pass

Mission Blvd. I thought about driving by the Barber Shop to see Nye and my heart began to race so fast I started trembling and I felt that queasiness again. I can't keep putting myself through this; it's not good for the baby either in my first trimester. This evening I'm going to figure out how to approach Nye and put this madness behind me!   I thought, 'I need to tell Nye that I'm sorry and get it over with. Yeah, I'm going to his shop right now and end this mess, I don't care who started it!' I drove past the intersection and got in the left lane and made an illegal U-turn headed to Coleman Highlands.

While driving, I thought about what I was going to say to my brother and changed my words at least four times and then I found myself entering a parking space right at the front door of "Kutz by Ziggy." Without thinking; I left my car so fast I slammed the door and didn't even think of locking it. As I entered the shop I scan the room looking for Nye and was greeted by a young man who looked too young to be working and he politely says to me, 'Hello, may I help you?" I realized the front booth was vacant and yet all of the latest barbering tools were laid out on the station as if someone just stepped away and I so desperately hoped it was Nye's station and that he was in the back, perhaps microwaving something to eat. "Is the owner here?" I asked while stretching my neck towards the back. Really I was hoping Nye would hear my voice and come out from behind the wall I was staring at, but... the young man politely told me, "No, I'm sorry he has stepped out for a few moments, is there something I could help you with, or would you care to leave a message for the owner."

By now disappointment started to overtake me, I felt like just sitting down in the chair in front of me, the one I was hoping was Nye's and letting the tears have at it, I felt so drained. I directed my eyes back to the young man and in a voice that quivered, said, "No, no thank you." As I turned to leave. "Who shall I say called on the owner?" While blinking back tears I found myself wondering just how old is this kid; he's acting so grown up, asking me the right questions. I quickly reached into my purse and grabbed a business card and handed it to the young man as I said, "Give him this, thanks." I turned to leave, hoping I could reach the door before the tears hit my face.

As I walked to my car the tears streamed down my face and I let them, I wanted to cry, after all... I want to see my brother and he's not even here.....I sat in my car and cried my heart out. All I could think of was I want to tell Nye how sorry I am but can't because he's not even here.....I cried until my phone rang. It was Wardell. He could tell I was crying and asked in a panicked voice if I were alright, had something happened to me! I sat there shaking my head 'No' and then it dawned on me, he couldn't see me so, I took in a deep breath and told him I was at Nye's shop and had just missed him....he told me to "Stay there, I'm on my way to get you!" I was able to tell him not to do that, I was alright now and was going to head home in just a minute. He made me stay on the phone during my drive home. He started telling me he had already picked Nicki up and was calling me to see if I wanted some ribs, he was around the corner from Adams' Rib to pick up our order he had phoned in from Aretha's. He had me wait until he picked the order up and he returned to the phone. He said he was worried about me being so upset and by me carrying his Patterson seed; he wanted me to be as rested and as peaceful as possible.

By now I'm pulling up in our driveway, Wardell had the garage door already up and he was standing there waiting for me with Nicki in one arm and dinner in the other. Ooh wee, I loves me some Wardell!

"Zinye"

I am so glad it is not as busy as it has been all day. I need to make a quick run home and get my oil for my clippers. I replenished the container yesterday and forgot to put it back in my bag. Good thing we only live several blocks away from here. I love the convenience of going home for lunch and when I need to get something like now. Let me get a move on so I can hurry back and clean my area.

While I sit at a red light, I notice a black Tahoe on the opposite side of the street. I think of Z. I stretch my neck to see if perhaps it's her driving... I couldn't catch the plate numbers.   Lord I miss my sister. I wonder why she's so heavily on my mind. Maybe Von is right, I might need to consider calling her. Nah, she probably hasn't forgiven me for not talking to her....Lord I know she has a right to be mad at me for severing our relationship, but I need to know if she's forgiven me. When she comes to me then I'll know she has no remorse. I don't want to extend my hand to her and she not accept my apology. I truly regret how I handled her betraying me. She might as well had taken a knife and cut my heart in half, cutting me out of her life like she did. Not needing me to help her make decisions was major to me then. Man, thinking of this now sure sounds stupid, but I was seventeen at the time. Young and really dumb, Lord please let her call me, I miss her so much...

"Zinora"

When we unwrapped the bag of food, the whole kitchen smelled of ribs and I forgot all about Nye and everything else. We all sat down and ate until one rib was left, we almost ate the whole thing, talk about tasty!

I straightened up the kitchen and headed towards the bedroom. Wardell asked where was I headed, I told him to the bathroom and then to lie down. He didn't say anything else; he just stood there looking at me so I kept going. I walked out of the bathroom and headed towards the head of our bed then I heard Wardell coming from the hall into our bedroom and he was saying, "I know, it has been years, but hold on, someone wants to talk to you." He was extending the phone to me so I could take it from him. I was trying to think who he could be talking too that we haven't seen in years and I put on my professional voice as I took the handset and said, "Hello!" "Hello Z; its Yvonne, how are you?" I looked at Wardell. He was standing in front of me bouncing Nicki up and down in his arms and I looked in his hand and noticed he was holding the post it note I had written Nye's phone number on Monday. I smiled and gave him a wink. Von is telling me how happy she is to hear from us and how delighted she knows Nye is going to be and I place my hand over the receiver and say, "Thank you." To my wise husband and he bends down and gives me a kiss on my cheek and he and Nicki exits the room closing the door behind them.

Von tells me they're expecting again in seven months which makes her due in October. I tell her how happy I am for them and she thanks me and tells me she heard about me expecting again and asks if I know when I'm due. I explain to her that I've not had the doctor make it official yet and I'll know after my appointment next week. She told me that Nye was on his way back to the shop and that we had just missed him by a few minutes, but she knows he's going to be ecstatic to know we phoned. She said that this last week he has been sharing with her that he misses me so much he can hardly shake the memories of the two of us growing up. I asked her point blank; did she feel Nye and I having a relationship would cause some issues with her because this twin thing we have going on is very strong.

She laughed and said, "Oh no, not at all, I have twin girls. It's amazing to watch them help each other as if they need no one else but each other. Remember I live with twin sisters, and they are incredible to watch." I told her that I had gone to the shop to see Nye, and I heard a beep coming in on her line so she puts me on hold and clicks over. When she returns to the phone, she tells me that was Nye calling to let her know that I had been to the shop, and he was so happy. Silence… I tell her that I want to see my brother and get a long overdue hug and as I speak the words, tears began flowing from my heart down my face…I hear this trembling voice coming from the other end of the phone say, "I understand."

I sit on the edge of my bed crying my eyes out to my sister-in-law and she tells me that she understands. I am so blessed to have her as a sister-in-law and so is my brother to have such a sweet wife. After several minutes of blubbering, I say, "Von, I need to see Nye as soon as possible, I've got to hug my brother and tell him how much I love and miss him. And I want so desperately to hold my nieces and let them know they are so loved by their Auntie Z, oh yeah, I want to give you a big hug also. I feel as though I could burst, I'm so happy!" I hear Von sniffling, I guess that's what you get with 2 pregnant women on the phone. Man oh man, I am so glad to be reunited with my brother and his family! Von composes herself and says to me; "I'll have Nye phone you as soon as he gets home. Is this number in my phone a good number for him to call?" "Oh yeah, this is our home phone number. And Von... thanks for being such a sweet wife to my brother, Daddy always said the Lord knows what woman the Rustin men need; and his words have proven to be true about you, I love you and can hardly wait to see you and get my hug." "Love you too and I'm sure that will happen real soon!" "I hope so, okay Von; I'll talk to you again soon, bye." As I clicked the headset to off, I lay all the way back on the bed and smile so BIG!

Lord I thank You for allowing forgiveness to flow in and through me. I realize that I need You and the powerful yet, precious Holy Spirit to strengthen me when I'm weak and to lead and guide me so that I will do the right things. The things that allow me to walk upright and bring glory to You; the things that will cause peace to live in and through me, Lord ...Thank

You! I'm smiling so; the joy inside of me right now is sooo, unspeakable!

As I lay here a melody springs up in me and I began to sing unto the Lord, one love song after another, ah, how sweet this truly is……

I hear this soft tapping on my door then it slowly opens, when I look to see who's coming through it; this little giggle three feet off the floor is heard. Wham! The door springs all the way open and it is Lil Kitten with the biggest, prettiest smile on an angels face. She's looking directly at me and headed my way. I raise up and she leaps up onto the bed, we hug so tightly, I love her and she loves me! Man oh man am I blessed. I look up and into the face of the finest man ever to live in Kansas City, MO. He sits on the edge of the bed and asks, "So; how did the phone call go?" "Oh Wardell, thank you for being such a wonderful husband, baby I appreciate you and your wisdom is admired by me. I think there is a pedestal with your name on it somewhere…thanks." He removes his shoes while I remove Nicki's and the three of us curl up in the bed and I tell Wardell word for word the conversation I just had with Von.

The whole time I'm talking to him, he is listening very attentively, then he rubs my arm while saying; "You know what me thinks? Me thinks us, Lil Kitten and her parents should get up and get Uncle Nye's address from Gam Ma and pay the Rustin twin girls a visit. That's what me thinks." Then he slightly turns my body towards him and adds, "What you think?" I let go of Nicki and throw my arms around his neck and say, "Me agrees!"

Nicki crawls to the edge of the bed and gets down on the floor and sits down. Wardell leans over to see what she's doing and asks, "Lil Kitten, what are you doing baby?"   Without skipping a beat, a little answer comes back at Wardell, "I put my twos on so we go bye, bye Daddy."   Wardell looks at me as I raise up onto my elbows, hunch my shoulders and say, "It's hard to believe she understands everything we say isn't it?"   As he gets out of the bed, he says, "Yeah, maybe that's where the baby sister talk came from. Baby we are going to have to brush up on our spelling around Lil Kitten," he hunches his shoulders and sighs, "I guess she's growing up!"   I pick up the phone and dial Mama. She answers on the second ring sounding out of breath. I ask if she had to run to catch the phone and she says yes and laughs. I tell her play by play how I went to Kutz by Ziggy and the phone conversation Von and I had. Then I asked for Nye's address because we were getting ready to pay them a visit.

I was so excited knowing I was about to see and hug my big brother; honestly, I had forgotten all about who started what, I was so close to getting my brother back in my life. I felt as though I was meeting my long lost brother I had lost contact with for over 7 years, you know like the people you see on television who had been estranged since birth or something. Maybe this is how the father of the Prodigal Son felt when he saw his long lost son coming towards the house after years of no contact whatsoever. I mean, my heart is racing! I went into the office and wrote down the address on a post it and Mama gave me directions.   She also told me we were all going to have Sunday Brunch over her house after church to celebrate her grandchildren meeting one another; she just had to witness them playing together. Mama was so happy her twins were being reunited!

Wardell drove us while I gave him directions on when and where to turn; it wasn't until we were parked directly in front of the house that I felt nervous. When I saw the beautiful modest home Nye and Von had; my heart leaped with pride. The house looked like Nye, you know what I mean…the structure, era, manicured yard, brown brick with a warm matching trim, and it looked so masculine like my big brother, strong and classy. Wardell unbelted Nicki; I was busy standing outside my car door, admiring the house. As we walked up the walkway, I could hear my heart beating fast. The double doors had large matching wreaths hanging and the colors were soft and inviting, um, must be Von's touch. Wardell rang the bell and as he stepped back from the door, he reached for me and hugged me real tight. I took advantage of the hug and drew some strength from him. Here he is holding our daughter in one arm and his wife in his other, man oh man, he's a pillar of strength, thank You Lord for my husband!

We can hear little laughter coming from the door knob, two different laughs to be exact. Then we hear fumbling with the door knob and Von saying, "Alright girls, you had better not open that door, what have I told you about the door? Huh, let me get it! Who is it?" I opened my mouth, but nothing came out of it, I just stood there with my mouth open. Wardell rubs my arm and says humbly; "The Patterson's calling."   As the door opens, we hear this loud, "OH MY GOD!" Von is standing in the doorway with her mouth wide open, now she and I look like twins; the opened mouthed ones!

I leaped up into her arms; the welcoming arms she had flung open wide just for me. We hugged so tightly and when our embrace ended, we both had faces covered with tears. The twins had grabbed hold of Von; each one had a leg in their arm and stared at me with a question mark on their faces. As I moved away from the door, I bend down and cup the cheek of Rachel, and then I reach over and cup Rebecca's little soft cheeks. I am stunned; they are so beautiful and have Nye's eyes. Wardell and Nicki steps into the house and as soon as he is completely inside; Von grabs them both and rocks and reals as she hugs them, then she extends her arms out for Nicki to come to her.

I reach for Rachel and she extends her arms to me making it real easy to be picked up. I tell her that I am her Auntie and Rebecca takes off running into another room. I notice Nicki is eyeing Von up and down and Wardell tells her, "It's okay; this is your Auntie too." Then Nicki almost leaps out of Wardell's arms into Von's and my lips become a magnet on Rachel's' cheeks, I hug her so tightly, she is so sweet! As Von tells us to come in and make ourselves comfortable, here comes Rebecca back into the foyer with us and she has a frame in her hand. She walks up to me and says, "Auntie Z," as she points to the frame.

Rachel eases her little arms from around my neck, points to the frame and says; "Yeah, Auntie Z." Then she squeezes my neck as tight as she can. Rebecca has turned the frame around and I can see the picture is one of me holding Nicki on my lap when she was a year old. Wardell takes Rachel from my arms and I reach down and grab Rebecca as she looks at the picture and looks at me with the biggest smile on her little face and puts her tiny finger on my chin and says; "Auntie Z." I grab and hug her so tight and swallow back tears, I love her so much, and I start on her little cheeks with the kisses.

Everybody is kissing on everybody, it's like a kissing booth in the room and we are all trying to get our money's worth!   Von tells Nicki that she wants to show her something and looks at me and nods for me to follow her. We all follow her through the formal dining room and into the great room. She tells us to have a seat as she walks up to the pecan sofa table next to the fireplace. The table is full of photos of our family and I'm guessing Von's also. She picks up the most recent picture taken of Nicki and when Nicki sees it, she says, "Wittle titken!" (Little Kitten) And she claps her hands while smiling. Wardell comes and puts Rachel in my left arm and takes Rebecca from my right arm. We have a loving good time for a good long while. We hug and kiss on each other and look at all of the pictures on the table, it was absolutely GREAT!!!

We noticed when Rebecca went to the bathroom, as soon as she returned to the room; Rachel took off to the bathroom. Both Wardell and I looked at Von and she told us they do everything like that except for eating and sleeping. She told us when they were infants they wore her and Nye out because they were never awake at the same time. Rachel is thinner than Rebecca and that's how everyone tells them apart, and, Rachel is the oldest by 19 minutes. Von shared her labor experience with us while the girls played together so well.

While we were talking I heard the garage door opening. I glanced at Von and she smiled and glanced over at me as she stood up. I stood up. She walked towards the door; I walked towards the door but stayed beside the wall. In walks Nye… he makes one step inside the door and reaches out for Von who is standing in front of him. He hugs her and kisses her on the forehead and says, "There's a black Tahoe in front…" I step all the way out from behind the wall and stand behind Von while he is speaking. He looks up at me. His eyes are filled with love and a smile breaks out on his face. Von stepped aside and I flew into his arms! Nye squeezed and rubbed my arms just like he used to when we were younger. He was silent while I said, "OhNyeimissedyousomuch!

He half laughed and said, "What, what are you saying?" I adjusted myself so I could look into his eyes and said, Nye I miss you so much, can you ever forgive me for shutting you out of my life?" I was holding onto his arm so tight and breathing so fast I had to stop and catch my breath. He pulled me close to himself and while hugging me so tight I could barely breathe, he says, "Z; I'll forgive you, if you forgive me for being such a stubborn mule." "Yes, yes, Nye consider it done, all done and over with! I love you so much and miss you terribly." We stood there, both of us crying and holding each other so tight. Nye says; "Z, I'm so sorry I shut you out, I was so scared I was going to lose my little sister…" He lets out a loud whimper and I could feel him trembling as I held onto him and I knew he was sorry, and then I let out a loud whimper.

The twins ran over to Nye and grabbed hold of his legs and started yelling, "Daddy, daddy! Don't cry

Daddy!" Then I heard Nicki, "Mommy, Mommy," I could hear her running towards me and then I heard Wardell say, "Woe! Lil Kitten, Mommy is alright baby; she's okay." And I heard Von sniffing as she reassured Rachel and Rebecca Daddy was alright. A real heavy silence filled the room. Wardell walked over to me and Nye and said hello to him as he placed some tissue into my hand. That was Nye and my queue to let go of each other and wipe our weeping eyes.

We all congregated into the great room and talked and laughed catching up on each other's lives for the past 7 years. Nye had 2 extra-large Pizzas delivered and we all ate. I went to the restroom and when I re-entered the room, Nye put his glass of Root Beer down on the table and walked up to me and grabbed my arm while saying to me, "Come back here with me, I need to talk to you." As we walked towards the back, he turned around and said, "We'll be right back, need to talk." Both Von and Wardell says "Okay."

We go into his office and Nye closes the door and tells me to have a seat. We both sit in the two chairs facing the desk and he scoots his chair next to mine with our knees touching. Nye grabs ahold of both my hands and starts... "Z, I am so sorry this craziness has lasted this long. I want to thank you from the bottom of my heart for having the good sense to come to me and put this behind us. To be honest...I never thought you would have let this go this long. I know I'm stubborn and allow pride to take control of me sometimes, but I, Z, I thought you would have come to the shop and told me completely off years ago. Now I want to admit that I took my big brother powers way too far; but when you told us that you had heard from the Lord and you didn't run it by me,"   Nye squeezes my hands really tight now as he continues. "Z, I was so mad at you. How dare you cut me out of your decision making and cut in front of me in line for our futures and get your answer before I do! I know that was stupid spelled backwards, but I'm being real about how I felt at the time I heard you had gotten an answer from the Lord and I hadn't. Z; I am so sorry..."   He looks deep into my eyes and I look into his, and we connected again. He reaches for me and I reach for him and we sit on the edge of our seats hugging....thank You Jesus! I finally have my brother back. "I'm so sorry Z, please forgive me." "I'm sorry too Nye and I need you to forgive me. You're right about me not putting an end to this mess sooner; I let stubbornness grab hold of me too and I entertained it." We both back up and smile at each other. He stares into my eyes, smiles, and his eyes are saying, "Thanks." Like in days past; I say, "You're welcome." With my heart, and Nye breaks out in the biggest smile. WE'RE BACK!

As we head back to join the others, I hear Nicki whining, "I want Mommy Daddy, I want Mommy." Wardell is patiently replying, "Okay Lil Kitten, Mommy will be back." When we fully entered the room, Nye tells Von he'll run the water for the girls' bath and makes an about face, headed to the bathroom. I thought to myself, 'Nye is a good husband too.' I glance around the room and notice Rebecca is lying stretched out on the sofa yawning and rubbing her eyes, and Rachel is standing on the floor, but at her sisters' feet, and both of them are watching Nicki. I shook my head, if that ain't me and Nye! Nicki almost leaps out of Wardells arms into mine and starts her whining again. Wardell gets up and tells Von how much he enjoyed spending time with her family, grabs my purse and we head to the front door. Here comes Nye, "Wardell, I promise next time we get together we'll talk, oh, wait." Nye is feeling his pockets and goes into his shirt pocket and pulls out a business card and hands it to Wardell as he says, "This is so we can keep in touch."

Wardell shifts my purse into his other hand and reaches in his shirt pocket and hands one of his business cards to Nye. Nye looks at the card and says, "Assistant to the Branch Manager, ah, that's good Wardell, I always knew you would do well." Wardell and Nye hug as Wardell says, "Thanks man." We walk to the door putting on our jackets and Von comes and stands next to Nye and he slips his arms around her and rocks with her as he stands behind her pressing the side of his face to hers. She folds her hands on top of his arms and while rocking, says "I really enjoyed you all and let's do this often, okay?" Wardell and I both say Okay at the same time as we step down and out. Ooh, I Mean!

I get in the back seat with Nicki and lay her down on my lap then secure the seat belt around her and hold onto her little hand. Wardell chauffeurs his precious cargo home; I am so blessed! I smile all the way home.

Both Wardell and I get Nicki undressed and in her pajamas, she is out and dead weight. I can't figure out how someone as small as she is; gets so heavy when she falls asleep. Lil Kitten turns into Lil Lead! Finally Wardell and I get to bed. It has been a long adrenaline-charged day for me. I tell Wardell word for word what Nye and I talked about and… without any clothing; I expressed how much I appreciate him.

Chapter Seven

Reunited And It Feels So Good
Party hardy, party down!

SATURDAY:

Wardell had to shake me to wake me this morning; 8:19 am and I have a 9am client, Mrs. Leanne Gordy. She has a little money and everyone in the shop must allow her center stage, no other conversations are allowed to go on while she speaks. I used to charge her more and more for her services in hopes she wouldn't come back; but one day during my prayer time I have for just my clients; Holy Spirit informed me she has no other shop to go to; we're the only ones that tolerate her. So, I take her early, before the shop gets full. I have her out in 65 minutes, I even walk her to the front door, hold it open for her and wave her off, whew, it's a relief to see her pull away! So, just thinking about Leanne Gordy makes me jump out of the bed and get my move on.

On my drive to work this morning Mama called me on my cell she had heard from Aunt Daphne and shared the good news, Donavan is getting married! Our prayers are being answered, she was so excited and I had to tell her about Nye and me in his office and promise to fill her in on the rest later. 10 am my cell rings again and this time it's Nye wanting to have lunch with me so we scheduled a time to meet at "Trina's Kitchen" for some good home cooked food.

Ahh, Lord I thank you for allowing forgiveness to flow too and through me.

We both pulled up in the parking lot at the same time. Nye waited for me at the front door and when I stepped up onto the sidewalk, he reached for me and we hugged. It felt so good to have my big brother back in my life, not that my life isn't full with my Patterson's; but having a twin brother and the twin thing going on in our lives for 17 years, well, it feels like my life is complete now, that's the only way I can explain it, yeah, I feel complete now, nothing missing; thank You Lord! Thank You!

Nye walks all the way towards the rear of the restaurant where it's quiet and we can talk. I just at this moment think about how easily I can follow him, I have always trusted Nye…as I sit down I realize my trusting him is why he hurt me so badly shutting me out. He looks at me and asks, "Wha?" I look him in the face, I look at how much we favor and feel as though I am looking at myself but a male version, sorta like when I look at Nicki and see a smaller version of me. What is so strange is at this precise moment; I realize although we look alike, we are different; it's hard to put in words but that's what I realize right now.

"Nye; I just this second realize we are the same, however we're different. I feel as though the time we have been apart has enabled me to step outside of our twin-ness and see you as a separate person. Maybe this is sounding like French to you but, growing up I always saw us as one. Do you think when Daddy prayed for us to be led onto the path predestined for us…our being apart from one another was in the plan?"

Nye is looking at me with wide eyes like he did the day he told me he was having lower abdominal pain and I started laughing. Again he asks, "Wha?" as he relaxes and a smile appears on his face. "Remember the day I called Mama at work and told her you were having female pain like me?" He gets a smirk on his face and smile while saying, "Do I …" Now he gets a serious look on his face and leans in towards me and says "Z…wanna hear something amazing about that story?….every time I stand in front of someone that asks me a question that seems really dumb, I remember myself that day and think, maybe they just don't know. Ump, that day often reminds me of my ignorance and causes me to have patience for someone else, some things we just do not know. I think it's so amazing how the Lord teaches us to produce the fruit of the spirit in the smallest, strangest ways." Nye leans back in his chair and smiles. The waitress comes bearing menus, water with straws and a smile as she states she will give us a few minutes to decide then she walks away.

When Nye's fish platter and my soup and half turkey sandwich arrived, he blessed it and we both dove into our food. He started; "Z to answer your question about us being apart being in Gods will; I have been thinking about our childhood this last week and sharing with Von my memories and I believe it was His will we learn to be twins without the Siamese syndrome. We could have found another nontoxic way of separating that wasn't so negative and painful; man oh man did I miss you. Last week I looked the word Siamese up; it refers to a language, see we have a language all our own.

We may not be joined physically but emotionally we were one. I really have been meditating about this and truly believe if we had gotten together and prayed about our futures we would have come to an agreement as to how we would have handled widening our circle without having a rift between us. I must tell you, I really missed my little sister, sorry, I mean my sister that I just happened to be older than." Nye laughs out loud as he looks at me. Ahh, this is marvelous, just marvelous!   As I smile I look real deep into my brothers eyes and tell him that I love him and always will. As he shook his head yes and says, "Me too!" We both got watery eyed.

He asked me about Nicki and said Mama told him and Von about me expecting again and he wanted to know when was I due and what did Wardell want because as he put it: "Us men tend to get what we want." I told him about my queasiness and how I thought it was associated with the Holy Spirit dealing with me about forgiving him and how I kept brushing Him off. My brother told me with tears in his eyes that he has been waiting for me to come to him. When he said, "Z, I realized how full of pride I am because I expected you to be the one to make me put this rift to an end…I'm so sorry."

He broke down; he sat there crying like a girl. I started crying and realized he looked like a girl, I began laughing so hard. He removed his hands from his face and looked at me; then he broke out laughing as he managed to say, "Wha?"   As I laughed. I told him he looked like a girl crying. He grabbed a few napkins, wiped his eyes and says, "Man how I missed you. No one can make me laugh and cry at the same time like you. I think we… Z; do you think we might be aliens?" As I wiped my eyes I said to Nye, "Leroy Junior and Paul Michael!" We laughed so hard we cried again.

As we left the restaurant, I told Nye I was looking forward to having brunch at Mama and Daddy's tomorrow after church and want Nicki to get close to her Mothers only brothers kids. He told me he was praying Rachel and Rebecca will adjust to another sibling and hopes Nicki will kinda break the ice for them. He said these last few weeks he realizes us not having other siblings made it difficult for us to let other kids in because we always had each other. What we went through should never be experienced by any siblings, the pain is too devastating. He turned and rubbed my arm and told me he loved me as I told him that I loved him too; I blinked back tears, I finally have my brother back, Lord You are so good to me!

I smiled all the way back to the shop. Nate asked, "So did you have lunch with Wardell today, you come back with a smile you didn't leave with. Oh, am I being all up in your business!" He was laughing and Shell and Sherry co-signed with, "Do tell. Yeah, do please." As I put my smock on I saic, "I just had lunch with my brother." Sherry stops with the flat iron in her hand and says in wonderment, "Not the brother you told us the other day that you aren't close with?" Shell turned completely around and looked me up and down and added, "Yeah, not that brother, the twin." I was looking up in my mirror at them, so I decided to give them an abbreviated version of Nye and I reuniting. So, I turned completely around and said, "Last night I extended an olive branch to Nye, my twin brother who I haven't spoken too in almost 7 years and he accepted it and today we had lunch together. I'm smiling because it feels so good for me to let go of un- forgiveness and grasp onto healing, love and relationship. The Lord is good yawl, just good!" I stood there smiling so big I believe they saw every tooth I own. Nate had completely stopped trimming his client's head and was listening to every word I said. I noticed his eyes left mine and went to the floor in a brief stare, then he looked back up at me and continued trimming. He was real quiet for the rest of the afternoon.

Sherry and Shell asked me a few questions, like; girl I can't see you letting 1 year go by without speaking, let alone over 6 years, how'd you let that happen, and what made you make up now, after all these years. I answered each question at length, watching Nate in the mirror as I spoke. Shells' client, Mary Howard told us that her mother and aunt had a rift between them and made amends just before her mother passed, it was such a beautiful reunion and her aunt was so glad they took care of everything before her mother left here. That shifted the conversation to sharing stories of healed relationships. After the shop was empty with the exception of Nate's client; Sherry shared with us how she had to forgive her son's father for leaving her for another woman of another nationality. Before she finished talking, Nate's client paid and left and I noticed Nate slowly swept his area and piddled around until Sherry packed up and left. He went to the back until Sherry left and I yelled, "It's just us Nate, come on out." He's 6 feet tall, big and buff keeping his body in shape for the ladies as he always brags to us, but when he walked into the room; he looked as though he was 9 or 10 years old, broken and in need of a friend.

I walked over to him and he never raised his head as he said, "I can't forgive my brother. I know I need too, I just can't. He owes me an apology, he was wrong, not me." As he spoke his last word, I felt his pain and have felt it for almost 7 years. I rubbed his arm as I said, "When you get tired of the weight from the pain; you'll forgive him." I turned around and slowly walked to my station, picked up my purse and left him in the shop. I heard Holy Spirit say, "Lock the door so he won't be disturbed." I did as I was instructed and left. I left headed to the store to get the drinks for the party then to the mal to get a birthday card and present for Clarence. Oh... I mean! The Lord is so good!

As soon as I sat in the car I glanced at the car clock; 5:48pm let me call Wardell and make sure he has picked up Nicki and let him know all he has to do is warm up the Lasagna if he's hungry. I have just enough time to power shop so we can make the party by 6:30. He told me he had already picked up the pops and juice boxes, Ma phoned him because she wanted them on ice early so they would be cold. He dropped the drinks off during his lunch. So off to get Clarences' birthday gift I go.

Ma and Pops have the parties early because we all attend church on Sundays, so our usual time to congregate at the Myer Street den is 6pm and we are usually all walking out of the door by 10pm at the latest, 10:30. Not just the Patterson's attend the

Patterson's parties; Linell Jr., Ronald and Clarence were five, four and three when the Patterson's moved into 9813 Myer Street and Ma was pregnant with Earl at the time. Two houses down from the left of 9813, was the home of five year old Paul and three year old Eugene Higgins and all five boys grew up on Myer Street until each one moved away, however their parents still live in the same homes and the guys and their wives keep in touch. Linell Jr. and Paul played football in school and both of them joined the armed services together.

Paul married Elaine and they have four children, Pauline, 11, Paul Jr., 10, Alvin, 8 and Regina, 7 and it is expected of the Higgins to be in attendance of all the Patterson's parties. Eugene and his family lives in Fairway Hills, Mo. which is the furthest from all us so they usually get to the party last. He married Rena around the same time Clarence and Wilhelmina married and they have two children Eugene Jr., 10 and Ella, 9. So with the Patterson's numbering 40 plus themselves, adding 10 more to the party, who's counting?

The party program is as follows: we sort of stager in and, by 6:30 we are all there and head from the den to the formal dining room for dinner and conversation. After we are all stuffed from the various tasty potluck dishes, then we start the dancing, and usually Barbara Jean, who is Linell Jr. and Adrianne's oldest and 11years old, along with Pearl, who belongs to Clarence and Wilhelmina, and she's their oldest and is 10 years old; along with Alexis, who is 9 years old and belongs to Phoebe and Allan, and yes she is their oldest also. The three of them get together in the den and start the dancing lessons.

They show us the steps to the latest dance and then Ella; Eugene Jr. and Rena's 9 year old daughter, jumps in before us older folk start to try and figure out the step. We have a ball trying to get it down like the girls show us. Usually Portia; Earl's wife, and Vedette get it first, and then me, Wardell, Samuel, Aretha, Phoebe and Clarence get it. The rest of them catch on later, but we have fun laughing at each other trying to get the moves just right. As soon as the dance lessons begin; the kids all stand around watching and laughing at us trying to catch on to the new dance. The young ones really laugh at Linell Jr. and Ronald because even when the girls hold their hands and go step by step, they still do their own personalized dance but let Linell Jr. and Ronald tell it; they are doing the latest dance and talk about funny, I mean! The youngsters get something to mimic later in the back room after watching us try and get the latest dance.

All of the Patterson females can get down dancing but the only males that can really flow are Wardell and Sheldon, Clarence is determined not to let us 'younger set' as he calls us, beat him at anything. He always brags about having all of the 'soul' in the family. Wardell lets him brag, but Sheldon; he goes word for word with Clarence and trust me by Sheldon being the baby; he is determined not to let his older brothers beat him at anything, you hearing me? All of that determination in the room is makings for a lot of fun happening, let me tell you! We have talked and laughed for weeks about the dance moves that go on in the "Myer Street den".

Around 8pm is when the kids disappear into the guest room Ma fixed up with a queen sized bed, that way when the three young toddlers (Marcel, 3 and belongs to Vedette and Markus; Jaylen, 2 belongs to Sheldon and Roxanne and Lil Kitten, 2,) falls asleep, they have a comfortable place to be. Barbara Jean and Alexis usually make their way back there and watch over the little ones while they all watch Christian cartoons and the latest Disney movies on the television Ma has in the room. There's also another room fixed back there, just for the guys, young and older. It has two screens for them to play video games on and an octagon shaped player table with 8 chairs for when they play dominos or Monopoly. Ma recently placed a high standing table in there for putting puzzles together.

My in-loves have 23 grandchildren and I'm carrying the 24th. Linell Jr. and his wife, Adrianne has two children; Barbara Jean, 11 and Linell III, 9. Ronald and his wife Imogene, have three children; Luther, 10, Raymond, 9 and Cedric, 7. Clarence and Wilhelmina have Pearl, 10, Tamara, 8 and Clarence Jr., 7. Earl and his wife, Portia have Patricia, 8, Jackie, 7, and Lil Earl, 5.   Aretha and her husband, Samuel has Sammie Jr., 10, Samantha, 8 and Serita, 7. Phoebe and Allan have 9 year old Alexis and 8 year old Myles. Wardell and I have Nicki and one on the way, and Vedette and her husband Marcus, has Markus Jr. 6, Marlena, 5, and Marcel, 3. Sheldon is the only Patterson to father a child out of wedlock, and his son, Sheldon Jr. is with Myra Henderson and he's 7 and seldom sees us or his father, but Sheldon married Roxanne and they have two sons, Jared, 5 and Jaylen, 2. So... when we have a family party you can see how full the rooms can be.

Ma and Pops sit side by side with their backs against the dining room table and watch us rock to the beat of the fast music. This serves a twofold purpose, one, they get good and entertained as we provide a lot of laughs for them and two; when one of the kids act up, Barbara or Pearl goes directly to one of them to tell on whoever it is. The odd thing is it's almost always Jared or Jaylen. Roxanne usually goes in the back room to straighten out the culprit, but it only lasts for a short while. It generally takes her 4 or 5 times going back there then Sheldon takes his turn and that's the end of it.

Ma and Pops stay glued to their seats, until a slow jam plays. Every once in a while they will give us a request to play something and when they do, Linell stops the pre-made music and plays the requested song from the particular CD they want to hear. It's almost always the same songs all the time; Pops request "Your Sweetness Is My Weakness" by Barry White or "Never Too Much" by Luther Vandross.

Those two are the only request he makes and while the song is playing; he looks Ma in the eyes and sings along with the song. Now Ma; she only has one fast song request, and that is, "I Feel For You" by Chaka Khan. Ma grabs Pops hand and sings along with Chaka on the part that states, "I think I love you," to Pops, then she winks at him. We really don't care what they request, we are going to dance to whatever plays and Linell doesn't mind changing the music players. Ronald asked Linell once if he thought about putting Ma and Pops music onto the pre-made CD, and Linell said he wanted them to know how special they were; that's why he announces "The following is dedicated to the world's best parents." Before playing their request.

When the slow jam time starts, that's when Pops gets up out of his seat, places both hands opened and out for Ma to join him and I mean he hugs her and closes his eyes while his chin rests on her chest and Ma closes her eyes and their slow dancing is like observing youthful love in the room. The first time I witnessed them slow dancing together, I understood why Wardell is so loving; he's just seen his father be that way towards his mother and thinks that's how he's supposed to treat his wife. In fact; all of the men in the family love us wives and they are so warm towards us and we have no problem reciprocating at all, in fact we love it!

Tonight the dance to learn is called, "The Strut." At least by Barbara and Pearls' definition. A few minutes after they were into the dance instructions, Pops and Ma told us to hold the horse; that dance was called, "The Temptation Walk," back in their day. Pops jumped up out of his seat and got in on the grove, right in step with Barbara and Pearl. I mean he was a strutin! Clarence got on the floor and followed Pops and caught right on. The both of them cut up on the floor, adding steps Barbara and Pearl had no clue about; I mean they busted some moves!

When the song had played out; no one was sitting in the room. We all "strutted" for over an hour, laughing every time Pops would holler out; "Watch this!" And he would strut his stuff, then he would come back with, "Yawl don't know nuthin bout that there!" We laughed so hard at Pops and I mean he performed for us. We took a break from all that fast dancing and sang "Happy Birthday" to Clarence and gave him his gifts and then we ate Caramel Cake; his favorite, and Vanilla Bean ice cream. After that, all the grown folk went back to the den with the slow jams ringing out and the lights dimmed.

Wardell took Nicki back to the guest room and he was back there so long, I went to see what was keeping him. As I turned the corner to the hall I heard him talking in a stern voice. "If I have to come back here again; this belt will be in my hand and I will use it on you, do you hear me?" I stood in the doorway listening and noticed Jared was standing in front of Wardell. His eyes are bulged as he looks at Wardell's belt around his waist. Wardell adds, "…You never, never… under any circumstances, ever hit a female, and your cousin! Boy, do you hear me?"

I peek over Wardell to see where Nicki is; knowing how Jaylen hits at her and she is the only girl in the room who isn't big enough to hit him back. I spot her standing next to her Daddy, holding onto his leg. Now Wardell gets on one knee and talks to Nicki, but I can't hear what it is he's saying. He kisses her on the face and stands up and as he turns around; he points his finger at Jared. He walks over to me and says; "I know it's not right to want to hurt a 2 year old, but she's my Lil Kitten." I grab his hand and we walk back to the dance room to get our slow dance on. I'm so glad Wardell is Nicki and my protector, oh how I loves me some Wardell!

As I'm being held oh so lovingly by my wonderful husband; I'm reminded of my first Myer Street Den party.

Because I was raised a holy roller, I had no clue what it was like to go to a dance let alone a non-church party. Nye and I were not allowed to attend school dances or anything that sounded worldly and with Mama being given to dreams, we were too scared she would find out if we had snuck into a school dance. To tell you the truth, Mama and Daddy kept us so busy, we didn't have time to even want to go to dances or parties. The few church parties we attended, all we did was eat, play games and somehow we always ended up singing all types of church songs. So Nye and I never thought we would miss anything if we didn't attend a party. Needless to say as soon as Wardell and I returned from our honeymoon, the Patterson's celebrated Ronald's birthday which was put off so Wardell and I would be in attendance. Since they only have parties for birthdays, they are serious about all of the family being present. There are 9 Patterson children and 2 parents, add Thanksgiving and Christmas; there is a party going on every month in the "Myer Street Den."

When Wardell told me on the plane ride back to the States, from our honeymoon that we had to attend Ronald's birthday party because the family postponed it waiting for us to get back, I asked him what the party would consist of. So, when I came over here for the party; I was so wide eyed, checking every move out. The dancing really mesmerized me, Nye and I would sneak and listen to worldly music on the radio, but to be in a room where I was feeling the drums bounce off the walls and rhythms of the music were pounding under my feet; and, I was *allowed* to listen! I tell you I was swaying and rocking and just-a-popping my fingers, I mean! I would pull myself away from Wardell when he would grab my hand pulling me towards the dance floor. I was so uncomfortable trying to dance and in front of a room full of dancers!

Then the slow jams came on. I couldn't believe grownups would hold each other like that in public. Because we had just gotten back from our honeymoon, every time Wardell touched me any kind of way; I would get so aroused, and when he held me in his arms and started to slow dance, oh my goodness! As soon as he placed his arms around me I told him that I didn't know how to slow dance as I shook my head 'No' at him. He walked over to the end tables and turned on the lamp lights, and then he went to the wall light switch and turned the ceiling light off. I heard a few men say, "Thanks" while Wardell slowly walked to me and held me real close to him and whispered in my ear; "Relax baby, just follow my lead." The man kissed my neck! I went limp like melted butter, and slow danced; we definitely did! Ever since then the lights get dimmed during the slow jams, its tradition now.

The last song is playing, "Let Me Make Love To You" by the O'jays. This is our signature ending song and we all know when the last bar is sounded; tonight's Myer Street Den Party has officially ended. The ceiling lights reappear and the women start clearing off the dining room table and head to the kitchen to help Ma clean up. The husbands clear all the plastics from the den, and Pops takes them to the receptacle outside while the husbands put on their father hats and head for the back rooms to collect the kids. By the time the kids have their shoes and or jackets on, the fathers slash husbands will have the cars warmed or cooled and ready for their families to take the ride home. Ahh, I loves me some Wardell

Patterson, yep... I love my Patterson family; I'm just blessed like that!

SUNDAY:

Wardell and Nicki came into the bedroom and while Wardell shook me; Nicki climbed up on the bed and pulled my eyelid up, asking, "Mommy woke up?" I get me a good, long stretch, and then I grab the eyelid puller and hug her while saying good morning. After I'm showered it's off to the kitchen to prepare some oatmeal and toast for my family. I cut up a few pieces of apple for Nicki and get her secured in her high chair while I finish breakfast. When Wardell finishes his shower we will be ready to sit and have Sunday breakfast together. "I hab a tister like Becca! Yey, I hab a tister like Becca!" I stand at the stove with spoon in hand and mouth gaped wide open, I mean jaw dropped! I am amazed at Nicki, and how she puts things together at her age. I put the spoon down and slowly walk to her high chair and softly asks, "Baby, where is your sister?" She puts another piece of apple in her mouth and hunches her shoulders; the I-don't-know, hunch. As I stand staring at her, I'm thinking, 'This one's a thinker! We have a thinker on our hands.' I run my hand softly across her tiny face and return to the stove.

We arrive just five minutes late for Sunday School, I am so proud of the Wardell Patterson's yey; only five minutes late! While on the way to church Wardell and I discuss letting Nicki go into the nursery during Sunday School this morning, well, more like Wardell telling me it's time. After what she said to me this morning; I think he's right, but she's still my baby.

I feel tears working up. Wardell gets Nicki free from the car seat and tells her that she is going to a room with other children like herself. He glances over at me and asks her if she would like that. No response from his Lil Kitten. My heart is racing so fast but I know he's right; I just need to cut this cord I have attached to her. As we step into the vestibule I almost whimper as Wardell goes towards the Nursery, not even giving me a chance to kiss her bye. I swallow real hard to keep the tears back; my baby is going to the Nursery for her first time. Then I ask myself, 'Who's having a case of separation anxiety here, the child or the parent?' Wardell loves her as much as I do so if he's okay with it…I guess I can be too, (sigh).

Wardell returns to the room less our baby in his arms and even though he smiles, waves and nods at fellow Sunday School attendees as he works his way to me, his eyes keep darting my way. I know him and he's trying to see if I am together after he left my baby in the Nursery. I paste a smile on my face as an indication to him I'm not mad. He steps in front of me and rubs both my arms while saying, "Lil Kitten is in good hands so don't worry, okay." I realize he wants me to not worry and I smile a genuine smile and as I shake my head, yes; I pucker my lips to give him a peck. He puckers back, we bump lips; mauh! And off we go into the sanctuary for some Bible teaching.

Deacon Cecil Cooke is our teacher this morning and after he prays he dives right into the lesson. Today we are studying **Proverbs 3:13-18** which reads; **"Happy is the man who finds wisdom, and the man who gains understanding; For her proceeds are better than the profits of silver, and her gain than fine gold. She is more precious than** rubies, and all the things you may desire cannot compare with her. Length of days is in her right hand, in her left hand riches and honor. Her ways are ways of pleasantness, and all her paths are peace. She is a tree of life to those who take hold of her, and happy are all who retain her."

Deacon Cooke absolutely broke down the Word this morning. I mean he explained to us the word 'happy' or blessed in some translations; in this scripture is like the word 'happy' or blessed, in the Beatitudes over in Matthew 5 and Luke 6:20-23. It simply means this kind of happiness is only experienced by those whose trust is in the Lord. This happiness far exceeds happiness as an emotion because joy and peace are attached to this kind of happiness and only the born again believer can tap into it by the spirit. Verse 13: **"Happy is the man who finds wisdom."** This describes wisdom as a characteristic; a trait that should be evident in the person whose life reflects Christ existing in them. Just as we see integrity and truthfulness in a born again believer, we should also see wisdom. Yeah, wisdom is a characteristic we should all possess as a spirit filled born again believer, just as Christ illustrated it in His life as He walked this earth; so should we.

"…and the man who gains understanding;" Deacon Cooke also shared with us that the person is happy or blessed when understanding is gained or found in a persons every day affairs simply because the benefits from understanding are insurmountable, matchless. **"For her proceeds are better than the profits of silver and her gain than fine gold."** Wisdom coupled together with understanding is worth way more than the value placed on silver or gold.

Then Deacon Cooke asked if anyone in our class had something given to them that was worth a lot simply because of the circumstances in which we received it made it valuable. Everyone in class had a comment on something they owned that is priceless to them; no amount of monetary value can be placed to it, due to the sentimental value it holds. Mainly because the story attached to how it was acquired increased the value. Deacon told us that wisdom and understanding can be compared to that precious sentimental possession because of what it cost us to gain it! …..Wow…. did I get a revelation!

I thought about Nye and I being in such a loving relationship with each other all of our lives and having a rift come between us causing such deep misery for me and how I had gone through being too stubborn and full of pride to be the first one to say, "I'm sorry". I was causing value or equity to be placed on the wisdom and understanding I was gaining. Now, today, I wouldn't trade my wisdom and understanding for what I went through and; I will definitely tell someone else that needs to be the first to apologize, to do so and cast the misery out of their life. The sooner you forgive, the better you will feel; it's just not worth the agony. Yeah…wisdom coupled with understanding… very valuable!

"…She is more precious than rubies, and all the things you may desire cannot compare with her." Because wisdom and understanding is very valuable to possess, the circumstances we go through to gain them, makes them become precious. Truly, nothing we can ever desire to possess, will measure up to the worth in owning wisdom and understanding, nothing!   Notice how Solomon made wisdom a person? We should posses wisdom as an attribute. She, in this scripture, is referred to as "SELF" wisdom really should become a part of us!

"...Length of days is in her right hand, in her left hand riches and honor." Deacon Cooke shared with us that living with wisdom and understanding deletes a lot of foolishness from our lives and, not having foolishness equals less stress and strife. Being stress and strife free keeps one a lot healthier and, can add days onto a person's life. Also; possessing wisdom and understanding, we will make good wise decisions and enjoy living a comfortable life and not live with our hands extended out begging, but we live with dignity and honor.

"...Her ways are ways of pleasantness, and all her paths are peace."   Wisdom is best friends with understanding and the two of them produces peace and peace produces pleasantness. Now there is an assurance you have, not arrogance; but an inner security you have that yields pleasantness. Family and friends will enjoy your company, you begin to like you, and, won't mind being alone. Hey, and who doesn't enjoy pleasantness?   Notice how all of wisdoms paths leads to peace.

James 3:17 states, **"But the wisdom that is from above is first pure, then peaceable, gentle, willing to yield, full of mercy and good fruits, without partiality and without hypocrisy."**   How true! What peace we often forfeit, excluding wisdom, not book knowledge but godly wisdom, wisdom from above, wow.... Then Deacon wrapped it up with, **"... She is a tree of life to those who take hold of her, and happy are all who retain her."**   Wisdom is a tree of life, when she's incorporated into our lifestyle, she is a characteristic we exhibit, not just as a show, but really own, inwardly, in our hearts. And, we deposit wisdom and understanding into our children and they deposit it into theirs, and so on.

This establishes a "Wisdom and Understanding" family tree to those who take hold of it. To retain means to keep in one's possession, to hold. Brother Pendergrass mentioned how sometimes we might have to take hold of wisdom and practice letting her have rule in us until we allow her a permanent position in our character. Deacon Cooke said that was a good point; if we need to add wisdom to our lifestyle after this lesson, we can start with a retainer on wisdom until she's rooted down in us!

I felt so good after that lesson, mainly because I know beyond a shadow of any doubt, that it was Holy Spirit's wisdom that kept prompting me to extend the olive branch to Nye. I think I smiled so much knowing deep inside peace is abiding where un-forgiveness once dwelt! Wow what a good feeling! You can hear me smiling as I speak can't you? Being set free is the greatest feeling….

After we were dismissed Wardell told me he was going to check on Lil Kitten and I told him after I went to the restroom, I would peek in on her. He asked me if I thought that was a good move. I told him I would be very careful not to let her see me. He smiled and said, "It's not Lil Kitten I'm worried about; baby, you might have the fit seeing her in there!" "Wha, I'm a big girl, I can handle it." I replied as I stood up to leave, of course he followed me. I was a little bit hurt Wardell thought I was such a baby about

Nicki, but in my heart I know sometimes I do baby her; he's right. It's like; she is still my baby, but.... I know, I know, she's growing up and I guess I must let her.

I opened the door to the Nursery just enough to get my head in the room and noticed Wardell holding our daughter in his arms; and he doesn't see his emblematical cord attached to Nicki, just mine! He's bouncing her in his arms as he smiles that 'I'm so proud of you' smile, ahh, I just loves me some Wardell. This lady approaches me and tells me that it's okay for me to come in. As I step into the room; she introduces herself as Sister Williams. I tell her that I was just intending to peek at Nicki because today was her first day in here. She told me that Nicki was adjusting to the other children just fine and that she suspected today was not the first time Nicki has been in this type environment. I smiled so big as I told her she was right.

I walked over to my favorite Patterson's and when Nicki saw me she smiled and reached her arms out to me. I took her as she almost leaped into my arms and I asked if she liked her class. "See baby Mommy?" Was all I could get out of her. She was pointing towards the baby lying in the baby bed as she spoke; her angelic little face has a big smile placed on it! "Mommy has to go get ready to sing baby; you have fun in here okay?" "Kay Mommy, lub you." She said as she almost leaps from my arms to get down. And off she goes, straight to the baby bed. She stands there watching the baby. I turn to Wardell who was standing next to me and says to him, "She didn't even kiss me bye." He says, "At least you got an I love you, don't be greedy Mommy." As I stood there looking into his eyes; I realized he was right. He puts his arms around me and guides me towards the door, leaving our Lil Kitten in good hands and I thought a real loud, "THANK YOU JESUS!"

Before Reverend Hall preached he requested the choir to sing Patiently Waiting by Hezekiah Walker.   The words go like this: **"I am patiently waiting for you anticipating that my blessings on its way. I am standing on your promises believing in your Holy Word, praise Your Holy Name."** It's an upbeat song and during the music only part; the choir sways to the music. The chorus states: **"While I'm waiting, I'll praise Your Holy Name."** Repeatedly and, we modulate until the whole choir is engrossed in the song, which infects the whole church.   When we uttered the last note, while everyone was still standing, clapping and praising the Lord; Reverend Hall stepped up to the platform and announced the title of his message this morning is, "Trapeze Faith." The whole church praised and blessed the Lord so, it took Reverend a few more minutes before he could begin the message. Talk about anticipation! The Holy Spirit had a treat in store for us.

Before I tell you what happened I need to explain what a trapeze is so you can get the full picture of what Reverend Hall taught us this morning. There are different ways to trapeze. There's a swinging trapeze, a flying trapeze and a double trapeze just to mention a few ways of traipsing. The reason anyone would use a trapeze is for entertainment. Some people that absolutely love flying are addicted to trapeze art. Oh yes it's an art these days and classes are available for the "air" lovers.

I'll describe how the "flying trapeze" works since that's the one Reverend Hall is referring to. The bar is very similar to the seat of a swing except the bar is thinner and very sturdy as it must be in order to hold an adult, and a moving one at that. The bar is attached to cable made of metals and these cables are attached to a stationary pole that makes the flying in the air possible. The point of traipsing is to catch hold of the trapeze and glide through the air from point "a" to point "b" without falling. A good circus act makes this very entertaining because they make graceful moves while in the air and sometimes there are more than one person traveling in the air at the same time. So keep that mental picture of catching hold of the trapeze in your mind while I share Reverend Halls' message.

First Reverend Hall read **James 2:14-26**. Then he back tracked to verse 18 and he parked there drawing us a mental picture of a trapeze. **Verse 18: "But someone will say, 'You have faith, and I have works.' Show me your faith without your works, and I will show you my faith by my works."** He said, "A trapeze is a short horizontal bar hung by ropes or metal straps from a support. It is an aerial apparatus commonly found in circus performances. However, today instead of being entertained, we were going to be encouraged.

Today the trapeze seat will be the things we hope for. Which is an answer to the various situations we are facing, trouble on our jobs, in our marriages, in our families, relationships or if we need healing in our bodies or perhaps our hearts or, maybe we are in financial need. Whatever we can think of that we need, the Lord can provide; that is what the trapeze seat will represent this morning. Now the cables, ropes and the straps that hold the seat, today, will be our substance. Our substance is what tie us to our belief in the Lord; thus making the seat things hoped for. Which is the evidence of things not seen, therefore it supports the trapeze seat. The number of cables, ropes and straps holding the trapeze seat depends on how much substance you have. Ah, let that soak in for a moment...

Whatever the circumstance, bills, health issues, relationship issues, job troubles; we all have them in common. Don't be dismayed about waiting on your trapeze seat to come with all of the answers, no, no; concentrate on the cables, straps and rope; your substance! The substance you possess doesn't have to be a lot, just enough to bare your weight when you grab onto the trapeze seat.   The substance is being supported by the Holy Spirit, we know He is here and has the ability to send the trapeze seat to us at the precise moment we can catch hold of it.

You see when we are in the Word, praising the Lord and praying, when life's troubles and worries appear, we become strong enough to wait, in faith....we wait, patiently, we wait, confidently yes indeed, we wait." Reverend Hall stood on his tip toes and stretched his neck looking and waiting as he spoke, as if he were waiting for a trapeze seat to come to him at any moment. Then he quickly turned to face the congregation and quoted the last part of verse 18 again; **"Show me your faith without your works, and I will show you my faith by my works."** He jumped down from the platform and he had all of us sitting on the edge of our seats!

He stood on his tip toes and began reeling back and forth looking ahead, as if waiting for the trapeze seat to come to him, still keeping his balance he shouted, "Show me your faith, show me your faith!" He shouted. Then he turned around real quick facing the Deacons bench and said, "Without faith, it is impossible to please God!" Slowly he extended his opened hands up while looking towards the ceiling trying his best to keep balanced while waiting on the trapeze seat. He says, "I will show you my faith by my works." Walking to the middle of the sanctuary, he stood still with his arms still extended he said, "When you are waiting on the Lord to come through for you, it's like waiting on the trapeze seat to come. You need to be sensitive to the timing of the Lord so you'll know at the precise moment when to extend your hand and leap out to catch hold of the answer you've been waiting for." He leaps forward and reaches out quickly to grab hold of the imaginary trapeze seat, and as if he caught it; he shouts, "Thank You Jesus!" Talk about a visual!

He turned towards the choir and said, "Timing is key when waiting on that trapeze seat to come to you, just wait on the Lord, learn to patiently wait on the Lord; He's the only One with the right answer. Praise Him! Praise Him! While you wait on Him, praise Him! Outwardly praise Him in the sanctuary and there's also a time to praise Him inwardly, making melodies in our hearts to Him, but praise the Lord while you wait because praise is an eraser for doubt; concentrate on Him and bless His Wonderful Name! I jumped up out of my seat and praised the Lord like I did in my bathroom Thursday night. It was me and the Lord at that moment, just me and my Wonderful Savior! I told Him that I loved Him, I blessed His Wonderful Name, and I let the tears flow like perfume being poured from me, all of a sudden I heard a loud, "Yes Lord" come from the depths of my soul... Ooh wee, the presence of the Lord was all up in Bethel Missionary Baptist today because He was sho nuff up in me!

All I can tell you is that I was not the only person who jumped up and magnified the Lord. When I opened my eyes and looked around the sanctuary, people were praising and worshipping the Lord all up in that church. All I could do was shake my head as I told the Lord how awesome He is to me! I MEAN!

I took my position in the choir stand and paned over the congregation looking for Wardell. He was standing with his arms stretched up towards heaven and he was worshipping as tears traveled slowly down his face. I love me some Wardell and he loves the Lord just as much as I do. My heart was beaming with admiration, knowing my husband loves and trust the Lord makes me love and trust my husband, I can't quite put it in words...I am blessed to love and be loved by a godly man. I just this moment realize this time last week I had so much un-forgiveness in me and now, today I have my brother back...I feel another praise about to break forth from me, thank you Jesus! Thank You! ....After I praised the Lord I sat in my alto section seat in the choir stand and worshipped the Lord; I just told Him how much I love and appreciate Him in my life as I sat and wept.

Booker, our pianist, began softly playing, "Hallelujah Anyhow," and the room was filled with worship. Today was incredible as far as service goes,

Sunday School and church service, wow what a time we had!

During the offering I saw my client, Faith Griffin walk by and give something in the basket. After she dropped her money, she looked up at me and gave me a short wave of the hand and, I believe she smiled at me, wha...Faith smiles! During the altar call, she came to the front asking for prayer and I closed my eyes and prayed a prayer of agreement with the alter worker; and also decreed the fallow ground to Faiths' heart would become broken and pliable to receive from the Lord. When I opened my eyes and looked where Faith was, I noticed she had tears streaming down her face. I rejoiced for her and stretched my hand towards her and pronounced healing and understanding be given to her, in Jesus Name! I believed it was done and began thanking the Lord for His Mighty Acts and Wondrous Works! I could already see Faith believing the Lord loves her and her loving Him back, I was so happy!

When we were dismissed I worked my way down to the pews and saw Faith working her way towards me. We embraced and she told me with a smile on her face that she was so glad she came to church today and she thanked me for sharing with her about the love of Christ because she pulled her Bible out when she went home after I did her hair and she began to read John in the New Testament and when she read it; she saw the love written between the lines. She hugged me and thanked me again and left church with a big smile on her face. That did me so much good, seeing her smile...wow, the love of God is truly amazing!

After I put my choir robe away I headed to the nursery. Wardell was standing at the door waiting for me, holding our daughter in his arms, yes I said our daughter, I'll let her grow up but she'll always be my baby now, always my number one! Nicki was so happy she paid with the baby as she put it; I was just glad to see she wasn't jealous; but then she is a Patterson and they are the most kindhearted people I know. I grabbed hold of her and walked to the car asking her to tell Mommy all about her class, and she did…all the way home!

We changed and headed over to Mama and Daddy's for Sunday Brunch as a whole family. I felt so good knowing Nye and his family would be there, I believe I smiled the whole ride over. When we parked in front of the house, I told Nicki she was going to see Rebecca and Rachel again today over here and she clapped her little hands and smiled just like I did; real big!

As soon as I washed my hands I heard the doorbell ring and Daddy say, "Lil Kitten I believe you're having company today. Let's see who it is." As I head to the front door instead of the kitchen I can hear the laughter from three little girls. Just as I walk into the living room I see the cousins hugging one another, nothing is being said, just hugging and tears began forming in my eyes as I stood waiting for my turn to get a hug. I bend down to snatch up Rebecca and I feel a hard Bop at my head, I look up and into the eyes of Nye. He had bent down to snatch up Nicki at the same time and we bumped heads. Now we are rubbing our heads and when we observe each other, we realize we look as though we are viewing ourselves in a mirror because we have the same hand movements and facial expressions. We laugh and reach to hug each other while holding onto our nieces.

After we embrace we notice Von and Wardell watching us and both of them are in amazement at our actions. I say, "Wha…" as Nye says, "Wha" we both quickly move our eyes to each other and break out in laughter. Daddy says, "Okay, it looks like the Siamese twin thing is back. Hey Unie! The Lord has answered your prayers; your twins are back together. Baby you hear me?" Here comes Mama into the living room, wiping her hands with her apron. "What honey…" She takes one look around the room and as water began to fill up in her beautiful eyes she says, "Thank You Jesus! My family is finally one! Lord I thank You!" Mama has both hands lifted in the air as she gives praise to the Lord. We all start blinking back tears and start hugging each other then we head into the Dining room. Von, Mama and I quickly exit to the kitchen to get the foods ready for our family reunion feast, and did she cook up a feast!

Mama has cooked all of our favorites. Daddy loves pork roast, Nye is a fish lover so she has baked tilapia and I cannot get enough of my mother's garlic mashed potatoes, she puts slivers of sautéed garlic in them, yum, yum! Not only does she have garlic mashed potatoes but she has baked yams, which I found out happens to be one of Von's favorites and a pot of mixed greens, steamed carrots, garden salad and she's cooking up the last of the hot water cornbread, talk about a feast! She told us that she cooked most of today's brunch yesterday so we wouldn't have a long wait after getting out of church. Her voice quivered as she spoke the words, "Out of church." She paused to collect herself and went on to tell us how blessed she is to have children that love the Lord; that warms her heart and floods her soul.

Rachael asks, "Gam Ma why are you sad!" While she runs over to Mama and gives her a hug. As Mama lifts her up onto her lap she explains the tears in her eyes are happy tears. Now Rachael doesn't let go of Mamas' neck and the expression on her little face is one of doubt so she rises up and kisses Mama on the cheek and says, "Gam Ma I love you kay." Every one of us grown folk says in unison, "Ahh". Daddy clears his throat and we all grab hands while he prays the blessing upon the feast on the table and the family surrounding it.

Mama informs the granddaughters they have their own table to sit at today and the giggles began, I mean! It was as though they were feeding off each other's giggle, it kept going and going and going…. Daddy informed us that Mama was spending so much money on food, tablecloths, glass ware and the little table and chairs set yesterday, he thought he was going to have to make two trips to the store; the back of his Silverado 3500HD was filled to the brim.

While we ate, Nye started telling us what church was about today then Wardell took his turn and while Daddy was sharing I found myself thinking about how wonderful this felt; all of us together and when I peeked over at the girls sitting at their own table I realized this is perfect timing for me to have another baby. I thought about how awesome Gods' timing is and thinking how Von and I are pregnant and probably due close to each other, and that thought made a big smile appear on my face. Just as I tune back in on the conversation, I hear Mama say, "Chile it was something to see!" She is laughing really loud and so is everyone else so I smile and look up at Wardell. He has a smile on his face and as soon as his eyes meet mine, he gets this question mark on his face as if to say, "Where were you?" I just raised my right eyebrow and winked at him. He gave me a sexy smirk and directed his eyes back to Mama.

Once again Daddy clears his throat and we all became focused on him. He sits straight up in his chair and his expression turned serious as he lifted the napkin from his lap onto the table he says, "God is so awesome, He has a way of taking what we feel are mistakes and a crooked place and He shows us in time, it was part of the plan that was predestined for us." Daddy shakes his head, smiles and looks over at Mama, deep into her eyes and continues, "Baby my heart would be pained listening to you pray for our children to become one again and I would consult the Lord for direction as to what could be done to answer your prayers. The Lord spoke to me after I spoke with Nye and told me to allow His will for their lives to become made manifested. It was difficult for me because I love my wife dearly and want her to want for nothing; but being obedient to the Lord is advantageous to the head of household.

I found out a long time ago that God has plans for me and my family and they are so wonderful, if I had done anything, I would have hindered something great from happening. So; I refrained myself many times from interfering with my children's reunion. And today...." Daddy is blinking back tears and his blinking has caused every one of us at the dinner table to start blinking back tears. He raises his left hand high and a "Hallelujah!" Comes surging out of his mouth, and before I knew it, my arms were raised and my eyes went to the closed position and I heard every one at the table praising the Lord. Hallelujah, Bless Your Wonderful Name and Thank You Jesus were the words of praise and adoration ringing in that room like a beautiful melody, I mean!

We praised the Lord so and when I opened my eyes I noticed the little people at their own table were sitting with their little precious hands lifted towards heaven and the same praise from the big table was coming from theirs. My heart swelled so seeing my baby and her cousins learning to give praise unto the Lord, I smiled so big as tears of gratitude traveled down my face….the next thing I heard was Nye at the piano playing 'Something About The Name Jesus' by Kirk Franklin and we all joined him in the living room and we sang our hearts out.

We went right into 'All Things Are Working' by Fred Hammond and into 'For Every Mountain' by Kurt Carr, then 'Rebuild Remix by J. Moss, then into 'I'm A Newborn Soul' by Hezekiah Walker and from there to 'Um Good' by Smokie Norful. While Nye was playing Mama sat next to him and when he played the last bar, she slid over and took control of the piano keys. She started with, 'We've Come Into This House' then she went right into 'The Blood' and Nye picked it up with the intro to Tramaine Hawkins, 'Changed' and Nye and I sang from the depths of our hearts unto the Lord….when he played the last note he jumped up from the piano, I followed his lead and we hugged one another and cried. The room was so quiet you could have heard a butterfly snoring as Granddad Campbell used to say. We all hugged and told one another that we loved and appreciated each other.

Now, when you have three children, under the age of four years old and it gets close to 5pm and; there is no whining; the spirit of the Lord has to be in the room! None of the girls made a fuss of any kind while we had our praise- a- thon going on. In fact they were singing right along with us, just an awesome time. Yes! Being reunited really felt good….

We all congregated into the dining room once again and warmed up the foods and ate some more however this time we added dessert; fried apple pies and coconut cake, yum, yum! While Von and I helped Mama with cleaning the kitchen, Nye and Daddy explained to the girls about praise and worship. It's just like Daddy to keep his motto going with his granddaughters: in all your getting, get an understanding. Von asked about Nicki and me meeting her and the girls at the park one day this week. So we decided to meet at Gateway Park, its midway for the both of us. Tuesday morning will work, this way the cousins can get acquainted and the Sister-in-loves can bond. I glanced at Mama because I remembered her telling me she had a dream and Von and I were at the park with the girls. She was smiling such a soft loving smile that I just had to walk over to her and plant a kiss on her cheek and rub her back. My Mama, my sweet lovable Mama, (sigh) I am so blessed to have her!

When we arrived home I noticed the oven light displayed 7:41pm and I let out a sigh. I am both gratified and fatigued at the same time. Wardell says for me to take care of Lil Kitten, he will put the dishes into the dishwasher. Nicki was so cooperative while I changed her into her pajamas she just yawned and why did she look like a little kitten to me; I couldn't resist kissing her and the kiss led to a hug, ahh; my Lil Kitten, ooh wee, I'm so blessed! Before I could get the covers over her she was asleep.   I stood over her smiling as tears swept down my dress; I couldn't help but think of how my life has been so enriched with my Nicki in it and...I can't imagine how much more enriched I will be with this new addition. As I think this thought I began to rub my belly, letting this precious baby know by my touch that she or he is already loved.

I hear Wardell come stand at the doorway and when I look up at him he has the biggest smile on his face and he walks into the room, stands behind me and hugs me so gently and as he kisses my neck he says, "Look at the first product of our love. She's as beautiful as the love we made to produce her, can I get an amen?" He rocks me in his arms and I can't help but break out in an enormous smile as I snuggle into his strong arms. All I can say is, "Umm." We both stand smiling, while looking at our first born for a few more moments and then we retire to our bedroom for some long, sweet lovemaking, ahh, I loves me some Wardell Patterson!

Chapter Eight

Ain't No Stopping Us Now!
Any way You bless me

I woke up just a few minutes before the alarm went off and felt so rested. I praised and thanked the Lord all the while I went to use the bathroom and even while I returned back to my bed. Ooh wee, I love the Lord! After I convinced Wardell there was not enough time for a quickie, I fixed his breakfast and while we sat at the table I realized I was eating out of his plate and I felt so bad, he never said a word, he just ate around me. I grabbed him a banana and put a Strawberry Yoplait in a zip lock bag for him along with a plastic spoon and told him, "Next time say something! You need your nourishment man." As he placed his arms around me he says, "It's not nourishment I'm in need of right now, it's time, or so my wife tells me." He gently kisses me as I try to loose myself from his embrace before he ends up late this morning! Whew!

After watching him leave for work I get into my prayer and ended up praising the Lord the whole while. I heard Holy Spirit say, "**Romans 8:28**", so I used it as my study scripture this morning. When we were twelve years old Daddy took me with him, by myself, to a Christian Book and Bible Store so he could get some church supplies and I picked up a Study Bible by the name of, 'The Quest Study Bible' and, I was so engrossed in it when Daddy came up behind me, he took a look at it and purchased it. He kept it for a good while then one day while I was doing homework, he came in my room and as he laid it on the night stand he told me it would really come in handy for me, and I could have it. So, as I remember, I still have that Study Bible and decide to find it and see what it says about Romans 8:28.

The Quest Study Bible has side-column notes on various scripture and it so happens, today's scripture has a note and it is as follows:
Excerpt from the Quest Study Bible

Do all bad events have a good purpose? (8:28)
No. There are three important qualifications to notice: (1) It is in all things- some good, some bad- that God can be at work. God can redeem things intended for evil, transforming them into good (see, for example, Gen. 50:20). (2) This promise is for those who love him. Those who are yet in rebellion cannot depend on everything achieving something good in their lives. (3) The good God desires to work is a spiritual, eternal work- preparing us for future glory. Also see is all suffering beneficial? (5:3)

I read **Romans 8:28-32** and it reads; **"And we know that in all things God works for the good of those who love him, who have been called according to his purpose. For those God foreknew he also predestined to be conformed to the likeness of his Son, that he might be the firstborn among many brothers. And those he predestined, he also called: those he called, he also justified; those he justified, he also glorified.**

What, then, shall we say in response to this? If God is for us, who can be against us? He who did not spare his own Son, but gave him up for us all- how will he not also, along with him, graciously give us all things?"

Now I have read this scripture quite a few times, but today it has a different light on it. I thought about what Daddy said yesterday at the dinner table, and I wondered why Holy Spirit waited until now to prompt me to stop this rift Nye and I had, why not three or four years ago? Why not a week after it started? But today this scripture reassures me, it was part of Gods plan from the moment Daddy prayed for us at the age of 17 for Nye and me to walk two separate lives and reunite at this point and time in our lives again.

I know without any doubt in me, that my life is where it's supposed to be at this point in time. The fact that we both went into the same line of business made me wonder if we could have collaborated on having a business together. However; after reading this scripture this morning; I know back then when we were 18 and 19; I would have done whatever Nye suggested and by him being so bent on me being the younger sister; he would have never allowed my input. We are twins however; we are two different people, wow Lord ALL things really do work together. You know what I realize; trusting God and waiting on His timing is difficult at times and that's really putting it lightly….but; it is definitely worth the wait! I am so glad I love the Lord and I'm saved!

I hear some pitter patter! As I close my Bible, I look towards the doorway, down where I know my baby will appear and she peeks her head around the door just enough to see me and she giggles and then takes off to the bathroom. I run behind her chanting, "I'm gonna get you!" As I enter her bathroom I hear, "lub you Mommy!" And as the words, "Love you too baby." Slips from my heart right out of my lips, the warmest smile appears on my face while I go straight to Nicki and kiss her all over her little angel face, oh how I loves me some Nicki! As I help Miss Independent wash her hands, I ask her what sounds good to her for breakfast and she smiles while saying, "Coco Puffs!" I'm not feeling coco puffs; I want some grits, bacon, eggs and some fluffy hot biscuits; yeah, that's what sounds good to me!

While the oven is preheating I make Nicki some Coco Puffs and start on the biscuits. I barely had enough buttermilk to make a small batch, just two nice sized and one little one for Nicki. While I get the grits going the phone rings. It's Wardell telling me to take Nicki over to Vedettes' at 1:15 and for me to meet him at the bank at 1:30; he was treating his beautiful wife to lunch today. He had already called Vedette and she's expecting Nicki, then he says, "Oh yeah I'm taking you somewhere nice so wear a skirt so I can see your beautiful legs, ok baby? Bye." And a "click!" I stood shocked, looking at the phone; he has never hung up on me like that before, what's going on?

The phone rings again and I answered, "I thought you had lost your mind man!" I hear, "Z; hello!" It's Mama! Oops. "Mama I'm sorry I thought you were Wardell. He called and told me to meet him at the bank and to wear a skirt then he just hung the phone up on me. I'm sorry, you calling me today? I already know what's going on with Nye and Von." I am smiling so big right now. "Well baby, can I talk to my only daughter and tell her how much she's loved and that I am so proud of her, huh, can a mother call and say that?" "Of course Mama, and let me just say that I am only imitating what I saw you do as a woman, wife and mother…Mama, you are the best ever! And I love you so much…" Now I'm crying like a pregnant woman! I mean!

Mama is sniffling over the phone and after a few moments I hear a soft, "Thank you Jesus!" "Mommy why you trying?" Nicki is asking. Oh my goodness, I have Mama and Nicki both tearing up with me this morning. If I don't get a handle on my hormones, this baby's going to be a cry baby! Mama says for me to tend after Nicki and to call her when I get a chance, she was a little under the weather and is lying in bed for a while.

When I lose Nicki from her high chair she hugs me so tight I can't get her grip to loosen so I finish cooking with her on my hip and we both start singing, 'This Little Light Of Mine.' I fix my plate and Nicki is sitting in my lap and she starts eating out of my plate and I see myself. This morning I ate out of her Daddy's plate the same way. I smiled and kissed her on the forehead, the saying about fruit not falling too far comes to my mind while I'm smiling. "Mommy, I pay wit Becca and Shell?" She looks up at me with Nye's eyes and my head automatically goes up and down indicating my answer is yes, then I think, tomorrow is our play date so I explain to her that we will meet her cousins tomorrow at the park and her little brown eyes lights up. We ate all of the food I cooked, Nicki even ate some of my biscuit after eating the little one I had made for her; man oh man did we eat!

I cleaned up the kitchen, took out the last of the ground turkey and started making my grocery list, then Nicki and I sang songs until noon and I mean she catches on quick to the words. We were ready and left the house at 1:05 headed to Vedettes'. I wore my jade green suit but with a black tube top under it. The skirt has a side split up to my mid-thigh and Wardell made me take it off the first time I put it on. We were attending a play one Saturday night. I thought he was playing when he grabbed me and told me he was not going to jail tonight because if I wore that skirt and a man looked too long at me in it; he was going to punch the man's lights out. I laughed but when I looked into his eyes, he was serious and when I asked if he was serious, he dropped his hands from around me and said, "Yes I am, your body is for ME to enjoy so, baby I will wait right here while you change into something more presentable for other men to see." I changed into a pantsuit. So, today I'm wearing the suit for the first time and, it's a little tight around the hips.

I pulled up in the bank parking lot a few minutes early so I decide to go into the bank and wait. I walk into the doors and a few of the Tellers wave at me. As I walk towards Wardells' office I can see the back of a females head and her hair is laid! He sees me approaching and stands up and waves me to come into his office. As I walk into the office, the lady stands up and turns towards me. I glance at her while Wardell walks towards me saying, "Rochelle; this is my wonderful wife; Zinora. Baby, this is Rochelle, a new trainee." While he hugs me I reach up and kiss his cheek and when I turn to greet Rochelle; this hefa has green eyes. I mean, her eye color is dark brown, but she looks at me like; 'You lucky dog'. She starts to twist her body while saying, "Zinora, I've heard so many things about you, oh no worries, uh huh, all good though." Then she gives this fake 'Huh,' while she smiles at me. I give Wardell a good tight hug and say, "Funny, I haven't heard one word about you, huh." Then I flash my fake smile at her and let her see me end it real fast, like Okay miss envy, catch a hold of this!

Wardell grabs his keys and we all walk out of his office, Miss Envy walking out first. She is a little taller than me, caramel skin tone that's smooth as a new born baby's. Her eyes are dark brown, almost black and I can tell she has tattooed eyebrows, extended eyelashes and, takes a lot of time applying her makeup, which I might add is matching her outfit. She has on a low cut light and dark shaded raspberry polyester blouse and her bosoms are being aided by a push up bra and the loud plaid tight short skirt is screaming, "Home to the Made" and, her wedge multicolored shoes looks comfortable. I watch her switch over to her desk and sit in her chair while Wardell goes over to Rita and inform her he's taking his lunch. I stand by the door watching Miss Envy and she is watching every move my husband is making; I feel my fingernails growing out real long and sharp and a fight coming up in me. Wardell grabs my hand and tells me that I will be riding with him and he has a surprise for me.

When we arrived back from our honeymoon, Wardells' 1996 Ford Focus had died so he called an Auto Broker friend of his and had him order a brand new Ford Mustang Bullitt GT. He told me from the first day it hit the market he has always wanted to own one. It was the first time he had a brand new car, talk about happy, he grinned every time he looked at it. The first month after he bought it and to this day he still washes it every two weeks. It's black on black with low profile rims and is real sporty. As he opens my car door for me he says, "So I see you're going to bail me outta jail this afternoon hey." I take a seat and flip the slit all the way open and say, "This is for your eyes only, I promise to keep the flap closed." I bat my eyes; he smiles and hurries to get in the driver's seat. Once he's all belted in he looks at me then down at my opened flap then back up at my eyes and makes his eyebrow go up and his famous smile appears! Oh, what can I say….

He drives us to the Hotel Phillips over on West Twelfth and parks in the valet, holds me tight as he steers me to the front desk. He has reserved us a room with room service and all… I stood at the counter with my mouth opened. He gets the key and off we go to our room. As soon as we step into the room he grabs me and starts slowly taking off my jacket and this man kisses my neck so tenderly I almost melt! He leads me towards the bed and there is a knock at the door, its room service already. We ate and made love and ate some more and while lying in bed, my husband told me that he loved me so much and how thrilled he was that I was carrying his seed and he went in detail about how he never thought he could father any children because of a severe case of the Mumps he had as a child. When he described how blessed he felt having Nicki and now another Patterson; he grabbed me and held me so tight, I thought he was getting emotional again.

Wardell is a very strong man and crying has only been displayed in church and only under the anointing. Lying here holding me ever so tightly; I know his heart is full of love for his family. I turned over to face him and I hugged my husband and I told him with tears in my eyes; that he was the best thing to happen to me and how privileged I was to carry his precious seed. We hugged one another so tight; I could barely breathe. We showered and when I pulled away from the bank parking lot, it was 3:17. I thought about Miss Envy and wished it was 4pm, that hefa!

I went home changed clothes and picked up my grocery list before picking up Nicki. We went grocery shopping and then I drove out to Nichols Road to visit Victoria's Secret; I had to pick up something I knew Wardell would love. I feel so sexy and loved; I believe I smiled all the way home! Miss Nicki sang to the store and back home, I mean! While the enchiladas were in the oven I phoned Nye. Mrs. Gibson answered the phone and we sorta re introduced ourselves. It has been an awfully long time since we met and it wasn't until I told her my picture was on the mantel, that she remembered me. She was "Sitting with the girls," as she put it, while Nye took Von on a date. Mrs. Gibson promised to leave a message to let Nye know his sister phoned. I don't know; maybe it's just me, but it sounded like she had an attitude when the word, "Sister" fell out of her mouth…just sayin.

We had a great dinner and while I was cleaning the kitchen, Wardell was supervising Nicki with her pajama changing and tooth brushing; the phone rings and it's Nye. He is laughing so I asked what was so funny and he told me Mrs. Gibson thought I was some woman trying to get with him. She said as long as they have been married, no woman has ever called the house to say she was his sister. Mrs. Gibson told Von to write down my phone number and give it to her because she was going to do a reverse trace and pay me a visit. Von was not allowed to attend the visit but her brothers were going to escort their mother to where I lived and make it very plain she was not going to allow no hussy to snatch Nye from her daughter! That was not happening on her watch! Nye said he was so tickled because she never takes up for Mr. Gibson and he was surprised to hear her want to fight some woman so Von can keep him. He told me that he knows for sure he has proven to her parents how much he loves their daughter.

I told him about Miss Envy and that Wardell had taken me to the Phillips Hotel and he was so happy that Wardell loves me and we are keeping the fires ignited in our marriage. I told him a little about Wardells' parents and how they are so much in love to this day after over 30 years of marriage. Nye shared with me how we are both blessed to have married into loving families because our parents show nuff love one another strong. We both laughed remembering how Daddy got into it with Brother Levi and how we never saw Brother Levi ever again after that day. We were both almost in stitches remembering that. I told him that I just wanted to check on him and Von is why I phoned, I didn't want anything in particular; he said, "Z, I missed you too, love you, bye." When I hung up; I felt so good having Nye back in my life. It's a little different now because we both have families; but, I don't feel as though a piece in my life is missing anymore, you know. I feel complete knowing no- thing is hindering my relationship with my brother anymore, it feels good being complete!

When I get to our bedroom, Wardell and Nicki are lying on the bed and he is explaining how having a brother is so much fun. She's just sitting there listening; I don't think playing catch and leap frog interest her. While I climb on the bed behind Nicki he says, "Ask Mommy, she had fun with her brother huh Mommy."   I lie down so I can look her in the face while saying, "Oh yeah, we had loads of fun growing up together. We walked to school together sang songs together and played so many games, oh yeah we had a lot of fun together." "Butter hit you Mommy." "Oh baby no, my brother; your Uncle Nye didn't hit me, he was a good brother."   "I want tister, peas Mommy, peas. I want tister like Becca and Shell, peas."

Her eyes are so sad and the little thin wrinkles on her forehead make me want to tell her okay, but I don't want to disappoint her. I do know we are going to find out what the gender of this baby is and have this conversation again. "Baby, do Mommy and Daddy a favor and think about having a brother okay, will you do that for us, please?" She turns from me and looks at Wardell, "Otay, I tink bout it." She is hunching her tiny shoulders and her little hands are up in the air while sporting the most serious look on her cute face and Wardell and I are smiling, thinking about how grown she looks. Wow, she is growing up!

We get some counting in with Nicki, she knows how to count up to 20, and two songs before we both put her down for the night. I take a long hot shower and when I enter the bedroom Wardell is reading a business magazine. I didn't say anything to him; I went into my closet and pulled out the bag with his gift in it I had purchased earlier today. I changed in the closet and when I walked into the bedroom; he glanced at me over his reading glasses and I notice his double take as his jaw dropped. This red number caught his eyes; sho nuff! I had my red sparkled stilettos on and I pranced around the bed modeling. He put the magazine and his reading glasses down on top of his night stand and watched me model for him. I said, "So; tell me Mr. Patterson; why haven't I heard about Miss Roach before today?"

"I have never told you about any of the trainees before, you happened to come into the bank today. Ugh, Mrs. Patterson; you don't have anything to worry about. These eyes loves what they see and always will, baby let me show you what I mean!" He rises up on his knees and crawls towards me grinning like he just won something. "Are you sure your new trainee won't start looking good when I get fat and out of shape?" He stopped in his tracks...I stand still looking into his eyes; reading them actually... he climbs out of the bed and as he stands, he says, "Zinora...baby, you, you are the world to me. I don't care if you weigh 600 pounds or lose a limb...baby I love you. You were made for me." He takes his hand and presses it against his rib and continues, "Baby this rib is short one because you were formed from it, you, not some trainee or any other woman, but YOU!" Now he is standing a few feet away pointing to his side. I step close to him and place my hand gently on his side and ask, "Here, is this where I was formed from?" Quickly he grabs my hand and pulls me up against himself and while he kisses my lips he moans

"Uh Hun".   The red number I bought today hit the floor!

Well; today I overslept again, Wardell is gone and I didn't hear his alarm go off. I open my eyes and praise breaks forth from me! I love the Lord for His tender mercies towards me and His loving kindness… I use the bathroom and get back into bed and began to sing unto the Lord this morning. I slip into worship and sing in tongues and in English. Nicki slips onto the bed and joins me with the melody but she doesn't know the words because I'm making them up as I sing. She figures it out and begins making up her own words. I listen as she says, "Jesus I lub you and Daddy and Mommy and Gram Ma and my Poppy and Gam Ma Fatterson and Poppy Fatterson and….." I can't take anymore; I grab her and hug her so tight and I began kissing my precious baby. I wonder as I look upon her if the Lord loves our praise and worship as much as I love hearing Nicki. I equate the Fathers' love is far greater than ours.   He is blessed by our praise and moved by our worship. Oh how my heart swells knowing my Heavenly Father is blessed by my praise! Ooh wee; I mean!

After we get cleaned up, we go into the kitchen and today we wolf down waffles, scrambled eggs and ice cold milk; um, um, good! Nicki ate a whole waffle and I ate …3. I'm ashamed to tell it, I have an appetite like a ditch digger!   As my Mama would say. Speaking of… Why didn't she call me back? I grab the phone, dial her number and there is no answer. I think…that is not like Mama, something is wrong! I run to my room and get my sweats on real fast and go get Nicki and throw a jacket on her and leave headed to Mama's house. Why didn't she call me back, if she had she would have left me a message, what's going on...Holy Spirit, what is going on? I franticly ring her doorbell and try to look into the window and as soon as I head towards the back door; I hear the front door slowly opening. I can feel my heart pounding as though it will jump out of my body and land on the ground! I say to myself, 'Now Z; calm down' as I slow my breathing down.

I have Nicki in my arms and she has her neck stretched as I do mine while we walk to the front door, both of us is wondering why Mama is not at the door. We slowly walk to the opening and there is no one at the door. I step up into the house and holler, "Mama... Mama say something so I know you're alright! Mama!" I get this little echo from Nicki, "Mama!" We hear this weak sounding, "I'm in the bedroom." We dart to Mama's room and she is lying down; under the covers shivering something awful. I walk up to her bed and Nicki jumps out of my arms onto Mama's bed and starts crawling straight to her Gam Ma. "Baby, Gam Ma is not feeling good today. Don't get too close, Gam Ma don't want you to catch this cold; okay baby." It's too late; Mama couldn't get it out fast enough. Nicki is already crawling under the covers with Mama and is kissing her face. Mama turns her head away from Nicki; but, Nicki takes her little hands and turns Mama's head towards her and kisses her face all over; like we do her! Mama smiles and brings her hands from under the covers and hugs Nicki.

"That works better than penicillin!" Mama says again weakly, then she lets out this deep tight chested cough. Oh no! I know that sound; she is full of cold. "Mama I'm taking you to emergency!" I go into their closet and find her robe that zips up and I go into her drawer and pull out a pair of thick warm socks. While pulling her up I realize she is burning up and so weak. I go to Daddy's side of the bed to get the phone but it's not there so I pull out my cell and dial her number and follow the sound. The phone is in the kitchen next to the stove. I notice there is some soup that has been heated and a bowl on the counter where almost no soup has been eaten.

I called Nye's house and he answered after the first ring. When I said Mama was sick; he said, "Okay; I'm on my way." He hung up. By the time I had Mama in my Tahoe; Nye pulled up with Von and the girls. I took one look at him and knew he was thinking what I was; Mama needs to be in the hospital. He went to her and asked how she felt. I walked over to speak to Von and the girls and she had a worried look on her face also. She told me that Mama has been having difficulty breathing lately and refused to see a doctor. I told her we were taking her to emergency and they will check her completely out before we bring her home. I hugged my nieces and Von. She told me to let Nicki stay with them until we get back. I didn't argue and Nicki was so busy clapping and smiling when we pulled off I wasn't worried at all about her; but Mama…….

While Nye was driving us to emergency I recalled all of the times I asked her over the phone if she had been running and she was so quick to tell me NO. I know my Mama, she believes in praying for healing; so do I; AND I believe in getting medicine if need be. We pulled up at the emergency entrance and Nye jumped out of the car and ran into the building. I slid under the wheel and by the time I parked and was removing Mama; Nye was there with a wheel chair and an attendant. Mama could barely sit up so Nye ran back into the building and a few minutes later he returned to where we were and he lifted Mama from the wheel chair... her arms were dangling, she looked so helpless; I broke down and cried. By the time I entered the entrance Nye had her stretched out on a gurney, and she was fighting for her every breath and I could only stand speechless, and spectate while my big brother prayed for our mother in her ear as he rubbed her hand.

A Doctor came swiftly and asked us how long had she been like this. Nye glanced at me and I said since yesterday and he pulled Mama away while giving orders to the nurses. Nye followed the doctor and I followed Nye. We stood in front of the double doors marked Authorized Personnel Only, where they had taken our Mama until the   doors stopped swinging; then he turned around and told me that we need to call Daddy. I stood tense, looking him directly in the eyes; I couldn't move and I felt as though I wasn't breathing. Call Daddy; oh my goodness, if something was to happen to Mama up in here; they will have to haul him off with a gun held to his head; he would tear this place up!

I called Daddy and stayed as calm as I could but he knew something was wrong when he heard my voice, he said, "Z?   Where is your Mama?" I said we're at Mercy Hospital, the emergency side, he said okay and hung up. Nye said it was a twenty minute drive from Daddy's job so we had better look out for him in fifteen. He held my hand and said, "Z; she's going to be fine." My brother grabbed me and held me in his arms; we never spoke a word, we were both praying silently. Daddy walked calmly in the emergency room and I took inventory of how he looked.   My Daddy is a good looking man for his age and he has taken good care of himself. I remember how young Mama looked to me last week when she was over and I realize my parents are still young and have a lot of living to do, they love the Lord and His work; so; I'm believing she is going to pull through this and together they will live a good rest of their lives! And it is so; in the Name of Jesus!

We noticed Daddy waiting at the desk so we walked over to him. He was calm but then Daddy is always calm until he attacks... When the nurse told him there was no news to report; he simply said, "Then I suggest you get some news to report to me; woman, that is my wife back there and I will burn this hospital down if I have too, tell me something and I mean NOW!"   "Sir; we are working very diligently to get information that is exact about your wife; all I'm asking is that you give us a little more time to finish running our tests. As soon as we know anything; sir you will be notified, thank you for being patient." She turned around and walked away before Daddy could say anything else. Nye told Daddy that he had already prayed and Mama was going to come through this alright. Daddy asked what happened; how did she get here. Nye told what he knew then I took my turn.

It turns out that Von was interested in medicine and knew a little something because she was going to become a Radiology Technician. She thought Mama was having some breathing problems and mentioned it to Nye; that's why when I called, he knew something was wrong with Mama. Daddy told us that she said she wasn't feeling well last night and he prayed for her breathing but she was asleep when he left this morning and had phoned her earlier but when there was no answer he thought she had felt better and was shopping somewhere, he felt really bad.

After an hour and a half, the same doctor that asked Nye and me questions came to update us on Mama's condition. She has double pneumonia and had we waited another hour, she may not have made it. Mama has a touch of C.O. P. D. and coupled with pneumonia is very life threatening at this point. They have started her on oxygen, antibiotics, an I.V., and extracting mucus from her lungs. They have her as comfortable as possible but not too; they want her to use her lungs and keep them strong. Daddy told the Doctor that we were praying people and with medicine and prayer; we believe she is going to pull through this. When he smiled at the Doctor, my heart rate slowed some; I knew he wasn't going to pull the Doctor by his chest and threaten him if Mama didn't get better! Whew!

I called Wardell while Nye called Von. He was worried about me being worried; he is concerned about the baby with me being in my first trimester. He told me to hold on and he went into his office and closed the door and my husband prayed for his wife and mother in love.   As I sat there in that chair I rocked as he prayed. I felt the presence of the Lord so strongly and it reminded me of when we dated, how he would pray for me before hanging up from our phone conversations, ahh, I loves me some Wardell! I felt like everything was fine after talking to him. I smiled and reached over and told Daddy that Mama was going to make it and take better care of herself; just wait and see. Then I patted his hand. He looked so worried and I have never seen Daddy that worried before so, I grabbed hold of his hand and gave it a real tight squeeze. He in turn, squeezed my hand while looking up at me and he smiled.

Wow, my Daddy is a very good looking man and his smile can melt away worries, no wonder Mama fell so hard for him. Daddy let my hand go and put his arm around me and said, "Z, I know your mother will be alright baby I will insist she quit that job. She only works because she is bored and I can't figure out why she refuses to admit it. She tells people that she works to pay for her car but that is not true. Baby we have trust funds for each one of our grandchildren and enough money in banks to pay her car off and pay cash for two more. I just don't understand...." He removes his arm from around me and leans forward in his chair and begins rubbing his hands together while staring down at the floor. In walks Nye and he stands in front of Daddy and stares at him.

Nye doesn't turn his head my way, just his eyes moves towards me. He gives me the 'go, let me and Daddy be alone' look, so I excuse myself and say I'll be right back. I went to the vending machine and watched them from there. Nye took my seat and talked to Daddy then he put his hand on Daddy's back and I watched my Daddy fight back tears as he rung his hands so tight and shook his head and shuffled his feet. Nye began ringing his own hands. I realized just this second that my brother is so much like our father; and I love them both dearly.

I eased over to the Rustin men and the gentleman sitting next to Daddy got up and let me have his seat. Before I could get seated here comes a nurse announcing, "Rustin family" and we all stood up. She explained to us Mama was going to be in the intensive care unit until her breathing improves so don't be alarmed; the tubes she is hooked up to are for her to get adequate oxygen and also remove excess fluids from her lungs. We followed her into and through so many doors and finally, Mama. My sweet funny Mama looked so frail and hopeless; I stood there in the doorway to her room unable to move. Daddy and Nye both took a side of her bed and Daddy kissed her on her forehead and Nye bent over and kissed her hand. When he looked back at me and saw I hadn't moved, he automatically came over and took me by the elbow; a gesture he was so familiar doing to me as we grew up; and he walked me to our Mama. All I can do is stand here; speechless....I deliberately stand over her and observe every tube and piece of machinery hooked up to her and I become numb; this time last week she was making me pancakes. Huh oh, I feel funny.....

I wake up in a hospital bed I fainted. Daddy was standing on one side of me and Nye was on the other. I tried to get up as I asked how Mama was doing. Daddy put his hand on my arm and told me; "lie back down and take it easy, your mother is in capable hands being here; you on the other hand need to take it easy carrying my grand child. You hearing me Zinora?"   I looked up at him and could see fear and compassion so; I lay back down. Nye says, "Wardell is on his way." I rose up again as I asked, "Why?" Nye spoke so fast I hardly finished my why. "You fainted and you're carrying his baby; come on Z!" I looked at Nye and he looked so scared; as he hunched his shoulders and blinked back tears. I knew it was Nye that had called Wardell, sensing something was wrong with me.

As I recline, I remember now the very first time I found out we had a strong sense of each other's feelings that was different from other brothers and sisters; we were in the 2nd grade. The teachers always separated us by making sure we had different classes but we would spend our lunch period together. They really thought keeping us apart would stop us from being close but when he fell head first from the big slide, he flipped over and hit the back of his head on the bottom of the slide, and landed flat on his back, on the ground. I was in my class and felt the wind being knocked out of me. I felt as if someone had socked me in the stomach and then came a heavy, hard pounding at the back of my neck. I looked out of the window because I heard noise outside from the children playing so I knew Nye was at recess.

I dropped my pencil and ran outside panicked. I knew Nye was in trouble, didn't know what from, but I knew something was wrong with my brother! The teacher was hollering my name to get my attention, but my heart was racing so fast as I ran out of that classroom, my brother was forefront in my mind right now. She followed me to the playground area still yelling at me to stop and her aggravated tone didn't even slow me down. As soon as I saw where the crowd was standing, my eyes commenced scanning the area for Nye's blue striped shirt I remembered he had on. I recognized his shoes as he lay on top of the sand on the ground. So many kids were standing around him, his shoes were all I could see and I ran towards him so fast screaming, "NYE, NYE!"

I shoved everyone standing near him out of my way. He laid there with his eyes closed looking as though he were asleep. I dropped to my knees and started praying, "In the name of Jesus; Nye, rise up and walk!" I didn't realize I was screaming at the top of my lungs until later, when the kids started telling what had happened. What was strange to me was how they looked at us after that, like we had super powers or something. And some of the kids would tease us and say things like; "If I slap you will your brother feel it?" Or "When he has to pee do you have to pee too?" Or the one that made me roll my eyes at them, "Does he belch when you get full?" Just dumb things!

Nye was always protective of me and if I was afraid to go around someone, he would ask, "Did they do something to you?" The first couple times I told the truth and said, "Yes." Nye would take me by the hand and march right up in their face and say, "Hey, this is my little sister and if you bother her again I'll beat the crap out of you; you got that?" Then he would almost touch his nose to theirs and give that look, a stare actually and after that, I would never so much as get a hello from that person. I was so scared he would hurt someone or get in trouble because of me; I just stopped telling him if I were bothered by anyone unless I really wanted Nye to help me.

As I lay here on this hospital bed, I'm picturing Mama in that bed with those tubes and I began praying silently for her. I heard Wardell ask for me and opened my eyes. I watched him as he walked into the room and spoke to Daddy and Nye as he stepped up to me and bent over and kissed me on my cheek and asked me if I were okay. I attempted to rise up but he put his hand on my shoulder and gave me a nudge as he shook his head "No." "Relax baby, what happened." Daddy spoke up and said, "She fainted and needs to go home it's hard for her seeing her mother like she is. Z; I will keep you well informed about your mother; baby go home with your husband and stay there, you hearing me?" Wardell spoke up, "Oh yeah! She hears you, yes sir; and, she's going to do exactly what you're telling her." He looks at me and says "Aren't you!" "Okay, okay; but Daddy promise me you'll let me know everything going on with Mama, promise." I heard my voice tremble and as Daddy started jingling his change in his pockets, he softly says, "I promise baby." Wardell helped me get up and he walked with me like I was cripple or something. I told him that I was alright but he insisted on holding me and helping me take each step.

During the drive home in my Tahoe; he didn't say anything but he kept glancing my way. I said, "I'm ok, I just fainted when I saw Mama with all of those tubes coming out of her." I began crying as I continued, "She looked so helpless, not the woman that laughed at me when she was teaching me to tie my shoes, or the woman that hugged me and told me she loved me every night before I went to bed; that's not my Mama in that hospital bed…" Silence the rest of the way home.

When we pulled up into the garage, Wardell opened the car door for me and stood there holding it while I turned to climb out of the car, he says, "Baby I can only imagine how I would feel if it were my mother in that hospital bed; but you are my wife and I am concerned about YOU right now. I need your faith to kick in and believe she's healed and concentrate on yourself and our beautiful baby you're carrying. Zinora; I will *NOT* have you lose this baby due to stress; now I bind that in the name of Jesus! Come on baby and lie down for an hour just for me; can you do that for me baby, huh?" He extended his hand out for me and as I placed my hand in his, I told him yes.

He walked me straight to our bed room and when I sat on the bed; he lifted my feet up and took my shoes off. He stood over me and said, "You had better be glad you fainted baby or else I would take advantage of you on our bed looking so sexy, ump, ump, ump." He smiles at me and raises his eyebrow. I smile and realize how blessed I am to be married to him. He asks, "Are you hungry; because I am." "Not really; but if you're getting something I'm sure I'll help you eat it." I smile and tell him about my breakfast. He sits on the edge of the bed and takes my hand and as he strokes it he looks at it and says, "I don't want anything to happen to you baby; you are a good mother to Nicki and a real good wife to me…I; baby… listen..." He looks up into my eyes and continues, "I will take care of you as best as I can; but you must take it easy; please." He reaches over and kisses me so tenderly and I feel my temperature rise!

"Are you okay?" Wardell asks while we lie on the bed exhausted. I roll on my side and look him in the eyes and tell him that I have never felt better and raise my eyebrow at him. We both laugh and as he gets up he says he feels like some soul food from "Soul'n It". We both go through our phones to call our order in; one of us has the number from the last time we ordered; we just can't remember who called it in. It's in my phone and after we place our order Wardell calls his brother Clarence and has him come pick him up so he can get his car from the hospital, then he'll pick up our order; Greens, yams, dirty rice, smothered pork chops and corn bread; now that's some good eating right there! I call Von to check on Nicki.

Von told me Nye had phoned her while we were at the hospital and told her I had fainted and asked if she was up to keeping Nicki for the day; without any hesitation she said, "Sure; Nicki is no problem. She's wearing an outfit of Rachel's and they are getting ready for a nap; let's see if that happens!" Von told me to rest and if Nicki needs to stay overnight; Nye would swing by and get some clothes and her toothbrush. She told me it was interesting watching the girls interact with their cousin and share with her. Von said it was good to see how they will accept another sibling and Nicki was a Guinea Pig and was totally oblivious of it! We both laughed.

After talking with Von I thought about how Nye and I had a hard time letting other kids into our circle. It always felt strange; like an intruder was trying to join our club but they had no clue as to the rules. We seldom had to tell each other what or how to do something and when other kids tried to play with us; we found it difficult to explain to them what to do. Kinda like today; when I couldn't keep Mama straight in that wheel chair; Nye knew to get her a bed. Also; when he wanted to talk to Daddy; I knew to excuse myself. I think I need to observe Nicki with the girls to see what Mama went through with the two of us. Mama… I called Daddy to check on her.

He said she was improving already; her temperature was decreasing and her breathing had improved some. He was going to stay at the hospital with her as long as he could and would call me in a few hours and give me an update. He sternly told me to stay home and rest and not make Wardell worry about me; then he asked about his Lil Kitten. I told him Von had her and he went silent for a few seconds, then he said he would love to be a fly on the wall and watch that; we both laughed. When we finished talking; I felt Daddy's relief and I know it's only because of prayer; it really does change things.

I prayed while I rested waiting on Wardell to come home with the soul food and Holy Spirit let His presence be known to me. He reassured me everything was going to work out just fine and I thought about my scripture study yesterday from Romans 8:28-32 and a big smile appeared on my face; Lord I love You and to prove it; I'll trust You!

Wardell came home with enough food to feed two families; we sat in the middle of our bed and ate almost everything; just the two of us! When he dosed off; I got up and cleaned the kitchen and paid some shop bills. When I slipped back into bed; I woke him. We talked about our future and having more children; I think Mama being ill has me thinking about my future and what goals I have long term and not just the next five years. Wardell and I wrote down our goals after we returned from our honeymoon and we have stayed to the plan up until now. He told me after I typed it up and posted it inside our closets; that this was not in stone; should we need to change anything, we will simply make the change.

This was said due to us not putting a number on how many children we wanted; he said he was a lot like his father and wanted to make all the babies he could afford and if he had to work extra jobs to provide; that was what he'd do. Today he tells me he does not want to lose any of his seed. He feels because we honored the marriage bed by us not having pre-marital sex, he should never lose any children because that was a desire of his heart.

The phone rings and its Daddy with an update; Mama is doing better and her breathing is looking as though her lungs are getting stronger also, her temperature is now normal. The nurses are all amazed and saying how incredible it is to see such a rapid drop in temperature. As soon as Wardell took me home from the hospital, Daddy phoned the church and asked the prayer warriors to offer up intercession for her. I actually heard a smile in his voice before we ended our conversation. The Most High God is AWESOME!

Wardell and I got up to go get Nicki from Von. When we went through the kitchen to the garage; Wardell asked me who cleaned the kitchen. When I told him I did; he sighed in disgust. I asked what was wrong and he sternly said to me, "Stay off your feet Zinora!" As we walked to the car I said, "I am not spotting Wardell; I just fainted." He glanced at me and sat in the car and waited for a few seconds before starting it up. He took a deep breath and looked at me and said, "Baby…today you faint; tomorrow you start spotting." I opened my mouth and he raised his hand up and kept talking, "If it looks like you might lose our baby; Zinora Ruth; I will make you stay home until after the baby is a year old, now I'm only trying to protect you…..Baby; just be careful, please, promise me that, please.." As I look at Wardell, I see his forehead is wrinkled and I know he's afraid and his eyes are full of frustration. So, I try and console him. I place my hand on his and softly say, "Alright honey; I don't want you worrying; I'll be real careful, promise." I touched his face gently and smiled; he smiled back at me and started the car.

When we walked in the front door to Nye and Von's, Nicki saw us and waved…she waved at us! No running chanting my wonderful parents are here; all we got was a wave. She was busy placing alphabets onto a board; a game Nye and Von has for the girls. Nye stopped Wardell in the kitchen while I went to the table where all of the females were. Von is supervising them as they are trying to see who can get the most alphabets in the right slot. As I take off my jacket Von asks how I feel and I tell her I'm ok then I tell her about how Wardell is acting. She laughs and tells me the story of when she fainted before she knew she was pregnant with the twins.

She said she had just sat down in her College Algebra Class when the room suddenly began to blacken and she felt strange. The next thing she knew, she was on the floor and her classmates and instructor were standing over her. She took the shuttle to the campus clinic and after the nurse took her temperature, it was when she said no to the question, had she eaten anything; she thought her fainting was a result of her rushing to class and hadn't eaten. They gave her some orange juice and she returned to class. Later that evening she told Nye she had fainted in class and after he went silent for a few minutes, he became a basket case. She said he paced the floor and told her they had to get married right away. She was like whoa just a minute, we don't know one another. He grabbed her and kissed her and said,

"That my dear is love and Yvonne I think you're pregnant and we need to take a run to Vegas tonight, what you say, will you marry me?" She told him to slow down all she did was faint.

He told her that because they had premarital sex the Lord would punish them with problem after problem if they didn't get married. She said he sat her down and told her that he loved her from the moment he set eyes on her and that was why he pursued her so hard. She told me the way he looked at her and held her in his arms, she knew he was telling her the truth and she was hopelessly in love with him, so she agreed to hop a plane to Vegas and they eloped two days later, on a Thursday. During their plane ride to Las Vegas she asked Nye what was going to happen to his Barber Shop he had just applied for now they were getting married and he told her the Lord was going to bless them because they were doing the right thing. Von told me Nye was so right; the Lord has blessed them tremendously and still is.

I was so stunned; Nye and Von had premarital sex! She noticed how quiet I was and asked if I had to digest the sex thing. I told her yeah, I never had sex before marriage and thought Nye never would either. Von moved real close to my face and told me that it was not planned; it just happened. I thought about the day Wardell and I kissed accidentally in the kitchen; if we had been alone, oh yeah... I shook my head; oh, now I understand.

She told me my fainting may not happen again; but for me to watch my diet and make sure I eat proper balanced meals. I remembered eating those waffles; all that sugar, so I made a mental note to watch my sweets intake. We stayed until after 8 pm; Nye cooked for Von and us; baked tilapia, broccoli, wild rice, salad and croissants. I can't tell you where the food I ate went to, because I ate like I hadn't eaten all day, I mean!

We both helped Lil Kitten get ready for bed tonight and she talked up a little storm telling us everything she did with her 'Tuzins'; (Cousins). We lay on her bed with her as Wardell read some of Emoni Moves to Grandma's House. He had to read quite a few pages before she doze off. We got in bed and talked about today's events and prayed that tomorrows new mercies will bring repair and rebuild. I fell asleep in my loving husbands arms.

Chapter Nine

At Last
The will of God!

We were both awakened by the sound of the alarm. Again Wardell reaches for me but today, I don't think about him being late to work; I touched and agreed with the man! He jumped into the shower and just as I was about to get in with him the phone rings; it's Daddy. He is at the hospital and Mama has improved greatly during the night and she's talking! I asked about his job and he told me he took a few weeks' vacation because he was not planning to leave his baby's side until she was one hundred percent. He asked me how I was doing and told me to take good care of me and Nicki. Daddy turned serious and said, "Z; the Lord is in this baby; I can't explain it but I know in my heart of hearts everything is going to work out for the best. Don't worry about your Mama; pray for her, all will be well, you'll see. Take care baby. Kiss my Lil Kitten and tell Wardell hey for me, love you, bye."

I was so happy I began to cry tears of joy as I sat on the edge of our bed. I raised my hands up in praise and adoration to the Wonderful and Powerful Holy Ghost! Wardell started getting dressed in silence and when I told him about Mama, his face lit up as he commented, "Good! Now don't you worry baby you hear me. Oh man, I'm sounding like your Dad. Seriously, take it easy for me today; please baby." "I will," was all I could say. Watching him get dressed had me fanning. When I realized I was fanning like Mama does about Daddy; I got so tickled! I ran to the garage with Wardell as he was trying to get out of the house and not be late. He told me he was going to pick up something to eat on his way to the bank and that I was not to cook; he was bringing home dinner. When he kissed me bye he rubbed my belly and smiled. As he slipped into his car he said, "I have a feeling it's a boy." He smiled so big and shook his head up and down; all I could do was stand in the door and smile; my man is oh so fine!

After I took my shower I went into the living room to get a scripture study in but I had a strong urging to sing unto the Lord; so I held my bible close to my heart and opened my mouth and these words fell out … **"There are so many things about the will of god, the things we can't explain because they seem so hard. We try to find the way that seems to be just right, but the way that we chose only lead us further from the light. If we could learn to accept the things we cannot change, and never question god; for we'll never know his ways."** I realize this is Hezekiah Walkers' song; Will Of God. A song the choir used to sing a few years ago and it has come up from my soul today; so I continue… **"There are many things about what God allows that we don't understand, but if he allows everything to be, it's a part of the master's plan. He knows what's best, and He won't put more on you, than you can, you can bear. His will is good, and, is acceptable, and, is perfect; yes it is!"**

I sang this song over and over; I felt each word apprehend my heart and my soul. I was surrendering to every word; I was surrendering to the will of God! I wept and I sang and I wept some more. Thinking of all the events that have happened in my life since a week ago Sunday; I saw the hand of the Lord in every tear, every thought and in every conversation I had. My heart felt as though it would burst; I was so full of thanksgiving and appreciation unto the Lord. To think He loves me so much He always has my best interest in mind; even when it doesn't look like it.

I thought about what Daddy said Sunday at the dinner table and about the scripture in Genesis where the fruit of the knowledge of good and evil was eaten and how Adam and Eve died spiritually.... **Genesis 3:4 & 5** says, **"Then the serpent said to the woman, "You will not surely die. For God knows that in the day you eat of it your eyes will be opened, and you will be like God, knowing good and evil."**

Being raised in the Rustin house, I learned to dissect the Word and I remember doing a study of good versus evil. The good in the Old Testament means to be or make; good, well or better. The New Testaments meaning of good is to benefit, profit, and have advantage. The evil in Old Testament means to spoil literally by breaking to pieces. You might say 'destroy', now isn't that interesting because that's what the devil comes to us to do, kill, steal and destroy by breaking us into pieces, wow! The New Testament meaning for the word evil is, worthless, as it relates to the fundamental nature of a thing, like our persons, double wow! The evil is set before us to influence us, so that we will never be who it is we were designed to be, and that we become worthless.

So, as I see it, before Adam and Eve ate of the fruit, they believed whatever happened was supposed to happen, no questions as to what was right or what might have been wrong; they accepted whatever was, was supposed to be. After they ate of the fruit, they questioned their every act; thus the spoiling or worthlessness coming into the picture. Dying spiritually causes us to battle with good over evil and most things we see as evil is simply supposed to be and; we need to learn to see its significance. I believe Paul brought this out so clearly in **Romans** chapter **7:21-25**. It states, **"I find then a law, that evil is present with me, the one who wills to do good. For I delight in the law of God according to the inward man.   But I see another law in my members, warring against the law of my mind, and bringing me into captivity to the law of sin which is in my members. O wretched man that I am! Who will deliver me from this body of death? I thank God—through Jesus Christ our Lord! So then, with the mind I myself serve the law of God, but with the flesh the law of sin. "**

Here Paul was describing the effects we have to deal with from eating of the fruit. If only Adam and Eve had **not** tasted to see. I realize some things in life we are to experience period. And, learning the difference when good and evil is in existence; well, I believe it is important to **understand** how to live being influenced by both! The most important lesson I've learned being separated from Nye all these years is that I trust the Lord like never before. All power is in His Hands and because I'm confident He only has the best in store for me; if I have to endure the bad with the good; so be it. When it is all over; the good will produce and bring forth the will of God, and; the bad will have taught me something and made the good worth enjoying.

There are times and circumstances when we need to, 'Bind, and Lose,' and that's when wisdom and understanding comes to play. We need to know what season we are in and what it is we are learning or being prepared for. Because we are born into sin, we need to become 'Born Again,' and learn to walk in the spirit, to know what it is we are supposed to do. If we remember that walking in the spirit is a lifestyle, not just a Sunday experience; we will trust the Lord is teaching us daily. We need to learn how to die daily so Christ can teach us how to walk in the spirit and mirror Him! Its a process and His grace gives us brand new mercies to experience our life in Him. Oh how I love the Lord!

I hear Nicki getting out of bed and realize I had better get my move on; I have my doctor's appointment this morning. We get ready and I fix us an omelet with onions, bell pepper, cheese and I threw in some crispy bacon bits and I mean! I had to make me two pieces of toast and finished Nicki's while we walked out of the garage door. If I don't slow down I just might get up to 600 pounds and see if Wardell meant what he said.

Nicki starts, "Tan I hab a tister like Becca and Shell Mommy, Tan I?" "Baby, do you think you will like a brother to play with?" She takes so long to respond; I look in the mirror to see what she's doing. My baby has this real deep thinking look on her face and I can't help but smile. I say, "I have a brother and we had a lot of fun growing up together." "You hab a butter Mommy? Where?" "Nicki, Uncle Nye is my brother, don't you think he looks like me?" "Uh yes!" "Nicki, baby not all brothers are bad to their sisters. I am sure your brother will love you just like Rebecca and Rachel love one another." "Mommy why Tan I hab tister." I glance back at her and she has her hands up and out as if to say, 'I don't understand why I can't have a sister' I laugh out loud; she is growing up and I'm noticing it more lately. Lord I thank You; I'm finally getting it! We have arrived at Vedettes and I give Vedette heads up about the 'sister' kick Nicki is on today.

This is a new doctor for me and after I filled out the paperwork I didn't have to wait long before being called to the back office. They wanted urine and blood and I waited for the doctor to examine me for just a few minutes. He verified that I am pregnant and told me both test confirms it. My due date should be around December 8th give or take a few weeks. Dr. Duke asked about my pregnancy with Nicki and he wanted to know if my pregnancy was easy or complicated, then he asked a lot of questions about my family history as far as the women and their health. I asked why all the questions and he said studies show twins are inherent and because I was one he needs more info. He asked me how was I feeling and when I told him I had fainted yesterday he said he was going to run one more test and would need some more blood from me.

He had me go into great detail as to what I was doing before fainting and after he listened; he told me to watch my diet and for me to make sure I ate balanced meals my hormones were probably off. It was very important for me to not be stressed then he asked the nurse to go get something he needed. As soon as she walked out of the office, he asked if I were a believer. When I told him yes, he smiled and told me to pray and believe more and worry less also that he prays for all of his patients. Then he told me so far everything was looking good he'll know more when the rest of the blood test results come back and he will go over everything with me during my next visit. He reminded me to stay in this room so I could give more blood and he left me waiting for the vampire. I felt so good when I left the doctors office. As I looked at my watch; I thought about how divine Pastrami would taste right about now!

I went to The Kra-z Greek and ordered a hot Pastrami with extra pickles and mustard. While I waited for my order I phoned Daddy. He answered the phone laughing and I felt so relieved because I know my Mama is better. He gives me the same update as this morning and tells me Pastor Stephens; his Pastor has been by and prayed for Mama and a host of people are praying for her full recovery. When I finished talking to Daddy I was smiling so big; and after I ate my Pastrami all of my teeth were showing, I mean!

I arrived at the shop to find it full and three walk-ins were waiting. I jumped all day and it was still popin when I left. I was so hungry I called Wardell to see what he had in mind for dinner. He thought for a few seconds and said fried catfish sounded real good. My mouth started watering; I told him that I would stop by now and get us dinner. It was 5:20 p.m. so by the time I pick Nicki up and get the catfish; it would still be hot for Wardell.

We ate everything in the bags except the paper it was wrapped in. Nicki ate two pieces of catfish and a whole hush puppy. I felt bad when Wardell asked what happened to the last piece of fish because I was holding it in my hand, getting ready to devour the last bite. I offered the rest of it to him but he insisted I finish it; after all I was eating for two; unquote! He gets up from the table and gathers all of the paper up to throw away. I told him I was not going to choir rehearsal tonight; instead I was going to see Mama for about thirty minutes and he stopped dead in his tracks. I told him the doctor said for me to watch my diet and that fainting could be caused by an imbalance in my hormones due to me being pregnant. He threw the papers in the trash and washed his hands, then walked to the phone and dialed it. I sat in the kitchen chair watching him, trying to figure out what he was up to. Nicki started singing and I couldn't hear so I got up and stood right next to him. I heard him say, "Okay thanks, be there in a few." He placed the phone on the counter and turned to me and told me to get Nicki's PJ's we were taking her to Ma; she will watch her while *WE* go to the hospital. I did as I was told.

When we walked into the hospital lobby someone called my name and when I looked, it was Mother Ball. She and Mother Wilson had come to see Mama and were told they had to wait until someone came down; only two persons at a time were allowed to visit in her room. I introduced Wardell to them and Sister Franklin walked up behind us; she had come from seeing Mama so one of us could go up now. Mother Ball politely told Mother Wilson she could go on up. Yeah; so she can pump all of the details of Mama being sick out of me. She is the kind of person that says lets pray about such and such but before praying she tells you every detail of what's going on first. What makes it so bad with Mother Ball is; she loves letting you know that she knows it all! I've got something for her today, just what I want her to tell everybody is all she's gonna get from me, ump I wasn't brought up in the church and didn't learn nuthin!

Well at least Mother Wilson knows hospital etiquette; greet, pray, bless and leave. She was back down and politely told Mother Ball she didn't mean to rush her but! While Mother Ball was upstairs with Mama, Mother Wilson talked about how she believed the Lord was going to completely raise Mama up and use her mightily. We were so encouraged after talking with her. I walked both Mothers to the door and Wardell went to the information counter. When I walked up to the counter he told me that Daddy was going to leave the room so we could both see Mama. The phone rang and the man behind the counter nodded at Wardell, returned the receiver and gave us both name tags.

Wardell held onto my waist until we walked into Mamas' room, then he let me go. I went straight to my sweet Mama and kissed her cheek while blinking back tears. I was so glad to see just three tubes in her; I know she's getting better! She smiled and told me not to start crying because then she would have to copy me and crying would make her hurt, so none of that. Wardell walks to the other side of her bed and kisses her forehead. He tells her that he is praying for her complete recovery and that his family was praying as well. In comes Daddy with a bottle of water in his hand. He walks over to me and kisses my cheek and nods while saying, "Hey" to Wardell.

We stayed for half an hour and left because there were five people in the lobby waiting to come up. I felt comforted seeing how attentive the nurses were to Mama and knowing Daddy was going to stay by her side made me feel as though Mama would rest better having him by her side and not at home by himself. As we stepped off the elevator and into the lobby, I sighed and smiled at the same time.

When we picked Nicki up she was having ice cream with Pops in the kitchen and when we went towards the kitchen, Ma pulled on my coat. When I looked at her she nudged her head towards the den so I followed her. She hugged me and held both my hands and said, "Z, Wardell phoned me yesterday right after he got the call you had fainted. He was so scared he asked me if you could lose the baby. Now I know your mother is in the hospital but baby, you are gonna need to pace yourself. Write down a schedule of what's important to do and do just those things. You're pregnant, have a husband that worries about you, a toddler that needs you and a business to tend to so be wise. If you are too tired to do what's on your list; let it go, it'll keep. Let Wardell see you taking care of yourself so he won't worry, okay." "Okay Ma, I will and thanks" "And Z, if you need me for anything, I'm just a phone call away you hear me?" I could feel the compassion I see in her eyes and the sincerity of her words and I moved my head up and down as my heart swelled from the love I felt from her. I gave her a tight hug and walked into the kitchen; straight to Wardell and gave him a tight hug. He wrapped his arms around me and gave me a peck on my cheek. Pops said that he was praying for Mama and told me to take care of myself. On the ride home I told Wardell that I was tired and was going to rest when we get home. He looked over at me and smiled.

Nicki was wired and cranky at the same time. I went to lie down and Wardell went in her room with her asking if she wanted to hear a story about a little boy who had four brothers and three sisters. She was all excited about the three sisters. As I lay on my bed I thought about my life this last week; and realized the Lord had all of the events that happened to me planned just like frames in a movie. The timing was unbelievable!   First the announcement which prompted the memories, then the Bible Study on forgiveness, hence the reuniting with Nye and now Mama being sick. It was predestined, just like Nye and me being separated all these years….wow.

Here comes my two favorite Patterson's. Both of them are jumping onto the bed with me. I sing, "Oh happy day!" Nicki copies me exactly and…the sing-a- thong begins. We sang and Nicki clapped her little tiny hands while Wardell beat to the mattress and I popped my fingers, we had a good time and finally Nicki started yawning and Wardell took her to brush her teeth and tucked her in. When he came back to our room I thanked him for being such a wonderful father and husband and I reassured him I would pace myself as Ma suggested and that I will get plenty rest. I shared with him about my new doctor being a Believer and he smiled that 'I'm so proud of you' smile and asked me some questions about the doctor.

He told me he wanted four children, two daughters and two sons so we wouldn't have an only child nor a middle child, that way his daughters would have a sister and brothers and his sons would have a brother and sisters. I asked him about how he felt growing up with sisters and brothers and what the difference to him was. We talked for a few hours and then that eyebrow went up! Now you know I loves me some Wardell, don't you!

I woke up with Wardell and got him off to work, then Daddy phoned and gave me Mama's update, she is less a tube today; the Lord is so good! Nicki was still on her tister kick the whole while she was getting ready and all the way to Vedettes. When I arrived at the shop Nate was there waiting for me. Because today is not a work day for him, I thought he was going to tell me he was leaving the shop but it turns out he wanted me to know our conversation last week stirred him to find his brother. We went to the back and he gave me a synopsis of his story.

His brother is almost two years older than he is and growing up, he idolized him, everything his brother Winston did was always admired upon by his younger brother. Nate fell in love with Alisha and they moved in together and were talking about getting married. He received a panicked phone call from Alisha telling him his brother had just left their apartment after trying to kiss her, she was extremely upset. He phoned his brother but only to get his voice mail. Nate left a message that Alisha was upset and for him to return the phone call. Winston phoned late that evening and told Nate that Alisha was lying because she was jealous of their relationship and if Nate believed her over his brother, then he was a fool.

"Tank told me he never thought I would let a woman come between us. I asked Alisha if she was sure he tried to kiss her and she told me I didn't trust her and our relationship went downhill after that. She moved out and Tank acted funny when I went around him, so I lost my woman and my brother. I ran into Alisha at a gas station a few months after she had moved out and she told me she had no reason to lie about my brother. I believed her and later that evening I went over Tanks place and told him what she had said, he had the nerve to tell me that he had done me a favor getting rid of her because she was wrong for me."

I interrupted Nate and asked, "Tank? The barber at "The Buzz" on Brockton Avenue?" He answers, "Yeah, Tank is his nickname. I became a barber because of him." Nate shakes his head "Yes" and continues. "I told him she was the love of my life and couldn't believe he would try and kiss my woman, so I swung at him. He moved out of the way and laughed at me. I left his place and have never spoken to him since. We take turns seeing our Mother because he owes me; you hear what I'm sayin?" I shook my head yes, he continues, "Z, my mother gave me Tanks phone number and I called him yesterday and left a message that it was time to open the closed doors and for him to call me back. I tell you it feels good to get that un-forgiveness off me but I'm not sure I can trust him again. Pray for me, and thank you for making me see *I* was the one in bondage not forgiving." We fist bumped while I tell him that he is so welcomed. While I worked I thought about Tank and Nate being brothers and I had never put it together before today. They are similar in build, both being big and buff and both have quiet dispositions, yeah they're brothers alright!

Aunt Daphne called, then Nye; wanting to meet me for lunch but I was too booked. The day was a busy one and that evening I stayed home with Nicki while Wardell went to Bible Study. After I put Nicki down for the night, I studied the last two verses in chapter 8 of Romans: **"For I am persuaded, that neither death, nor life, nor angels, nor principalities, nor powers, nor things present, nor things to come, nor height, nor depth, nor any**

other creature, shall be able to separate us from the love of God, which is in Christ Jesus our Lord." (Romans 8:38 & 39)

I realized that Paul understood the love of God and when you truly understand His love, you can't help but love Him right back! The word 'persuaded' can mean convinced, confident and even converted. So to be confident, convinced and converted that nothing could ever happen to someone who loves the Lord that will be able to make them want to be separated from Him; I truly think this is the ultimate we can give unto the Lord. When He has our undying love, He has our trust and obedience, and that my friend means He has us! When you think about love; the greatest proof of being loved back is knowing the person you love will always be there for you, regardless of what goes down or how; nothing separating you says it all. Like my Daddy would say; I can show you better than I can tell you! I mean!

Wardell came home and gave me a recap of the Bible Study and then he told me that Faith was there tonight. When he kissed me goodnight the fires ignited, ooh wee I just can't get enough of this man!

We both woke before the alarm went off and wondered what we could do to pass the time, um, oh well there's no better way to start the day! When I aided Nicki getting dressed she started the sister talk again and I decided to listen and not ask her to think about playing with a brother. I'll wait until we get the ultrasound and know for sure whether she'll be sharing the rest of her life with a brother or a sister, we can prepare her then. Daddy phoned me while I was on my way to the shop, Mama is doing very well and she has started medication for the C.O.P.D. The doctors want to make sure she has a compatible dose. She's being moved from ICU into a room. He was so happy.

The shop was jumpin today! Wardell phoned to see if I was doing alright and Aunt Daphne called again, she's planning to come take care of Mama when she gets out of the hospital and stay for a week. Oh my goodness listen to this….a tall cute older man came into the shop with his son and he looked around as he walked up to me and asked if his daughter was ready. While he spoke his eyes were scanning the shop and then he asked where the braider was. I called Sherry to the front and while she came forward he said, "My sister, Roberta, phoned and informed me she had dropped my daughter Gail off at the beauty shop earlier to get her hair braided and for me to pick her up at 4:30. Oh by the way I'm Leon."

He extended his hand to Sherry then to me but his eyes were on Sherry most of the time he spoke. She checked her book and was very patient with him asking him questions about who was his daughter's appointment with, what time was the appointment and with all of her questions he was getting worried so he decided to phone his sister and he realized he had the wrong shop. Sherry knows the lady that braids over at Braids by Bobbi so she gave her a call and asked how close was she to finishing Gail and that her father was on his way to get her. Well, when Sherry gave Leon directions to Braids by Bobbi she apologized to him for the mix-up and when he said, "I believe our meeting was in divine order." Everyone in the shop froze. Then he asked Sherry for one of her cards, that's when we all gave each other the Um, git it Sherry look!

When my work day had finally come to an end I sat down in my chair and thought about what sounded good for dinner tonight and I realized I am very blessed. I have a wonderful husband, beautiful baby and a great family and shop family. I am going to get some food for my family and stay home tonight and enjoy the people I'm blessed to have. While getting up my phone rings and its Wardell telling me he has a taste for some pork chops and gravy and he knew just where to get it. He wanted to know what I had a taste for. I smiled and told him I will help him eat whatever he brings home and later on I was going to let him know what I had a taste for! I could hear him smiling through the phone as he told me he loved himself some Zinora.

On the drive to pick up Nicki all I could think about was how good the Lord is to me. I am so glad His Word is available and meditating on It helps me to understand my rights as His child. I smile so big while thanking the Lord for all of the great things He has done for me and my family and I am especially grateful for the prompting of Holy Spirit to heal me of un-forgiveness because I am so free. Uh oh, I feel a praise breaking forth!

EPILOGUE

The doctors sent Mama home that Saturday and Daddy hired a lady to come once a week and cleanup for her until her breathing is better. She needs to stay clear from chemicals, smoke and sprays of any kind. It turns out her growing up around cigarette smoke weakened her lungs and the pneumonia weakened her bronchial tubes, her body couldn't handle it. Mama told me that she never opened the front door for me and Nicki and she believes an angel of the Lord must have. I thought about it and believe she's right because the door opened so slowly and the angel waited until we walked away from the door before opening it; that's confirmation to me that my Mama still has work to do for the kingdom of heaven!

Nye and I try to have lunch twice a month so we can have some twin time, it is so good having him and his family in my life. He wants me to help him with the music for the musical in May. Wardell and Nye went over Phoebes' to watch a fight with her husband Allen and he has bonded with the rest of the Patterson clan. Von and I meet at the park on Tuesdays for an hour and we watch the girls interact. It is so amazing to watch the twins, I feel as though I'm watching Nye and myself from a projector. They are so much like us it's just amazing. One thing is for sure, Nicki is breaking the ice for their baby brother or sister. She is so eager to have a 'tister' to play with until she doesn't mind having to barge in on whatever they are doing and it is so heartwarming to see how easily the twins allow her some of their space, almost as if she belongs with them!

Well, when we went to church Sunday, Faith joined and has been coming faithfully ever since. Wardell says that Brother Haywood has been eying her and the way he's been following her every move, he'll be saying something to her real soon.

Now Nate, man oh man! He talked to his brother and apologized but he still hasn't regained the relationship they once had but Nate is okay with that because…he has regained contact with Alisha and they are planning a wedding in September. Now that's some deep love there, I mean!

Sherry and Leon are dating and he's talking about marriage. Sherry is afraid of being hurt again but we are all praying she gets her healing and allow Leon to be Leon. Their kids get along real well with each other and with her sister's kids also. It's good to see Sherry happy with Leon and he looks at her with so much admiration.

I haven't had any more queasiness and I believe it's because Mama prayed for me. I seem to eat all day as though I haven't had anything to eat at all. I keep saying I'm not going to eat anything else after I eat this, but before I realize it, I'm opening my mouth to eat something else. I just hope I don't get too big because I really don't want to find out if Wardell meant what he told me. It seems as though I can't get enough food or enough of Wardell these days, this pregnancy is definitely different.

You know, when you feel in your heart you are exactly where you're supposed to be; it is so fulfilling. I am so happy I forgave Nye and we restored our relationship, as my Mama says, "The Word of God will work, if *you* work it!"   I mean!

SUMMARY

Is it clear to you that the person in this story is free now? She has allowed the un-forgiveness to flow out of her. One of the definitions of forgive is "to release." To forgive is a choice of releasing. Let me say that again, to forgive is a **choice** of releasing! You will definitely know you need deliverance and healing in the area of un-forgiveness. The question is: are you willing to surrender to forgiveness? Are you willing to let the matter completely go? Are you willing to become defenseless and transparent? The choice is yours like in the story, often; we are not the originator of the offense or insult. When you are the offender, put your pride in check, and do what must be done, out of "humility." Humility is not hard to walk in; all you have to do is remember you have made mistakes and often they were done unintentionally. So, you can relate to being the offender, and that alone is humbling.

When you are injured by offense, you don't feel responsible for initiating restoration. However, you must extend your hand in love and humility, and reconcile your relationship. Work out the reasoning part first because your mind will tell you the offense was done intentionally and you should just write the person off! So deal with the why you think they offended you, but, you must be honest. Go all the way back to the beginning of your relationship with them and work your way up to the offense itself. Most times it will jump out at you; the motive behind the offense. It will take time and don't settle for, "She has never liked me from day one that's all." If that is true, why did you keep going around her, and since this incidence happened, deal with it and deal with it now! If these type offenses happen often, be honest and ask yourself, "Why do I attract these types of people."

Let's look at forgiveness and compare it to emptying the kitchen trash. It must, absolutely, must, be dumped daily, or, the consequences are unbearable. You have a storage area inside you, and, just like a trash bag, all the negative, harmful words must be emptied out. Not by cussing someone out, or scheming to get even. Make the choice to forgive and not carry that weight inside you because un-forgiveness is weight. Un-forgiveness also causes resentment. Resentment is the source of "artificial respect". Yep! The source of being phony! Resentment breeds bitterness and hatred. Bitterness alters our true feelings and obstructs our ability to make wise choices. We become suspect of anyone we meet for the first time, for fear of being offended again.

Let's accept the fact that being offended is a part of life. It is going to happen! It's amazing how Jesus told us in Matthew, chapter 18, and verse 7, that in this world, offenses will come. Yet we don't prepare ourselves for them. We must equip ourselves for handling offenses in a positive, mature way. It may sound like an impossible task. However, we are reminded in **1 Thessalonians 5:15, "See that no one renders evil for evil to anyone, but always pursue what is good both for yourselves and for all."** This scripture tells us forgiving is doable! Now we may not want to do it, but it is doable, and, it takes the mature to do it......What's so surprising is, when we are born again, we think we become exempt of offenses. Forgetting we will be offended, for the gospel sake. We need to be capable of handling offenses because, they are sure to come.

Luke chapter 17, verses 1-4, Jesus teaches us how to handle offenses. **"Then He said to the disciples, "It is impossible that no offenses should come, but woe *to him* through whom they do come! It would be better for him if a millstone were hung around his neck, and he were thrown into the sea, than that he should offend one of these little ones. Take heed to yourselves. If your brother sins against you, rebuke him; and if he repents, forgive him. And if he sins against you seven times in a day, and seven times in a day returns to you, saying, 'I repent,' you shall forgive him."**

Offenses must be confronted. For some of us, when we hear the word, "Confront," we imagine the police cars surrounding the house, or the gurney carrying someone off to the hospital, because many of us do not know how to confront without violence. We suppress our feelings for so long and when we let the top off, we lose a volcano, and the mess that comes with it. If you are angry, wait until you can express yourself without being defensive. Go through your mind, frame by frame; ask yourself, "Why did those words hurt me? Was it the tone that bruised me or the words?" Get to the root of your hurt, write it down on paper if you must, but find the reason you are so upset, so offended.

It could be the other person stepped on a memory land mine; they reminded you of someone else. Or, perhaps a hurtful past experience. Be honest, is it their fault you live in a land mine field? It's time to get rid of the land mines! The offense must produce deliverance and healing! When we realize un-forgiveness infringes upon our worship, we should leap at the choice to forgive. So, let's make it a practice of emptying out our container of offense on a daily basis.

Forgiveness, like manners, is a staple of life to the born again Believer! Just as we learn to say, "Please, yes and no thank you," forgiveness is just as significant. **Matthew 18: 21& 22** says: **"Then came Peter to Him, and said, 'Lord, how often shall my brother sin against me, and I forgive him? Up to seven times?' Jesus saith unto him, 'I do not say you, up to seven times, but up to seventy times seven".**

Many of us read this and we think, "That's a lot of forgiving I have to do," and, some will even multiply 7 X's 70 and try to keep track. The point Jesus was making to us is, the more you forgive, the easier it becomes. Wait now! Don't get me wrong, the pain of being offended doesn't get easier. It still hurts, and, the closer someone is to you, and they offend you, the deeper the hurt is. What Jesus is saying to us is, once we understand the **advantage** of forgiving, it's no longer our duty to forgive; we simply **choose** to forgive. So, find a formula to forgive that works for you and use it as often as you have to. Be willing to forgive. The act of forgiveness takes a willingness, to submit to transparency. The transparency then causes a releasing. The releasing causes us to experience liberty, a liberty that can only be experienced from the release. Find a formula to forgive that works for you and use it daily, as often as you have too.

Let's really look at this. In the story, the brother needed to forgive his sister for, what he saw, was her betraying him. She didn't include him in running her decision by him. After 17 years of her sharing her ideas, he felt betrayed and left out. This may sound petty, but we have been offended by far less. Be honest; how many times have you said, "It's the principal!" If he chooses to forgive her, he now has to take a long hard look at his own, "Raw" feelings. This is submitting to transparency.

Reading this, it seems so easy to do; doing it requires you to remove all the layers of blame, and take responsibility. Now that the brother has submitted to transparency, he sees that his hurt did not come from his sister not considering his opinion. Now that he takes the responsibility for his feelings, he realizes it was childish of him to punish her, for not being included in her decision making. He can now let go of his hurt, thus, the releasing. Here comes the liberty! He is now able to admit his regret; he is no longer bound by hurt, guilt or fear.

Guess what, do this a few times and the light will come on. The more I forgive, the better I'll feel. Now, I know when Holy Spirit shows me my true self, it is for me to know the truth and be made free from it! I understand now, when I forgive, I am forgiven! Wow! I am no longer contaminated with the resentment and bitterness. It's over and done with. When I see that person who offended or insulted me, or when their name is dropped, I am no longer disturbed. I am free, and this liberation feels so good! I will not let anyone ever again, take it from me. Thank you Jesus!

Let's get a visual; imagine every time someone says something that offends you a 5" X 7" blanket falls from the sky and covers your chest area to protect your heart. By the end of the week, you can barely move because of the weight from the blankets. Even though the blankets are used to protect you, the protection used is weighty and soon you are unable to move. The blanket is un-forgiveness and it comes to our aide as a means of protection, however, if we don't DEAL with un-forgiveness, it hinders us from getting around.

We learn to deal with un-forgiveness at an early age. We find the blanket protects us and by the time we become teens, we have the protection system down. Because of the weight from the blankets, we need to learn our own personal technique from the Word that will free us from un-forgiveness.   Un-forgiveness is very unhealthy and, it causes us to be skeptical of people for fear our feelings will be trampled on.

Can you see how the weight of un-forgiveness holds **you** down, not the person you refuse to forgive? Find a way daily, to examine the blanket, fold it up and put it away in your testimony chest.   Remember the choice is yours.   When you realize un-forgiveness produces unproductive thoughts, you understand its a waste of your time!   (Philippians 4:8). So, when the question arises; Who ME, 4Give?   Just smile and say…certainly, certainly, certainly Lord!

WHO ME 4GIVE?

WHO ME 4GIVE?

www.ingramcontent.com/pod-product-compliance
Lightning Source LLC
Chambersburg PA
CBHW070436120726
47910CB00003B/814